WHEN LONDON SNOW FALLS

WHEN
LONDON
SNOW
FALLS

HAYDEN STONE

Entangled Publishing
644 Shrewsbury Commons Ave
STE 181
Shrewsbury, PA 17361
rights@entangledpublishing.com

Embrace is an imprint of Entangled Publishing, LLC.

Edited by Heather Howland
Cover design by LJ Anderson/Mayhem Cover Creations
Cover photography by Laifalight/Shutterstock

Manufactured in the United States of America

First Edition June 2022

embrace

WHEN LONDON SNOW FALLS is a contemporary queer romance between a music-loving barista and an indie rocker. While an overall fun read, the story includes elements that might not be suitable for all readers. Mentioned are the illness/death of a parent, family conflict, homophobic parents, anxiety and panic attacks, depression, a possessive ex, alcohol use, and past drug addiction. Readers who may be sensitive to these elements, please take note.

For my friend A., who liked to have a laugh, too.

Chapter One

There's no such thing as bad weather, just unsuitable clothing.

So they say, anyway. Whoever they are, wherever they are, they sure have a lot to answer for. Like the literal arsehole raincloud that burst open with passion over London about three seconds ago on my way to the café. In moments, the late November rain soaks my wool winter overcoat and my favorite thrifted cotton velvet jacket—which is usually quite warm when not absorbing water like a towel.

I probably look like a waterlogged cat after a bath. Or three vigorous baths.

Squelching into the stockroom of the café where I work in London's Soho, I hang my coat and jacket and find some paper towels to mop the worst of the deluge from my hair, combing it with my fingers more or less into place.

If there's anything I learned as a member of the Renfrew family growing up, it's that appearances matter. Always. Doesn't matter what the weather is or if you're working at a café or attending a posh dinner party.

I also learned that, sometimes, the indoor storms that

catch people off-guard are the toughest.

Thankfully, my phone still works, confirmed after a quick check. I've got five minutes before my shift starts to call my friend Emily, over in Wales, and our two-year-old daughter, Carys.

The phone rings four times before Carys answers, peering into the phone from Emily's lap. "Daddy!"

At least my soggy appearance hasn't put Carys off. I can't help but brighten when I see her. Carys's hair floats in a cloud of baby fine waves and she has an intense gaze with her blue eyes like mine. Her fingers grip the screen and the phone moves wildly about, leaving me a little motion sick. Emily's laughing.

"You need to hold the phone like this to see Daddy properly," Emily explains, holding the phone for Carys. "Hi, Charlie. We tried answering the phone together."

"Success, I'd say. How're things? I have a couple of minutes before my shift and thought to say hi."

"Good—"

"Play wif me," Carys demands.

"I wish I could. I have to work today."

"I'll play with you," Emily tells Carys quickly. She eyes me through the phone screen. "You look terrible, by the way."

"Thanks. Trying out a new look. I call it River Thames chic. Take that, Oxford Street. Like it?"

"Love it. You'll be a hit out there with all the boys."

I laugh at that. "You know I have no time for that." Not anymore. And probably never again.

The phone gets yanked again by Carys. "Play now?"

"Let's go get your stuffies," Emily tells her.

The phone swings wildly. "Bad dawg!" Carys calls offscreen in a triumphant cry.

"Bad dog?" Last I knew, Emily didn't have a dog.

There's a loud *thump* as the phone drops on her end and

then the sound of shuffling. Carys giggles wildly while Emily retrieves the phone.

I run a hand through my wet hair, amused despite the headache pressing behind my eyes. "Hell if I know what most of that was."

"The abridged summary is that her dog stuffie, Mr. Ruffles, fell in the mud at the park yesterday when Carys dropped him. Then when we were home, we sat together and watched him go around and around in the washer. She refused to move or let me leave, either. Like this was my fault."

"Laundry trauma lasts a lifetime, Em."

"It wasn't you sat on the floor for an hour. At least she agreed to read stories." The smile in her voice gives her away—she's not as bothered as she's trying to convince me she is.

I laugh, something bittersweet caught in my chest. It sucks they're so far away, and I don't get to Wales as often as I would like. They're my true family. Emily and I weren't ever together, before or after Carys, but we are close friends, and equally devoted to our girl. Even with the big ups and downs of having had a child young, something neither one of us bargained on. The truth of it is that we're both wild for Carys. She comes first, today and always.

"I'll be there for Christmas. I know it's not soon enough…"

She gives me a pointed look. We've been over this before. "We're fine, Charlie. And you're about to be late for work."

Emily always was the stable one. I'm kind of like the one misfiring synapse in someone's brain—some genius moments and some moments we could all do without.

"Talk later. Love you both." I blow a kiss as I hang up.

If I can't be there, I do the next best thing, which is send them everything I make to support them, outside of school costs.

Today is my last shift of my usual thirty-hour week. That's

on top of studying full-time at University College London and going to band rehearsals whenever we can squeeze one in. Those are at least a bit of an escape from the usual hectic pace, though we've been ramping up the frequency as we book more gigs. There's also the weekly check-in with my therapist and, when they get their way, Sunday dinner with my family.

It's…a lot.

Lately, I'm so exhausted in lectures that everything goes in one ear and out the other. I've usually either rushed to class from the café or needed to go straight to a shift or rehearsal right after. At night, I try to go through the lectures again to figure out what I've missed. The term's been a total muddle.

I rake my hands through my hair a third time for luck, grab an apron, and head into the front of the café.

The screech of the steamer does my head in. Never mind the strip lighting. While I'm warm and dry indoors today, give me November gray and rain. For my headache, dark and dreary lighting, please. And silence.

But the customers queuing for their Saturday morning coffees don't care about the state that exhaustion and Friday night's left me in. I'm not sure if it was the single pint I drank that packed a wallop, the lack of proper sleep for days, or the press of what might be a migraine from too much stress. Or maybe it's that last night's gig still rings in my ears. Luckily, most of the customers so far this morning are regulars. There's little talking, punctuated with occasional nods and gestures at the pastry display.

"Your order'll be up in a couple of minutes," I say in the brightest customer service voice I can manage to the woman I've just finished helping at the counter.

Jasmine pauses beside me with a ruthless grin. "You sure you don't want to be on food orders, Charlie?" Behind her, Lars smirks at the espresso machine as he wipes down the steamer for the next drink, doing a poor job of pretending not to listen.

I shudder at the thought of frying eggs—frying anything, really. Any sort of greasy or fatty food is out, too. Brioches. Croissants. And never mind salads. Too leafy. The offensive crunch of celery, and the tyranny of raw vegetables on an unsuspecting stomach. It's a total nightmare. The till is the safest here, even with the glare of the lighting overhead. Safer yet would be the luxury of lying absolutely still in my own bed with the pillow pressed over my face, but I need the pay. Every penny counts.

"Fuck no." An involuntary shudder ripples through me.

They're convinced I'm hungover. Which has happened before, sure, but I haven't had time or money for drinking in a long while. Maybe I'm coming down with something. Like malaria. Or dysentery. Or the galloping consumption, which would be at least useful for my English literature essay, and appropriately Victorian. Maybe I can get a sick note and an extension again.

"Let me know if you change your mind." Jasmine flounces off in a cloud of curls and irreverence. Bloody typical.

Beyond her, the café's full of university students and tourists. It's the students that I especially notice, mostly head down over their textbooks and laptops. Like I should be, because I'm always way behind with my assignments and studying. That'll be me the moment I'm done with my shift tonight. The closest student has a daunting stack of economics books, enough for my blood to run cold as an English student. At any rate, exams are breathing down my neck as I get the last of the term's assignments in. Plus, I've got two assignments to finish up over the holidays on a special extension after some passionate groveling to my tutors.

Another group of students, a trio of guys, talk about their big night out plans for later tonight. Dinner, drinks, dancing.

Sounds amazing. Sign me up. Except I've got no cash for a big—or small—night out, loads of homework, and precisely no dancing lined up. My band has a gig later but it's work, too, so I'll already have less time to study than usual on Saturday night.

With a sigh, I squint against the light for the next customer. They're somewhat man-shaped at first glance. He says something that I don't quite catch. He's nothing but a dark silhouette with far too much bright light blasting my eyes from behind him.

Then he slides cash—*cash!*—across the counter in an offhand way. Like we do this routinely and have the drill down.

Now I'll need to do sums. Perfect.

"What sort of wanker or monster uses cash these days?" It tumbles out before I can stop myself.

"A wanker or monster that's lost his wallet and bank cards. That sort," says the shadow mildly. Scottish accent of some kind. "Also, criminals and people who want to stay off the grid. You'll just have to guess which sort of monster I am."

Frowning, I lift my head and look at the customer more closely. Screw the bright light.

He's about my age, early twenties. Lean. Lip ring. Bleached, streaked, and disheveled blond hair. Multicolored jumper under a leather jacket with matching long scarf. He's grinning. Very fuckable. I haven't seen him here before, but he looks familiar. But from where? He's a face out of place, without context.

"Sorry. Didn't think you'd hear." Bad habit, me running my mouth off and sticking my foot in it. Jasmine's entertained on a regular basis. Emily's taken me to task over it for years. I really do know better. Current me is only bothered enough to serve hipsters hot drinks in a passable enough way to pay the bills. I've got more important things to worry about. Like

Carys and Emily. And tuition. Real world worries.

"My hearing's not bad. Youth and all." He stuffs his hands deep into his jacket, smiling, a bit bleary-eyed. Even still, he's appealingly lickable. I *can* take a moment to imagine that, even if it isn't Friday night—the only night of the week I allow myself to interact with potential hookups. The guy won't know. And I can delude myself for at least five minutes.

"Spry. Good. I like that. But..." I glance down at the cash, crumpled from his pocket. It's the side with Jane Austen demurely facing out, a reminder of my reading and essay waiting at home. *Wuthering Heights* waits for no one, least of all me. "Only old people carry money. How did you get money if you lost your wallet?"

"Old people!" A laugh follows. "I'm here for a coffee, not an interrogation about how I manage my money. Or about what I keep in my wallet. But like I said, I could be a criminal or someone keeping off the grid." He leans in ever so slightly, a mischievous glint in his eye. "Maybe you shouldn't push too hard."

Thank God he's amused and not offended. And that my manager is nowhere in earshot for this exchange. Lars and Jasmine are lapping this up, from what I can see out of the corner of my eye. I never get flustered by customers, so no doubt I'll be hearing about this after.

"Sorry." My face burns. "None of my business, is it? You're right."

"Well, it is your business if you're calling monsters out on their monstrous affairs. Never mind their wanking." If anything, his grin broadens. The effect is devastating. "I could've paid in change. For all you know, my pocket is full of pennies."

My face burns even hotter at the thought of him in any number of compromised scenarios I can vividly imagine. *Focus, Charlie.* "Please don't," I beg. "It's too much to count.

If you've ever worked retail, you'd get it, I swear. I haven't got time for that."

He pretends to consider. "So, what you're saying is that you want to hurry me along?"

"No! Oh no. I mean, no, of course not. Take your time. Shit. I'm sorry."

He laughs. "I'll stick with paying with the ten-pound note, then. Since it's less counting for you."

I'm wrecked from the week and my headache continues to press behind my eyes. And yet some weird part of me thrills at this rather odd conversation with this new customer. "Thanks. That's very humane."

He leans against the counter, eyebrow raised. "I hate to be obvious about it, but you could enter the amount into the cash register and it'll tell you the exact change. No need to count anything out," the young man says helpfully. "Completely efficient. Unless…you like counting?"

"Oh no. You should see me cash out sometimes. Better thought—maybe you shouldn't. It's probably frowned upon, keeping a customer in the shop at closing, actually."

At least he'd be interesting company if he *was* there when I closed the shop.

"Especially if I'm a criminal." His eyes dance.

I peer at him. "*Are* you?"

"Could be. I mean, you don't know, do you? I could be an accomplished thief."

"True," I say. "But also, I don't know if you're the off the grid type. Do they wear leather jackets, colorful jumpers, and bleach their hair? You seem very city to me. Like you've escaped from Shoreditch or some other hipster enclave."

"Depends, I'd say. You can't assume anything in today's world, like where one keeps their hipster enclave. City or country, who can say?" He shrugs.

"You're not going to make this easy on me, are you?"

"Afraid not. This is far too much fun."

Clearly, he's having a great time.

And something weird has happened: I'm smiling, too.

"What would you like?" I ask at last, after a long moment passes where we just look at each other.

"An Americano the size of my head. And that brioche." He points, then gazes at me, probably memorizing my description to tell my manager what an arse I've been, which would be a fair point, because I *have* been a bit of an arse, calling him a wanker out of the blue. He nods at a man standing further back in the queue, absorbed by his phone. Longish hair obscures his face. "And, for the record, my bandmate spotted me the cash."

I hesitate. He's in a band? Something odd like a moment of conscience rises. Or maybe it's something else, lower and more primal. Get a grip. *Maybe dating austerity measures have taken more of a toll than expected.*

"How about you keep your tenner? Your drink's on the house. I insist. For probably being the worst sort of service person in Soho this morning."

"I think I had worse counter help somewhere else last weekend." He laughs. "If it makes you feel better."

"It really does," I agree solemnly. "I like to be at least one rung up from mediocre."

"You might be at least adequate, if not competent," he assures me merrily.

"I aim for purely serviceable."

My face flares with heat. Did I really just say that?

He taps his fingers against his lips, smiling. "That's very interesting."

"I'm full of wonders."

"I agree. You do seem full of wonders. And there's a lot to admire about a man who can think on his feet."

Something in my gut thrills, a secret part of me that

actually does care very much about what other people think. What *he* thinks. And that secret part of me is all-in with the rare attention. It's got to be the banter, even with feeling rough. There's something brilliant about the unexpected simple pleasure of trading nonsense with a stranger on an otherwise dull morning.

If only I could figure out why he looks so familiar. I must have seen him play at some rock club. Maybe at some armpit of a dive in Camden or off in the far-flung reaches of Brixton. If only I could remember which gig. Obviously, he's hot. And distracting. That's two points for science. It can't be a past hookup because I wouldn't forget him.

Forget all of that. I need to get through the next few crucial seconds without shaming myself by pushing my average-to-subpar social skills over into total disaster.

Of course, nobody's particularly arsed about the ex-virtues of one Charlie Renfrew.

"Right, where were we?" I flail about in the conversation, unsettled by his rapt gaze. Quickly, I look down, anywhere but at him. The tenner is still on the counter. "You're not paying. I insist, man."

His gaze only gets more intense, if that's possible. "I feel terrible about giving the staff a hard time and coming away with free food and drink, and you get nothing out of it," he says. "It's a tip, then."

"No tip. Besides, I've got a gig later and I'll get cash from that. And I wouldn't say I got nothing out of this. I learned about the criminality of hipster monster enclaves, probably in urban settings. I mean, that's good stuff, right?"

"Right." He's looking far too amused. "Gig, huh?"

"Yeah. My band." Unnerved, I'm fresh out of witty banter, or even the non-witty banter I'm also very capable of providing.

"What's your band called?"

"Err, The Screaming Pony."

He grins broadly at me, nodding his approval. "Good name."

"Thanks."

"Well, I guess I'll need to find some other way to spend my money." He's about as irreverent as Jasmine from a couple of moments ago. The cheeky bastard. He pockets the money. "Thanks."

"You're welcome. You can come back and spend it some other day." Hopefully when I'm not on shift, because I'm fairly certain I've made an utter arse out of myself. No need for a repeat performance.

Quickly, I make myself busy by neatening things around the till.

He doesn't move.

Why doesn't the arsehole step to the side and wait for his order like any other sensible human? I glance at him. "You can wait at the other end of the counter. You don't have to watch me clean."

"I know."

Our gazes linger, and despite my head aching and my embarrassment levels being at an all-time high, I don't want this moment to end. At last, we exchange nods before he steps back and heads to where Lars does his thing behind the counter.

Then, it hits me why he looks so familiar but out of place: he's Ben Campbell, the frontman of one of London's hot upcoming bands, Halfpenny Rise.

Oh, help.

He's fire on the guitar, of course. And vocals.

And he's even more stunning in person than in the gig photos I've seen online or in the couple of live shows of his that I've caught around London.

Bloody hell. I've made a complete fool of myself when

I ought to be licking his boots. Or have him lick mine. Whatever. I'm not fussy. As long as there's someone licking something, I'm in. Especially if it involves music. And him.

My eyes widen. Wait. Fuck, did I actually just tell *Ben Campbell* about my band?

There's no way to come back from the disaster I've made of taking his order, never mind asking him about what it's like fronting for Halfpenny Rise or how to play lead guitar like he does, in a way that tears my heart out and shoves it into my mouth for the finale under some epic pyrotechnics display.

At any rate, Ben Campbell's now safely over in Lars's queue to pick up his drink, at the far end of the counter behind the pastry display. And Friday, the authorized night for fun, is nothing but a memory. The window for fun has closed.

"I would rather like to order a coffee," says a silver-haired woman curtly, with no time for my waywardness. She stares hard at me, as if she's had a private tour of my thoughts from the last five minutes.

"Sorry," I say, for the third time in five minutes, springing into action like a semi-competent barista.

Focus. Onto the next customer if I don't want to get fired. Getting fired would ruin the balancing act I've got going on in my life. Forget distractions, even the temporary kind.

Even distractions as dangerously tempting as Ben Campbell.

Chapter Two

Cold rain pours down on me again as I rush for the bus after working a long shift, shivering and starving. I'd give anything for a steaming hot drink about now. The coffee I made earlier during my shift at the café is long gone. It's past proper dinnertime now. The Saturday afternoon shoppers are going home, and the people headed out for the night in the West End are off to theaters and bars. Because their windows for fun are wide open.

Anyway, none of that matters right now.

I'm late.

At least it's not terribly far from where my band's playing at tonight. Some private holiday party for the something-or-other society of artists. Or was it publishing? Designers? I can't remember.

I don't have time for this gig, but I'm strapped for cash. On top of the usual I send Emily every month, I've got to buy Carys a new stroller since the axle broke on the old one. My student loan only goes so far, along with the money from the café, even with working nearly full time. Despite being permanently skint, there's absolutely no way I'm asking my parents for help. I've only got about a year left at uni before I finish my English degree, and they've already told me loads of times how useless that'll be when it comes to a future career.

But I don't have time to think or worry any longer about strollers or money or the fact I've just spent three years of my life working toward a degree that won't improve my situation.

Once onboard, I text our singer, Briar, that I'm on my way. I wolf down the tomato and cheese sandwich from work with a quick scroll through stroller reviews on my phone. Three stops later, through crawling traffic, and I'm in East London arriving at Shoreditch Town Hall. At the small venue for the Saturday night show, I weave through the queued crowd.

There's no separate way into the basement where we're playing that I can see. Or maybe I don't know how to find it, so I've got to come through the main entry like everyone else.

"I'm with the band," I say apologetically, cutting in line amid glares. I gesture at the guitar in hand as my alibi.

What I ought to be doing instead of rocking out tonight is reading *Wuthering Heights* for the essay due on Monday. I haven't had a chance to start, not properly, and I really want to dive in with a big pot of tea. I tried starting last night, only to wake faceplanted in the book, strange dreams of a severe but super sexy Mr. Heathcliff and haunting landscapes dancing around my brain like sugar plum fairies.

My friend Aubrey, who owns a bookshop despite only being a couple of years older than me, sold me a second-hand copy yesterday with a student discount. We met in a lecture a couple of years ago before he had to drop out and run the family business.

At this rate, I'll have to drop out of university too because I either can't stand to think about the future loan repayments or because I'll drop out from sheer exhaustion between studying and working around the clock. I can't help but feel wistful seeing how happy Aubrey is now, with an amazing new boyfriend and loads of plans. Weird what love does to a man, I guess.

That's not in the cards for me. At least not anytime soon.

"I'll vouch for him," says Briar, blond hair up, wearing a flowing knee-length cotton dress on the other side of the surly-faced person ready to check tickets at the door. Briar smiles at me and ushers me in. "You look like you had a swim in the Thames, Charlie."

"I keep telling people today it's part of my new look. It's how I freshen up for a gig. Wild swimming. New routine. I'm gonna set trends like an influencer."

I slip past the ticket attendant who still eyes me with suspicion, and I attempt what might be a winsome smile. Whatever works to get me in.

Briar glances over her shoulder at me as we hurry through the spotlit venue to the back room turned greenroom. The ceilings of the historic building are low, with exposed pipes and red brick walls, the floor not quite level concrete that's been painted gray. The basement is a collection of oddly laid out rooms.

We go past the main room with the stage, dance floor, and tables to the side. Festive decorations are in clusters on the walls. There's a bar in the next room. Colorful art posters hang on the wall.

"And I thought *I* was fashionably late," she says. "We're up next for a quick sound check. They put us at the end. Get out of that wet coat and scarf."

I don't need to be told twice and wriggle out of my sopping scarf and coat, down to a black T-shirt and jeans. I rake a hand through wet hair. "Do you have a cloth so I can wipe down my guitar?"

"I'll find one." Briar goes to Jackson, her boyfriend and our drummer, who is always prepared for just about anything. Of course, he delivers. I quickly check the tune before hurrying after the others.

The rest of my bandmates are already headed for the stage. Gillian beelines for her keyboards. Matt picks up his bass guitar. There's no time for chitchat as someone yells, "Doors in ten!" We get in two songs during our sound check before we're chased away, long enough at least to make sure everything's sounding like it should and our kit's working.

We dash off and then the doors open. Before long, the opening band is playing.

Meanwhile, I've pulled *Wuthering Heights* out of my bag and try to read in the greenroom before our set. The only way I'm getting through this whole book, or at least attempting to get through this book, is to read in five-minute bursts here and there over the weekend between everything.

Sometimes—just about always—I've got to do what I must, but it doesn't leave time for much else.

Our set happens in the blink of an eye.

Briar's voice is dreamy and lush at the same time. All eyes are on her. I support her on vocals and on lead guitar. We've got something special, even if we aren't some big—or let's face it, small—rock band.

Playing music is the way I feel alive these days, the most like myself. Something like happy amid everything else. On stage, I'm free from all the stresses of everyday life. For most of an hour, there's no worries about my tuition, or money, or Carys a country away. It's bliss, and I'll play every minute I can get.

After we leave the stage to a roar of cheers from the crowd, I join Jackson and Briar for one drink at the bar, buoyed by our set.

Finally, I have a chance to breathe. This is the last gig before the holidays. We've been burning the candles at all ends. Especially me.

We clink our pints and drink. They lose themselves in each other, which doesn't help the conversation. They're kind of disgustingly sweet, even after two years together. He's a bear of man, as fierce on drums as Briar is ethereal in her singing and performance.

I should have brought *Wuthering Heights* from the greenroom to the bar.

Instead, I stand there looking longingly into my pint, trying to remember the last time someone looked at me like Jackson looks at Briar. Or like Aubrey looks at Blake. I swear it's been so long I've forgotten what it's like.

Don't even think about that.

Someone puts a pint down next to mine, as if on cue. I glance over.

A bright-eyed man smiles at me. He looks very wholesome, a boy-next-door type. Possible vacuum salesman. "You were great up there."

Unused to the compliment, I fidget with my pint, turning the glass in my hands on the bar. "Uh, thanks. It's not just me up there, though."

Taking compliments is definitely not my strong suit.

"Your band was great," he corrects. Still smiling. Admittedly, he's kind of attractive. He's a few years older than me, in a smart suit too formal for tonight's party. He's close, leaning in, like he's interested in more conversation.

Shit.

"Uh, thanks," I say again. "I'm glad we could play this... event. Are you a designer, or, um, artist? For whatever this is tonight?"

"Fundraiser for the Queer Art Society," he says smoothly. "And the answer is none of the above."

"I suppose zero out of two isn't very good, is it?" I consider him. Not really my type—he's too clean-cut.

Even so, if I wasn't so damn tired, I'd be up for a night's fling, which nicely dodges the dating ban, but I can't even manage credible banter. Hell, if we even tried to hook up, I'd probably fall asleep in the middle of everything. Some hookup.

And that's about when I remember Ben Campbell looking far too delicious in the café earlier. Talk about temptation on legs. I'd stay awake for him.

"I'll help you out. I'm in communications," says the man. "For an art charity."

"Right. Thanks." That explains the too-slick suit and tie he's wearing.

"Can I get you a drink? My name's François."

"I probably shouldn't. I need to get back to Heathcliff."

He blinks. "Your boyfriend?"

"Something like that," I say apologetically. "It's a bit complicated. His estate. My lack of one. My mother's beside herself."

That last bit at least is true.

God, Charlie, you're hopeless. Though I can't just say I don't date. That always leads to an awkward conversation.

"It's a shame Heathcliff is so…demanding." I do my best to give an apologetic shrug, swirling the last of my lager in the glass. It's not exactly a lie.

"Good luck with that," he says.

"I'm gonna need it, believe me." I down my drink and set the glass down with some finality, and straighten, still holding the glass. I'm about to make excuses to leave.

And then my heart stops. Possibly my lungs quit working, too.

Ben Campbell saunters past, flanked by a couple of his bandmates. He pauses by me, long enough to hold my gaze until my face sears. He gives me a wink and a cheeky grin. Shameless and bold. "Great gig."

I nearly die on the spot. My beer sloshes.

Just like that, he's gone as suddenly as he arrived.

I gawp wordlessly after him. *Oh. My. God. Ben Campbell just watched me play.*

I try to pull it together and fail miserably, staring.

"Heathcliff's a lucky man. Good night." Communications Francois slips into the crowd to try his luck with someone else.

How exactly am I supposed to return to my room in Finsbury Park and my reading and essay now? Totally unfair, universe. Out of sorts, I make my way out for home, wondering if I'll ever see Ben Campbell again.

Chapter Three

The morning shift goes by in a blur of lattes and pastries, the ever-present clatter of crockery the inevitable soundtrack to my café life. It's Saturday once more, though I had a patchwork of shifts during the week around my exam schedule. Now it's back to the usual weekend routine again.

My only escape from all of it the last few days was the occasional lewd daydream about Ben Campbell, including the details of how I embarrassed myself in front of him last weekend, because my brain loves reliving moments of peak shame in excruciating detail, punctuated with distracted memories of equally peak hotness. Even through all of that, his easy grin stays with me, imprinted.

God, Charlie. You're hopeless. People like Ben Campbell definitely aren't for you. Especially when you keep making an arse of yourself in front of him.

I wipe my fingers on my black apron before wiping down the counter at the café. The routine's all muscle memory now, no thought required. Which is good, because I'm seriously distracted right now.

Luckily, between uni, café work, the band, and Carys and Emily, I had very little time to think about anything else this past week. Certainly no time to spend wondering how far those freckles might go down his neck and beneath his collar. Or what he might look like without all of his wintry layers against the late autumn bluster. Or if he's warm enough, or if he needs my help to chase off winter chills with a few kisses. After all, I'm selfless like that.

The dating ban's going just great.

At any rate, with the term wrapping up, Friday night saw me out hitting a rock club for a friend's gig and having a good time for a couple of hours. Till I woke without enough sleep for today's shift, regretting my poor life choices again as I struggled through the morning routine. When did I become such a lightweight? Probably since I don't go out often these days. Once in a while, I'll let myself have a Friday night—and only a Friday night—out for fun, and I've got to make every moment count.

"God." I down a pint of water as Jasmine and I stand behind the front counter. Everything aches and my mouth's packed with cotton wool. Like, I know full well London water is dodgy and full of pharmaceuticals and who knows what else, but adding cotton is a step too far.

"God speaking," says Jasmine. "You'd think you'd learn by now. Gonna rethink the point of your existence, Charlie?"

"You'd think." I take over the till with a grimace. Unfortunately, that means dealing with people again. People mean even more talking. This is far more than my brain can bear this morning. "But I'm not gonna. I've got things to do. No time to waste."

Which is why I have the ban.

I'm busy, but I'm also admittedly scared of opening up to someone and being vulnerable. Like sharing about my time spent in therapy, or time spent wrangling medications to find the right ones or the right doses. Or the right combination. But to be fair, there are things I've done in the past that were just plain old shit judgment, and I still don't quite trust myself.

It's true that some of my situation is self-inflicted. Sure, it's not good to drink like I did on Friday nights once upon a time, but it's a far cry better than how I used to spend every night off my face. That's addiction for you. Now, I'm clean, but I've not forgotten.

Clean's not always easy, especially during the holidays with my family. Christmas is coming up fast, and stress is high, so letting loose for a little while by going to a rock club when I can on a Friday night is fair play. Besides, it's technically market research for the band about what's happening in the local music scene.

At any rate, music keeps my head above water. And so does work at the café.

So far, it's a quietish Saturday morning.

Customers come at an easy pace, which makes me look almost functional. Brilliant, because the manager is in this morning, and I'm hoping not to embarrass myself in front of her. Better not relive last Saturday's episode again.

The café is dotted with shoppers and students sitting at worn pine tables, stained dark with time, and mismatched painted chairs. Colorful artwork by local artists hangs on brick walls. A couple of customers have the prime seats by the fire on the old leather sofa: a fab place to be on a cold day like today. Others sit in front of the large windows. A few of them are students from my course. They're laughing and talking about all of the fun things they will do over their holiday break. Everywhere I look, people wear layers of woolen things like pullovers and hats and scarves. Coats hang from the back of chairs, and the windows are fogged up with condensation from the heat inside.

I'm not getting a break. Not until I go to Wales for a

couple of days. But I'll probably spend more time traveling there than with Emily and Carys.

Attempting to be useful, I start wiping down the counter. I can handle this. *Simple tasks, Charlie. Simple tasks. Work up to the bigger tasks.*

After a couple of minutes, I clue in that someone's watching me. Sixth sense or something like that. I glance up.

Oh God.

It's him.

Ben Campbell, the hottest guy I've seen in forever.

He's brilliant, his blond-streaked hair tousled in a way that I could imagine burying my fingers in, looking just as hot as last week—possibly more so. His coat's unbuttoned, hands stuffed in the pockets. He's smiling, cheeks flushed a delicious pink from the cold outside. Who knows how long he's stood there watching me. Unfortunately, it's long enough for him to watch me gawp.

Act cool. Like he's any other person.

"You're making a habit of this?" I ask him archly. Time to save face, despite my thudding brain and heart, the adrenaline already going. "Hope you've had better luck with your wallet this week."

"Aye, I have." He pauses to pat his wallet in his rear pocket, conveniently over his arse. The tease. Ben's eyes are very blue and his grin is irrepressible. There's something entirely appealing about it, and even more appealing about him.

All I know is that I can't look away while wiping the counter clean of invisible dust again.

"It's my phone this time," he says. "Gone."

"Hmm. Shame. Sounds expensive."

Casual, Charlie. Be casual. Beat him at his own game.

"I suppose that's what insurance is for. I'm not sure if it's more or less of a hassle than canceling my bank cards, though." He looks forlorn. Hell, he's positively wistful as he sucks on his lip ring.

"Do monsters get insurance coverage these days? It's so hard to keep up with the trends."

He flashes a grin. "In some circles, aye. We do."

"At least you have phones. Sure beats roaring to each other from the tops of skyscrapers. Very modern. I'm keeping to my story that you're an urban monster and not an off-grid one."

"The best crimes and Americanos are in the city, it's true."

"So you've admitted to doing crimes, then."

"Only under pressure."

"Maybe you just wanted to come clean. For your conscience, you know. After last Saturday."

"Well, there is that. I couldn't stop thinking about my monstrous crimes. Kept me up at night. You know how it is. Or the mean coffee that your coworker made. Or, you know, other things."

"Right, coffee." I stand there like a fool, cloth in hand. Well, it should have been obvious already that he was flirting, but this is confirmation of his queer card. "So, er, what can I do for you this time?"

A fail on the smooth front. Jesus, Charlie. He's here for a coffee, like everyone else. Don't get excited. This is harmless chatter, nothing more.

"I came to see you." Ben looks entirely too pleased with himself. "I've been by the café a couple of times this week and you weren't working. I asked last time when you'd be in and they said Saturday morning. So here I am."

I nearly drop the cloth. My fingers tighten to literally get a grip. "*You* came to see *me*? I mean, wasn't going to the gig last week suitable punishment enough?"

"I need to know something." His expression shifts from

playful to serious. "Something I've not stopped thinking about since the last time I was here."

"Yeah?" I lift my head, intrigued and yet already horrified about what I might say next. I can't trust my tongue. Or words. They're in cahoots. What on earth does he need to know that I could tell him?

"What kind of services do you offer?"

I splutter, my cool facade in tatters. "Services?" I put my cloth down with a slap on the counter. "What do you mean, services?"

"Well, last week you told me you were the worst sort of service person in this part of London." He tilts his head, hair falling in his eyes, which gives off an air of mischief even with his deadpan expression. "And I want to know what services you aren't offering, so I can avoid asking for those. Spare us some awkwardness and all that."

My brain throbs a dull drumbeat. All I want to do is stand here and admire him. That's free, too. No harm in looking. Today he's got on a fuzzy green jumper under his open coat. I'd love to slide my hands under that pullover, feel the skim of soft wool and skin. Definitely, absolutely fuckable.

"Well?"

"Coffee services, mainly." I gesture widely at the café. It's hardly Buckingham Palace or something posh, but we've got real cred with the bohemian set of Soho and university students. My lips twitch. "If you've noticed."

"Oh yeah? What else? I bet there's more." His grin glows. "Great gig, by the way. I would love to talk to you about the show sometime, in addition to any services you're offering."

Out of the corner of my eye, I can see Jasmine's shoulders shake with silent laughter. Because it's best to embarrass oneself in front of an audience, of course. But I'll take the high ground. I'll show him. And Jasmine.

"Coffee and music are the services you can buy," I say

gamely in an effort to recover my long lost chill.

"And the services I can't buy?" He grins, unrepentant. "I bet you've got a lot of talents that could be…useful."

Oh. My. God.

"Bold." I give him a challenging look.

He shrugs. "I know what I want."

So do I. I consider him, all appealing angles and blond hair that doesn't obey order and gravity. God, he's tempting.

The drumbeat in my skull is echoed by the drumbeat in my chest. The adrenaline again. He must hear my heart thumping away through the din.

Don't get tempted. You can't. There's no way that's ever happening.

"Before my manager flays me, what can I get you?" I try to sound nonchalant.

"An Americano, I think. Please." His smile thrills me from the inside out. He's a bit devastating like that, charming with a hint of the wicked about him. It's a heady combo.

I nod. "As you wish. You're in danger of becoming a regular, you know."

"It's a risk I'm willing to take." He looks solemn but the glint in his eyes gives him away. "You never know what might happen."

"I bet you say that to all the boys."

He laughs with delight. "You might think so, but I actually say surprisingly little sometimes."

"Calling bullshit." An unfamiliar pull at the corners of my mouth turns my rare smile into a mirroring grin. "I guess we'll just have to see if you ever come back. Or maybe the questionable service has driven you off." I try to look convincingly casual, leaning against the counter. "That'd be bad for business. Hell, it could even jeopardize my job if I'm driving the customers away."

"I'd hate for you to lose your job."

I shudder involuntarily at the thought. It's hard not to think about my tuition shortfall because I put sending money to Emily before paying for university.

"God, me too."

"Well, I suppose I should let you get back to work then. Still would love a chat sometime about the gig."

The day I talk to the lead singer of Halfpenny Rise about *my* gig is the day I die of mortification. Clearly, I need to divert him. "You might need to buy something else to justify all this time at the till with me."

He considers the display case. "Hmm. Then I'll take a chocolate chip cookie."

"Just a cookie?"

"Two cookies, actually. One for each hand. I need to keep my strength up."

"Good thinking. That's important."

I give him the cookies in a paper bag. In return, he gives me his bank card and I ring him through, feeling strangely lighthearted.

We smile foolishly at each other as I pass him his card back.

Looking costs nothing, right? No one will catch on and it doesn't bother anybody. It's way safer than a conversation, least of all about my gig. If I can have something to fantasize about, it'll make all of this that much easier.

Light-headed, I hide another smile before anyone sees and go back to work. Then there's a rush of customers and when I have a chance to look up again, he's gone. And, God help me, I want to see him again, and more.

Chapter Four

So much for heady Saturday fantasies about Ben Campbell. Sunday, by comparison, is far more real. At least I've got a solid eight hours of sleep behind me after a positively demure night in working on homework. I'm gonna need my strength.

The morning starts early with me in my pajamas, eating bowl after bowl of cereal while I try to get through three long chapters of literary criticism in tiny font, and I think it might actually kill me. It's drier than yesterday's toast left out overnight, stale and brittle. No comparison to *Wuthering Heights*.

I'm exhausted by ten o'clock but there's still lots to do this morning.

I clean the flat in record time, do a pile of laundry while studying, and call Carys and Emily. I transfer her five hundred pounds to help with their bills. Then, I dash for the bus to the station and the train out to my parents. At least the train ride gives me more time to try to catch up on my readings.

And my growing collection of totally inappropriate Ben Campbell–related fantasies, God help me.

Hours later, I'm at my parents' table for Sunday lunch, a permanent routine that only leghold traps, the flu, or alien abduction could stop. Unfortunately, none of these things happened on my way to Richmond. Not even a well-timed rail replacement train delay.

Instead, I'm at the broad oak table beneath deep beige walls and a tall, coved ceiling in ivory. On the walls there are antique portraits of stern-faced men and women to keep a wary eye on the diners, doubtless to report them to the authorities—my mother, in this case—for any foul play before lunch, such as unauthorized snacks and other contraband.

We're not posh, certainly not aristocrat posh, but posh enough for it to be uncomfortable, despite my years of practice and the burden of expectations and more in the Renfrew family, who're down for a generous helping of tradition and then some. I've never had much time for tradition.

My phone buzzes in my pocket, and I sneak a peek. It's my older brother, Michael.

Sorry, won't be able to make it after all. Lawyering emergency for trial tomorrow. Please tell Mum and Dad?

Traitor, I text back with a frowning emoji.

There goes my ally in all of this. I could hardly declare a barista emergency where someone urgently needs me—and only me—to make custom premium macchiatos or gourmet sandwiches, post-haste. Though lurking in the café for another glimpse of a certain bohemian rocker wouldn't be a bad way to spend a Sunday afternoon.

Next time, I promise I'll be there, texts my brother. *Good luck.*

I sigh and lift my head.

"Is everything fine, Charles?" Great Aunt May asks. Though she's pushing eighty, she's got surprisingly good phone game and was a quick study when I taught her emojis and GIFs a few months ago on her new smartphone. She's sent me some howlers since.

"Michael won't be able to make it. Work."

"Such a pity," she tuts. "I will mail him a picture about my feelings."

A grin appears on my face, unusual in this room. I lean back in my chair, absently fidgeting with my tie. "I hope you do, Aunt May."

Behind Great Aunt May, at the end of the long room, a fresh Christmas tree beside the hearth is decorated like some sort of feature article in a traditional home magazine. Each ornament is perfectly styled to impress. Fresh boughs decorate the mantle. Ribbons and ribbons, pinned to the built-in bookshelves, of Christmas and seasonal greeting cards flank the hearth.

It does look nice if you're into that sort of thing. I'm not quite the target demographic. My nod to the season is hanging a candy cane from my desk light in my room back in Finsbury Park.

Earlier, I set out ten place settings for the guests to my mother's exacting instructions.

One of those guests is my cousin Delores. She's somewhere in her forties. Right now she's talking to my Great Aunt May about her spirited career in accountancy, which makes me want to weep. To be fair, Delores isn't having a great time either reliving her trauma of the past work week and stories of her tyrannical boss, so I don't think weeping is strictly off the table for anyone.

"And that's when the auditor stepped in." Delores pauses, as solemn as the portrait behind her. "We couldn't leave till midnight."

Great Aunt May gasps. I grimace in sympathy. That really does suck for Delores.

"Charles," my mother calls from the adjacent kitchen.

"Excuse me." I stand up, smoothing my shirt out of reflex.

No comments today on my appearance is a rare win.

Part of me is more than tempted to put a fork in my hand to get out of this since Michael bailed. One night, I swear I'll sneak in under the cover of darkness to paint the dining room oxblood red, or better yet, an over-the-top sunshine yellow, just to break the monotony of beige in here.

Charlie Renfrew, black sheep at your service.

I've done the rounds to be social, poured drinks, which the outrageously gendered roles in the Renfrew entertaining routine permits me to do. In fact, demands. I like getting to work in the kitchen, but my mother won't have it. Especially not on a Sunday when people are over.

"Hi." I slip into the kitchen, where my father is carving the roast. The only other authorized carver is Michael. "What can I do to help?"

My mother lifts her head. Her dark hair is perfectly coiffed, even with the cooking, and she wears a spotless apron. "Charles. Would you ask everyone what they would like to drink with dinner?" she asks.

"Everyone still has their drinks from before. Aunt May's had two G&Ts, dreaming of summer," I offer by way of explanation, but she's not having it. "And the food's not out yet, which is when I was planning to do the rounds again."

"Dinner's served in two minutes. Please make sure everyone's seated and do pour the wine. Did you ring Michael to see if he's stranded at the station? He's late. I wonder if I should hold lunch," she muses as she dresses a salad. "Maybe we should wait."

"He just texted. Lawyering emergency. Can't make it. Regrets and all of that."

She tuts like Great Aunt May. Clearly, the tut is genetic and passes down through the generations. I probably do it too.

"Lawyering emergency?" Mum asks finally.

"Yes. Coincidentally, I swear I have a barista emergency at the café..."

Which is about when I have an unbidden memory of yesterday's exchange at the café with Ben. And how hot he looked with that colorful striped scarf and bleached blond hair. He could probably wear rags and still look good, all angles and more charisma than what's healthy or tolerable when ordering a coffee.

A sigh of longing escapes me.

"Go pour," she says sternly, gesturing at the door with a wooden salad fork, bringing me back to the present, despite my best efforts to will myself elsewhere. "Everyone else is here?"

"Everyone else is here," I confirm with a nod, finally straightening. "Seated and ready for lunch."

The rest of the guests are family friends and a business associate of my father's. Laughter bubbles from the other room among the din of conversations. My parents both love dinner parties and they have it down to an art. Michael's enviable absence is muddling Mum a bit, and she's somewhat put out. But Michael's the good son, so he can get away with it.

Mum shakes her head at me. "And remove the setting for Michael."

"Will do," I call over my shoulder as I head back into the lion's den to follow her instructions. Wine's poured. Now, everyone has three drinks at the ready, including their water glasses, cocktails, and the freshly poured wine.

Showtime.

My father carries in the roast to the usual coos of satisfaction. Plates are passed to the left. Gravy is ladled. Everything is characteristically bland and I go wild with the pepper. Silently, I pass the pepper mill over to Delores, who follows suit.

Dinner conversation soon unavoidably and unfortunately turns to Christmas plans.

Mum looks at me. "You'll stay the week, won't you?"

I blink. "No. I mean, I have plans too."

"What plans?" She frowns.

"You know what plans. Remember? I've told you before. I'll come for Christmas Eve dinner, then I'll go to Wales to see Carys for Christmas Day. Then I've got work back in London."

"Charles. It's Christmas." Mum's dismayed. The thin line of my father's mouth tugs ever so slightly downward. He strokes his salt and pepper beard, perfectly groomed. "Christmas means family."

Inwardly, I sigh. Here we go. Outwardly, I hold my ground.

In therapy, I've gone through the importance of staying calm in these situations. "Yes. Which is why I'll see you and everyone here, then go to Wales."

"Charles, you can't do that—" Mum starts.

My face burns as I ball up my fists, the promise of a panic attack gripping my stomach.

One, two, three... I count.

"Of course I can do that. I'm going to do exactly that, Mum," I say flatly, even if I'm somewhat breathless. "Go to Wales for Christmas with Emily and Carys, who are also my family. Carys is my *daughter*. Nothing you say is going to change my plans."

"You can't."

"Watch me." I look at my mother, jaw set.

"You don't even have the decency to marry Emily and yet you call her your family." Mum sniffs her disapproval.

"I'm not in love with Emily. Plus, this isn't the 1950s. She's a good friend. And my family. And—"

"Don't tell me anything more, I don't want to hear it—"

"I'm gay, Mum. And attracted to men, for the record."

I can't believe we're having this fight. Again.

"You're just going through some selfish phase. Yet another of your self-destructive phases like you're having some perpetual tantrum and not thinking about us—"

"Let's talk about who's actually being selfish here—"

Mum's face turns red. My ears burn. Everyone stares at each other in awkward, paralyzed silence. Nothing like some casual homophobia at the table and denying Carys's existence to ruin another family gathering.

There's a clatter, and Great Aunt May cuts her off, the only one who can get away with that. "Oh no, I've dropped my cutlery. Charles, would you please get me another fork?"

Great Aunt May has no problems with dexterity. She's nimble, an athlete back in her day.

As I rise, she catches my gaze. She's slightly turned away from my parents. There's a hint of mischief in her pale eyes.

"Of course." Grateful, I bolt to the kitchen. Drawing a deep breath, I rake a hand through my hair, then grip the counter to do the breathing exercise that my therapist taught me.

Stay calm. Stay fucking calm.

That's not strictly part of the exercise. My stomach's in knots. I pull out my phone.

Nightmare, I text Michael. *Mum's pretending she hasn't heard me talking about going to Wales to see Carys. I hate Christmas so much.*

There's a surprisingly quick response.

Hang in there. Keep with your plans.

I don't think she'll ever accept Carys, I text back. My eyes sting for a moment before I will the tears away. Not here. My shoulders are tight.

I'm sorry. I hope she comes around one day too.

With a gulp, I slide the phone away and find a fork. One

piece of cutlery at a time, I'll get through the rest of Sunday lunch. When I bring Great Aunt May her fork, she pats my arm.

After cake, I make my round of goodbyes and retrieve my guitar from the study off the entry, where it was tucked away out of sight so it wouldn't offend anyone. I tug on my black leather lace-up boots, find my wool coat in the wardrobe, and wrap a generous gold scarf around my neck. With gloves on, I take the guitar and my bag with some uni reading and open the door.

No one comes to see me off.

In the gray mist, I walk the fifteen minutes to the station, pushing away the heaviness that Sundays usually bring when I come out to Richmond, like I'm trying to briskly outwalk the ghosts of my personal history.

I've got headphones on over my ears, playing some old tunes from The Stone Roses, and I feel freer. I tug up the lapels of my wool coat against the sting of the weather. Out here, December's late afternoon gloom hangs low. On the platform, I shiver, guitar in hand and backpack slung over my shoulder.

Once the train arrives, I huddle down in my seat. The air con's probably on, because that would be just my luck today. I spend about three minutes on my readings, too out of sorts to focus. Instead, I give Emily a quick call to check in and get a glimpse of Carys to cheer me up a little. If only they weren't so far away.

There's a moment when I think of Ben. I bet he doesn't have family drama like this. What does he do on Sundays?

Chapter Five

Next Saturday, after another week of final essays and exams and weird opening and split shifts, I'm admittedly on the lookout for Ben as I work.

It's silly, I know. He's provided great material for the occasional self-indulgent daydream because who doesn't like lusting after rock stars? Especially when they don't know they're being lusted after, which is really for the best.

Around London, I've seen posters for his band's gig last night. For a wild moment, I thought about going, but I decided in the end that might come across as too weird, even though he went to my gig. Plus, I can't afford the ticket right now, with Christmas coming up on top of everything. I've got rehearsal tonight for the third time this week anyway, which means less time to do all of the things that need doing.

Which is fine. I'm not on the market for dating in my self-imposed exile. I'm broke. I'm too busy. Besides, I'm no good with relationships, and I don't have time to get good at them. Not till I've finished my degree.

What would be the point of meeting him again other

than to give a spike in my libido? Even if I went to the gig, he wouldn't know I was there, and only in my wildest fantasies would Ben Campbell pick me out of a crowd and think to himself, *right, I'm having a big night out with some random barista.*

In fairness to me, I do make a mean latte. One worth remembering.

Plus, who says I could even get a ticket from a scalper? It was a sold-out gig. I couldn't keep myself from checking for tickets, despite the loud voice of reason. Why did I do that? I don't know.

Past me would have drunk to oblivion to not worry about it but current me has supposedly turned a page and, again, I can't afford to drink like that even if I wanted to.

Outside, it's sleeting sideways. There's the promise of snow today, and the Saturday shoppers stay warm for the moment in the shops, hunting for the perfect last-minute Christmas or Hannukah or other festive gift. Though they ought to be frightened by what flurries might do to London transport.

To be fair, there're a lot of times the tube or train schedules get messed up, even without snow. Hell, the wrong kind of leaves on the tracks and that's it—public transport becomes a distant memory, and everyone panics trying to get home on the last buses and tubes. But even with the threat of foul weather, right now the café has a lengthy queue to the door as people apparently want to warm up more than they want to go home.

I'm only in a partially tragic state for a Saturday morning with a tension headache. I may be running on adrenaline and biscuits, but I'm determined to prove to Jasmine that I can function like a pseudo-normal human. And, let's be entirely honest, in case Ben comes in again.

This week, I caught myself nearly an hour into a uni

lecture before I realized I hadn't taken in anything because I was too busy daydreaming about him, which was way more important than seeing what Heathcliff and Catherine got up to in reviewing my notes for the exam.

What's it like kissing a guy with a lip ring?

With a break in the rush, I speculate while I clear tables. Back and forth, back and forth. Bussing isn't my favorite thing, but someone has to do it. And sometimes I entertain myself by thinking of stories from my classes, the cost of studying literature, or song lyrics.

Inside the café, the windows are steamy with condensation from the warmth inside and the chill outside. The tables are mostly full at this point. Some are tourists traveling during the lead into Christmas, some are locals that I recognize. I gather colorful mismatched mugs and place them expertly on trays, ferrying them back for the others to load into the dishwasher.

Once the empty tables are clean, I neaten up the free magazines and flyers by the café entry, beneath an anemic string of Christmas lights from Poundland, and check out the community noticeboard for events. My band, The Screaming Pony, has a poster up to play another show after Christmas.

We've been practicing extra to make sure everything sounds as good as it can. It's a bigger gig than usual for us, and a lot's riding on us to not fuck it up. We're out of luck for extra rehearsal time, now with the Christmas break coming up. Some of my bandmates are scattering to go home to spend the holidays with family outside of London. While I fret over the lack of rehearsal time leading up to the gig, my wandering thoughts are pulled back hard into the present by a wallop of reality.

"I think you might be the boy with the thorn in his side," says a voice that's becoming familiar.

Lilting, even.

Startled, I turn. No reasonable person lobs a Smiths reference out of the blue. Of course it's him, because the universe isn't done toying with me yet.

"And you're this charming man?" I counter without missing a beat. "Settle the fuck down, Morrissey."

Ben laughs, slouchy gray hat over blue-streaked blond hair. This Saturday's jumper is a pale pink with a white rabbit appliquéd on the front. His long striped scarf is a million colors and looped over his leather jacket. It's stunning, like him.

I take a moment to absorb the sight of him. He's definitely the best thing I've seen this morning. This week. "Why'd you say that, anyway?"

"Call it another hunch."

"You saying I'm some kind of crank?"

"Nope. I'm saying nothing like that. Though you were frowning at the posters."

"I guess that happens sometimes."

He looks at the posters too, also taking in the one for The Screaming Pony. I could die of embarrassment.

This is your redemption arc, Charlie. Don't fuck it up. Pretend to be cool.

And if I can't be cool, I sure as hell can create a diversion.

"Huh. Well, then. What'd you lose this week?" I make a show of straightening flyers that don't need straightening, so I shuffle paper around rather uselessly. I'm focused on making the postcards line up perfectly straight to the edge of the ledge where they sit, deliberately not looking at him. As if by looking over and acknowledging his existence, he'll disappear in a puff of fanciful imagination, leaving me little to wank over later.

"I tried something different this time. Think I found something instead," he says lightly.

"Yeah? What's that?" I lift my head to peer curiously at

him.

"You'll need to come with me and see."

I blink. He's watching me, posture relaxed with his hands in his pockets. He looks dead serious. And, I might add, hot. He gives an enigmatic grin.

"What, now?" I ask. What's he on about? "I'm working."

"You must get breaks." He reaches out to adjust a flyer, too. Helpful and civic-minded, so that's a win for café banter.

"Usually," I concede, glancing around the café. Curiosity is getting the better of me.

Why is he even here talking to me? What on earth does he want me—me of all the people in London—to come and see? He could have his pick out of a million baristas.

Most of the tables are full—students at laptops, shoppers relaxing into their chairs, and other people catching up over a coffee and cake. "Depends on the state of the queue, actually. And if there's anyone around to cover."

He peers at me before looking over at the counter while I glance over at Jasmine where she's restocking pastries in the display.

No queue. Only one person waits to pick up drinks.

"I don't see a queue. Do you see a queue?" he asks.

"Well, no. Not exactly. But there could be a rush at any minute."

Which really is a pathetic cover because it's a lull right now.

Fine, then. I'll indulge this for just a moment. No harm done, right? I'll spare a minute to see what he's on about. And then I'll get back to work and the million other things I have to do.

"Right. Wait here a minute." Brusquely, I remove my apron.

He grins. Cat, canary, all of that. If I look carefully, there'll be feathers floating in the air.

I squish my apron into as small of a package as I can while I stride over toward Jasmine. Whatever bait this is, I'm apparently all in. My legs had started walking before my brain could catch up.

"Catch." I toss my balled-up apron in her vicinity.

She laughs at me. And catches easily. "Go, already. I'll cover for you if anyone asks."

"I'll return the favor sometime."

"He's cute," she whispers. "Good luck."

I roll my eyes. The last thing I need is an audience. The smile is tough to suppress, though.

It's a perfect morning for no managers.

I return to where he's waiting patiently, still by the community noticeboard, making an impressive show of thoroughly taking in the posters and pamphlets. He should be well up on North London events by now.

"Well, here I am. Now what?" I put my hands in my pockets.

"Good, good. Thought you might have lost your nerve. You're dragging your feet a wee bit, I think."

"What do you take me for?" I scoff. "I can't just walk out on my job. The people need me."

"I'm so glad you're a responsible employee."

"That's me. A model of modern responsibility."

It's not even a lie.

His laugh thrills me, and I shiver, and it's not because of the threat of a London snowpocalypse. The adrenaline-seeking part of me is in control, but this is harmless.

He'll show me something silly and nothing else will happen. And we'll go our separate ways and that'll be that.

"C'mon, then. Time's getting on. Especially if you're expecting a phantom queue."

"Now, now."

He leads the way outside, still looking rather pleased.

Outside, the sleet has officially changed over to snow, falling lazily in tufts, transforming the street. Traffic hisses on the wet road as it starts to stick on the pavement. I've come out only in my thin black pullover and jeans. I'm underdressed for the occasion.

The wind blows wet snowflakes direct from the Arctic onto the nape of my neck and ruffles Ben's fringe as he turns to face me in front of the café, a broad smile on his lips. I shiver.

For once, my brain draws a blank as I fully take stock of him. In the daylight, pale freckles cover his nose and cheeks, pink with cold. And he looks so genuinely pleased to have me come outside. He stretches his arms out in the falling snow.

Yeah, he's definitely hot.

Even a cynic like me can see the beauty in this rare London snowfall, this moment before it turns to grime in gutters. Right now, there's an unusual charm in Soho, muffling the city. But all of it pales in comparison to him, and he's glorious. Something sexy and playful.

"Thought you might need to see this."

"You might be right," I concede.

"Naturally." He grins, looks up at the sky, then at me. He sticks out his tongue to catch a snowflake.

"Naturally," I echo, flushing at the sight of him.

I can imagine a thing or two he could do with that tongue.

He unwinds his colorful scarf and puts it around my neck, pulling me close. The wool is soft, though damp. The shock of the chill of snowflakes melting on the nape of my neck, of his closeness, gives me an uncontrollable shiver.

I stare intently at him. His body radiates waves of heat. There's that inferno Dante promised. Hell will be so much more fun than my hectic schedule.

"Kiss me," he orders with a grin.

"God, you're demanding. Make me leave my work, come

outside, now a kiss. What's next?"

"Well, that's up to you, isn't it?" he says teasingly. "I can't wait to find out, personally."

"Oh yeah? What makes you think there's something more?"

"Oh, you know. This and that."

"Is that right?"

"Yes."

I shiver, a combo of cold and lust. His gaze is unwavering. I can't look away either.

And of course I kiss him, because, fuck, I've been wanting to do that since he first turned up three weeks ago. His lips are hot and soft and delicious, far better than my daydreams in lectures or anywhere else.

I'm kissing him because I want the kiss as much as he does, and I'm kissing him not because he's the singer from an up-and-coming band, but because—well, because of the way he looks at me. On the basis of what exactly, I don't know. And this can't lead to anything else, but an impulsive stolen kiss, his mouth against mine, is a Christmas gift come early that I'll take. His mouth tastes of mint and snowflakes, too.

God. Help me.

"I might need another. Since you got me out here," I manage, reeling.

"Mmm, good idea. Need to make sure that first one was real, and I didn't imagine it."

Is he feeling this too? He must be feeling this chemistry. It can't be all in my head.

Stop thinking.

I indulge in another long kiss, because he started this, and, well, I'm greedy and short on kisses. Everything falls away, the sleet, the road noise, even the cold does little to cool the heat rising between us. He's radiating warmth, my fingers catching his.

We lift our heads after who knows how long.

Blood rushes in my ears, the cold forgotten because we're sparking some sort of fire between us out here on some random London street. Then we kiss yet again, hungry for more, our bodies responding to each other.

One kiss. Two kisses. Three.

My heart careens like a wild thing in the cage of my chest, beating so fast that at any moment I could grow wings and take flight. His fingers move to my biceps, the warmth of his hands encircling me, gently at first, then more firmly. Like the burn of his hands will leave a permanent tattoo through my too-thin clothes.

"Wanna hear something outrageous?" he asks. His eyes dance.

"I live for outrageous."

"I need you inside me. Like, five minutes ago." He's nonchalant, teasing.

My eyebrows climb at that. "Is that so? A bit forward, Morrissey."

"Afraid so."

I'm not the sort to turn away from a chance sexual encounter, in full disclosure. But there are rules. Parameters. Like it being Friday night, say, rather than being propositioned in the middle of a Saturday morning shift at the café.

The prospect thrills me. A shiver runs up my spine.

Right. A hookup tonight. I can do that? I can do that. Something to look forward to later before rehearsal. Or after. Or...

I'll worry about that later. I've got Ben in front of me, right here, right now. That's what matters.

Chapter Six

Naturally, I've been hard for about five minutes. Which feels like a lifetime.

The arsehole probably noticed when I kissed him. God, even slightly rumpled he's looking more tempting than ever, and he's got on that grin like he's already seen me naked. What exactly does he fantasize about, anyway?

It's time to take charge of the situation.

"Well, I only have five minutes and four hours to go till the end of my shift. Not that I'm counting down or anything." I grip his arse. Firm.

More kisses follow, eager as our mouths seek each other.

"That's a terribly long time to wait," he laments, teasing me. "Like, five minutes and four hours too long."

"Yeah, agreed. Totally unreasonable."

"Mmm. We better do something about that, then."

"Great idea."

The burn of his lips remains rough on mine when we lift our heads and dare to look at each other, two strangers kissing in a snowy street. It's like the taste of him feeds something

I'm dying for, something impulsive and wild. Something that's well outside of the usual *uni-work-Carys-band* routine, a challenge I don't want to ignore even though it's well past Friday night, past the window for fun.

"Let's start with the five-minute option to fuck, then. It's festive. To welcome the new year and all that." His blue eyes are bright with mischief.

Festive? I can pretend to be festive if that gets me laid.

"I bet you say that to all the baristas."

He flashes that grin that does me in. "You're the only one, actually."

"I'm impressed."

"And I'm intrigued."

Time is counting down—time that can't be wasted. Jasmine can only provide cover for so long. But I'm having way too much fun, so why not.

I take his hand, our grip tight as I lead him to the back of the café and unlock the door. I flip on the lights. All the better to take in the glorious sight of him. We head into the crowded stockroom full of boxes and shipping pallets, shelves brimming with equipment, and bags of coffee cups. The thundering inside me has returned in full force. As he looks around, I take a moment to slowly draw in a deep breath to steady myself. His hand is warm in mine. My fingers tighten, and he does the same in response. There's something about that small gesture that makes me dizzy.

Our gazes meet.

"I'm gonna ride you till you come over your boots," I tell him, rubbing against him, skimming his mohair sweater with my fingers, the softest thing. In here, like this, he seems a lot less celebrity and a lot more real. And warm. "So get ready."

Ben unfastens my belt, giving me a level look. The buckle rattles a sharp metallic sound in the quiet of the stockroom. "You terrible man, Charlie Renfrew. I know who you are."

"You don't know the half of it, I'm afraid."

His hand is already inside my trousers, fingers teasing a path down to my cock, which is caught up in the cotton of my boxers, more than ready. He's terribly distracting, and I gasp at the thrill of his fingers. All my questions will be rather shit from this point out.

"Your gig, by the way, was brilliant. You're wicked on guitar." He smiles as his fingertips trace the length of me, then tease my balls. I desperately suck back air. There's no oxygen in this room for a comeback. "Those fingers aren't just for slinging lattes. And you're fucking hilarious."

"Bloody hell." I press my cock hard into his hand. He holds me firmly. I thrust.

"Never underestimate someone who pays in cash." His gaze is unrelenting. God, he's glorious. The dark streaks through blond hair a tangle of shadow and light. The angles of his face. The distracting fullness of his lips as he licks them. "Believe me."

"Suck," I command, gripping his wrists.

He goes to his knees and then I'm in his mouth—deeper and deeper—until I gasp, his tongue merciless against the urgency of my cock. An unrelenting heat blazes from the promise of his mouth, far better than any of my daydreams since that day he first appeared at the café.

I push. He yields.

Clutching his hair, I shut my eyes to give myself over to his mouth while his hand continues its rhythm at the base of my cock.

When I can't take this fantastic teasing anymore, I haul him up. We both hurry to unfasten his jeans, awkward in our lust as we shove down boxers to our knees. Clumsy fingers brush against each other.

He rubs his bare arse against me. "What do you think about me?"

"That's easy. The hottest guy I've seen. And on guitar too," I gasp. "Halfpenny Rise is fantastic."

He laughs, pleased, pressing against me as he bends into the chaos on the table.

I'm fumbling for my wallet—praying I haven't lost it—and find a lubricated condom and Ben's continuing to tease me and somehow I get the damn thing on—and then I press one finger into him and another.

"Oh fuck, please," Ben begs.

"You want me?" I taunt him, my fingers relentless.

"Fuck—Charlie—"

"You gotta fucking wait."

So I tease him, because I can, and in response he presses back against me, because he can do that, too. It's intoxicating, fucking Ben, a high worth chasing, a high that bucks and cries out in my arms. He's lithe against me, responsive and electric. My other hand works his cock till he seeps with pre-cum, and then I slide gradually inside him, then all in, and soon enough I'm fucking him incoherent. Pure heaven.

As he shudders and gasps for more, I squeeze my eyes closed, gripping him firmly. His breath is my breath.

"Ohh—harder—" Ben begs. His body spasms in response. God, I could come right now. Gritting my teeth, I groan as he takes me inside over and over.

My fingers are a vice on Ben's skinny hips. I'm thrusting against him pressed over the table as bags of coffee jostle and dance and fall. His skin burns against mine like a summer sunset, or maybe this is what a supernova feels like.

Coffee beans spill everywhere. They clatter and bounce off in a million directions. As we try to keep our footing, we step on the coffee beans and it smells like French roast and Ben, an intoxicating custom blend.

The wire shelf against the table rattles rhythmically, metal jangling with the beat of us, animalistic and raw.

We're gasping and I clutch his hair and he sobs out. God, this would be a terrible time to get caught.

I stuff a hand against his mouth to stifle his cries.

"Too fucking noisy," I grunt against his ear. He nips at my fingers in response. It only urges me on.

And we're locked together while I work the length of him while I ride. My clothes are suffocating, my skin damp with perspiration. Beneath me, he writhes and moans, the quickening of his breaths more ragged and more desperate. And the more incoherent he is, the more I want to make him come, to feel as alive as I feel right now as we blur together, like this is a thousand Friday nights rolled up together in one, and I can do anything, be anyone. Like I've stolen a page from someone else's life.

Ben convulses back against me, thudding against the table. As he calls my name, I smother it against his lips, his breath hot in my hand, and oh the ecstasy of this moment— and hell, that's about when he comes impressively over his black leather boots. And his jeans, and the floor, and the table, too.

About then, it's all too much for me. My arms are wrapped around Ben, frantically pulling him upright. A raw cry escapes him, urging me over the edge at last, and I come in a blind rhythmic heat.

There's nothing but him and me, no café, nothing else, and I chase that moment as long as I can, gasping out nonsense against the nape of his neck as his chest heaves under the wrap of my arms. His skin is hot against my lips.

My eruption at least has the decency to be contained and he feels incredible. I don't want to break this moment. Instead, it would be better to live right here in this moment. I close my eyes.

Blood rushes in my ears and I hold on to him while I reel, still rocking slightly, the thrill of him so close. His cologne or shampoo smells of cedar and mystery.

"That's five minutes, I think," Ben drawls, biting my wrist, the slight pain bringing me back. With reluctance I at last open my eyes, letting reality slide in once again. Sacks of coffee, a stack of pallets, and a shelf overflowing with takeaway containers of different sizes surround us. Overhead, the lights flicker and hum. Cold starts to register against my skin, a shock compared to the warmth of Ben.

He stands in the midst of all the stockroom chaos, a brilliant sight, all mussed-up hair and rumpled clothes.

"I think... I think we might need to do that again later. Once you lick up this mess you made," I declare, and find a tissue. We attempt to neaten up. I deal with the condom. After some quick effort, we look almost normal.

He's flushed and grins. "Good. 'Cause I like cream with my coffee."

"You can count on that," I assure him breathlessly, watching him in frank admiration. "Ready to get out of here?"

"Yup." Ben meets my gaze as he adjusts his cloud soft pullover. "Done. Till you next provide, that is."

"If there's anything you can count on me to provide, it's cream with your coffee."

"Probably not a good time to tell you I'm more of a tea-drinker," he says.

"Probably not."

"Still need cream, though."

"Point taken," I say. "Fuck, that was hot."

I catch his jaw, a hint of stubble pleasingly rough beneath my fingers, and thrill as he leans into me, closing his eyes. His mouth melts against mine, still tasting of mint, his hands hot in the small of my back under my shirt. Having Ben so close makes it all too tempting to start all over again. Goose bumps cover my skin. Judging by the shiver that runs through his body as I hold him, he's also caught up in the daze of our lust. I'm still trying to catch my breath.

"What time are you off?" he asks, tilting his head.

"Oh, I'd say about two minutes ago, but officially three o'clock."

Ben straightens and I grasp his arse through his jeans. "How about you come meet me outside of our studio later? It's just around the corner. We'll be done by then." He gives me the address.

There's a split second of hesitation, but only for a split second. There was something I was supposed to do later, but it can't be important. It's not for hours, anyway.

Five minutes of sex only gets a man so far. And after that, it would be ridiculous to not have a follow-up, right? Then we'll get that lust out of our systems and get on with things as usual.

"Can't wait." Reluctantly, I let him go.

The end of the day can't come quickly enough. Somehow, I drag myself back to the café, entirely distracted through the rest of my shift. And Ben disappears off to do mysterious Ben things until we meet.

If he turns up.

Best not get my hopes up about that, at any rate. I don't exactly have a great track record with guys turning up, even for hookups. Besides, it's just one night. Nothing more, even if he does show up. That's the rule. He doesn't need to know anything else about me.

Chapter Seven

When 3:00 p.m. arrives, I have a not-so-small panic as I hang my apron in the stockroom where Ben and I had our tryst just a few short hours ago—a stockroom it took me a good hour to completely clean afterward. What if I'd imagined the whole thing? A hallucination from sex deprivation and far too many lattes? What if it's a side effect from flocks of owlish hipsters with oversize glasses wanting special variations on their achingly affected orders, trying to outdo each other and do in a barista's head?

What's wrong with me? It's nothing more than lust. That's it—a lust-related altered state of reality.

As I stretch my arms overhead, my lower back aches from the relentless way I'd done Ben—or my hallucination earlier. The cascade of coffee beans that had spilled across the table and the stockroom floor provided proof as I'd cleaned it all up that I hadn't imagined the whole thing. At least, the manifestation of my hallucination was messy. God, the mess. Fucking heaven. Remembering that will get me through some cold winter nights.

No wonder I don't get laid nearly often enough. Too much thinking.

But never mind all that—what's important is figuring out what's happened to Ben. Because odds are he was real. And I could do with more sex. I need to get going in case he arrives and doesn't see me and then thinks I stood him up. What sort of arsehole would I be if he thought that?

No guarantee he'll turn up again next Saturday, Charlie. Christmas is coming and everyone will be out of their routine. Including and especially you. Hurry up. Limited-time offer.

After grabbing my coat hanging from the corner of a metal wire shelf holding boxes of supplies, I hurry out the side door, crunching through the snow-covered alley to the pavement in front of the café. It's precisely 3:02 p.m. when I leave. I tug on my coat as the brisk wind cuts through my clothes. It's a short walk to Ben's studio, but I'm already late.

God, I better not be too late. I should have left early, had Jasmine cover.

There're too many people around to run through the crowd or to easily spot Ben. The narrow street where Ben's studio is heaves with a pestilence of shoppers seeking bargains. Outside the studio, I stop short. I check my phone for the address, check the buildings. I'm in the right place. This has to be it.

But there's a problem.

He's not here.

Shit. Oh shit. I *am* too late. It's 3:05 p.m.

Chewing my lip, I stare futilely at my phone, as if through sheer force of will I could set the clock back to 3:00 p.m. I wouldn't be late, standing alone out here.

Before I have time to launch into a full-scale panic, I remind myself that even if I had Ben's number, there's no guarantee that he hasn't lost his phone again in the last few hours, given his track record. I try to make myself breathe.

My chest feels tight. Like I'm being smothered. I look left and right and oh God, he's left already—

But that thought's cut short with a tap on my shoulder.

I spin, breath stuck in my throat.

Ben stands there on the worn concrete step outside of the studio door, looking terribly amused, like he knows perfectly well how he gets to me.

He reaches out to brush snow from my hair. "Hi."

"I was worried you thought I'd stood you up," I blurt, too worked up for witty banter. There's no wits left to rub together, just jumbled-up nerves and angst, and the few remnants of my former social skills.

Breathe.

Snowflakes drift down to land on his striped wool hat, melting as soon as they land. His eyes dance. "Had the same thought," Ben says. "I was a little bit late getting out. Probably got here around 3:04, I'd guess. The commute was fierce."

"Comedian."

"You don't even know the half of it," Ben says. "I once thought about doing a stand-up routine, but I don't have the chops or the thick skin for comedy. I've got the late nights down, though. I'll stick to gigs."

"Fuck, I hope so. Your fans—never mind your bandmates—would be devastated if you didn't turn up," I quip back, stuffing my hands into my pockets to retrieve my gloves for London's chill. Probably should have done that sooner. "Never mind all the ticket refunds and bitter reviews online. You'll be panned on social media."

Ben laughs, then leans in, sea-blue eyes dancing. "But tell me this: would you have been devastated if I hadn't turned up, Charlie?"

"Um…" My face warms, which I hope is enough of an answer for him. How embarrassing. I haven't reacted like this over someone in ages. Years, in fact.

He reaches out a hand, catches my jaw, and moves closer, his lips a fraction away from mine. And in that moment, everything but him and me falls away. I don't think I'm breathing, but I close that electric distance as the hair on my arms stands up at the thrill of him.

We kiss.

His mouth is soft, far better than any brioche that I've tasted.

I suck on his bottom lip. He makes a sort of feral sound, shudders in my arms. I'm not sure if it's a gasp or a groan or something entirely otherworldly, but he's just as caught up as I am. His fingers dig into my wrist. I press against him, close enough to smell his cologne, and quite possibly a hint of crushed coffee beans from the stockroom, but that might well be my overactive imagination.

I catch his jaw to kiss him more deeply, the thin leather of my gloves pressing against the radiating heat of his skin. Ben responds just as hungrily, teasing me right back, his lips brushing mine.

Right now, there's no street. No London. No shoppers weaving around us as the snow falls. Just us, and the rise of our breath cold enough to see when we finally pull away.

Eventually, I come back to my senses, dazed. I look at Ben, who's flushed under his freckles.

"I'll take that as a yes," he whispers.

"Arsehole," I murmur back affectionately. This man. He's playing with me. Fine. Two can play, right? For the sake of the evening's entertainment. "And you? Would you have been devastated if I hadn't turned up?"

"Absolutely," Ben says without a moment of hesitation, dead serious. He runs a hand through his blond hair, his knitted wool hat in his other hand.

I shiver. He's gone and done something funny to my insides. I don't know what that is exactly, if it's the first siren song of a new addiction far stronger than caffeine, a new sort of high that comes from tasting him, of thinking back to our earlier break in the stockroom. He's something else. Euphoria courses through me, both terrifying and thrilling. It's not a comfortable feeling, like I'm outside my skin and raw and—

Just fucking stop.

One night. That's it.

Someone brushes past me, and I realize we're standing in the way of the stream of shoppers moving past us and someone trying to get into the studio.

"Rehearsal was all right?"

"Yep," Ben says. "Getting ready for our next tour soon. After the holidays."

See, there you go. Reality and real life.

And then we're off in a snow-covered London. Ben takes my hand. Startled, my instinct is to pull away, but he smiles, and I let out an unsteady breath.

Snowflakes drift down, stilling the hum of the vast city's frenetic heartbeat, quieting things down even at this time of day. The snowfall is fresh and bright, too soon to be browned by traffic and smog. Right now, it's magic, and maybe it's the snowfall that's brought Ben to me. Or maybe Ben brought me the snow. Whatever it is, this combination is intoxicating.

And then an alarming thought sinks in: I just hope when the snow melts, it won't take Ben with it.

• • •

Soho is bustling.

Which is a fair point most of the time, it being small but mighty and packed with history. Add snow, and it's more chaotic than usual. Traffic still snakes by, but enough snow's falling now that it's starting to officially alarm the commuters who are alarmed enough in the first place, and there's a fraction less traffic than usual as people start home to escape the snow. Give it another hour with snow falling like this, and traffic will come to a standstill. I can only imagine what it's doing to the tube and trains, but Ben and I are on foot. It's the only plan we have so far. It's the only plan I'm capable of.

We're walking. Holding on to his hand has kept me tethered to the earth. Otherwise, I'd probably drift up somewhere into the clouds, past the smog and pigeons and airplanes. I'd float high over London, looking down, and if I was up there with Ben, I'd be a happy man indeed. Like this, there are no troubles to deal with or problems to face. A brilliant distraction, even if it's temporary. Especially because it's temporary.

My hangover's now a distant memory, probably also helped by the fact I drank a couple of liters of water after getting back from our stockroom tryst. Jasmine made me eat something solid—soup and a sarnie, she'd said, to keep up my strength. Her grin had been big enough as though she'd been the one getting laid. Clearly, she'd known what we'd gotten up to. I pray she hadn't heard us. Well, even if she had, I'm not sorry. Ben is far too hot to be sorry about.

Just one night.

He squeezes my hand and I come back to reality as we walk.

"Where are we going?" I ask, coming out of my daze.

"Small detour to Denmark Street," says Ben. "I need strings."

We pause on the corner by Soho Square Gardens, a small green patch in the heart of Soho overlooked by buildings. People move around us like water around a boulder in a stream. We keep moving, just enough to stand next to a black wrought-iron fence marking the entry to the square. A broad area marked with pavers and dotted with snow-covered benches is inside the park gate. Beyond that is an expanse of trim lawn. In the summer, people bask and hang out here. Now, in the snow, no one lingers but us. The sensible aren't sticking around.

Ben kisses me then and I groan softly, all too eager to respond in kind. My body reacts quicker than my mind, left at least three minutes behind.

And my cock's already stirring, though this really is no place to carry on and get arrested for public indecency. We're both greedy for kisses though, and I catch his wrists in their leather cuffs. Usually, I'm not one for public displays, especially out on the street, because who knows who's watching, and even though two men kissing shouldn't be an issue, unfortunately to some people it still is. But it's the middle of the afternoon on a busy street and no one is paying us any attention when we straighten.

"Strings?" I ask.

"Strings," Ben confirms. "For my guitar. I used my last set after the gig last night. Broke the E."

"It happens to the best of us," I say. "Nothing else broken, I hope. From last night or...earlier."

Ben laughs, shaking his head. "No, mate. My arse is just fine. More than fine."

My face warms and I grin—grin!—foolishly at him. "Excellent news."

How appalling. I'm practically giddy. Most unbecoming.

He steals another quick kiss and then tugs my hand. "C'mon."

We make our way up Denmark Street, a haven of guitar shops and music and kit that fills any musician's heart with joy. Denmark Street is a true holiday year-round as far as I'm concerned, an escape from the rest of chaotic London. It's early, but already the afternoon light has begun to fade.

"I've got to admit I'm a bit nervous being here with you,"

I say. Maybe it's a funny thing to admit to someone whom I'd been screwing relentlessly a few hours ago, but still.

The reality of this is starting to sink in: *Ben fucking Campbell.*

All right, so he's not like David Bowie or Alex Turner or anybody like that. But for the indie rock scene, Ben Campbell and Halfpenny Rise are a big deal. As for me, I have mates and we jam weekly in a rehearsal space using stolen time carved from my schedule, because it's the only thing I've got going these days. I dream of touring one day, but Halfpenny Rise has an album out and have toured the UK. Meanwhile, we're trying to save up for a proper demo.

"People come to Denmark Street all the time." He grins. "Nothing unusual about that."

"I think it's the *you* part that's the new element."

He pauses, looking uncharacteristically uncertain. "Is that a problem?"

"Oh no. No. It's great, believe me. I just can't get over it that I'm here with you. And earlier. And all of it," I say, shaking my head. "This sort of thing happens to other people and not me. You…you're like some sort of high."

Ben laughs, obviously thrilled. He squeezes my hand again. "You're not so bad yourself, Charlie."

"God, how embarrassing. That was far too earnest. I have a surly reputation to maintain. People will talk."

"Aye? Why the surly reputation?" he asks curiously in his soft lilt, reaching out to adjust my scarf. It's a genuine question, and he's gazing at me in a way that I know I have his full attention. When was the last time someone looked at me—really looked at me—like that?

"Part of my sunny disposition?" I ask.

"Go on. I won't judge, believe me. I'm far from perfect, too."

I shrug. My natural prickliness is a survival skill, I've

been told. For reasons, of course. But I'm not going to get into them with someone I'm just seeing once. Listening to my life is terribly dull and uninspiring. It's time better spent doing other things that actually matter—like Ben.

"Oh, I don't know. Just a lot on. Uni and work and my band. And...other things. Probably not things for a...a drink, or whatever we're doing."

"Mmm, a date after the first hookup. I love it."

"We're probably going about this all wrong. I mean, sex is one thing, and a date is quite another." I shudder with alarm at the thought of a date, even with Ben. Dates are guaranteed disasters. I definitely don't have time, even if he actually wanted to go on a date with me. There's my family and the band and uni, never mind work. I mean, I have Carys to care for as my top priority. There's no time for me or what I might want. Maybe one day there'll be time for want.

And yet he's so very tempting.

"I'd love to go on a date together," Ben says with a drawl, eyes dancing. "And learn about you."

"Shit. Already? Let me keep my illusions a little longer. Please." *A date. I can't do a date.* "What if we call it a drink?"

"We can call it a drink." He laughs. "Well, I *did* come by weekly to see you at the café because I was curious. You're hot, and talented, and I want to know more. Is that so hard to believe?"

"It is when it's me." I glance away. He doesn't know the first thing about me or my mistakes that I'm trying to make up for.

"Ah, c'mon. Don't sell yourself short," Ben says, squeezing my hand, looking seriously at me. "Life's hard enough as is with people wanting to do that for you. Last thing you need is to be hard on yourself, too."

"Well...old habit." What to say that doesn't sound completely ridiculous? "You know, that life thing's intense sometimes."

Understatement, Charlie. Seriously.

"Oh, I know about that. Well, think on it and let's go into the shop and I'll get some strings and then you can tell me where you'd like to go next. How's that sound?"

"It sounds great," I admit with a smile.

We go in. Soon, Ben's browsing strings and chatting away to the man behind the counter. I take the opportunity to absorb the sight of him instead of the music gear that would ordinarily hold my attention. New priorities today.

Ben's bundled in colors from his woolly hat to his striped scarf over his black leather jacket. He has an easy energy, magnetic, falling into conversation with strangers like it's the most natural thing in the world. They're laughing and I'm smiling as I watch him. Maybe he's flirting, but I think that's just the way he is: open. It's a remarkable thing.

How does someone move through the world with such ease? Like there's nothing to lose? I'm desperate to hold on to this moment before he inevitably disappears, because it's too impossible to dare dream that this is anything more than a fantasy, some kind of extra Friday night manifestation due to a warp in time and space somewhere. Because gorgeous, funny men don't happen into my life. It's too dangerous to hope for more, even with our obvious chemistry. But it's even scarier to think this isn't a dream, but my actual life, and now Ben's the new wildcard.

After Ben buys his guitar strings, he turns to me. "Wanna go for a drink?"

"A drink?" I ask, as if I've never been asked for a drink before. It's taking a long moment to grasp the idea that Ben Campbell wants to spend more time with me. I glance at my watch, memory flooding back: I've got rehearsal later. But… we've been practicing for ages. And frankly, there will be more rehearsals, but only one afternoon with Ben.

"Hold that thought." I text Briar that I can't make it as he watches me curiously, and I smile. "Yeah. I'm up for a drink. Let's go."

Chapter Eight

After another stomp through the snow, we end up at the Crobar in the late afternoon. It's a tiny hole-in-the-wall rock club in Soho famed for its metal music. All kinds of acts have played here, from tiny upstarts to festival headliners. Though neither of us is a metalhead, there's a lot of technical finesse in heavy metal with its roots in jazz. We're both more of the rocker sort, with Ben definitely having far more chops. I'm casual, jamming with other uni students and the occasional gig—he's the real thing, a true showman. He's got a couple of albums and tours under his belt. The blues influence with his guitar-playing's obvious, and God, his fabulous voice. There's little wonder why his band has already been successful.

The last few hours have been surreal, like I've woken up in someone else's life. There hasn't been time to take stock. Not really. But I'm enjoying the impromptu holiday from the usual. Even if it's a Saturday. I'll catch up on everything else tomorrow, including mundane things like laundry and readings, though uni's now just out for the Christmas break. Meanwhile, curiosity's got me in its grip. I've already established he's more than hot. He's intriguing. And he must be feeling the same, because he's here with me and didn't stand me up after the stockroom tryst. Which was more than hot. But he's funny too, and talented, and I can't help but wonder what pints with Ben Campbell might be like.

We're snug in the dark cavern of the bar, which is moodily black and sticky in the day as we work on our pints, second round in. The lights are low. Framed memorabilia hang on the walls, spotlit like the bar. Others have sought refuge here from the snow and from shopping, and maybe transport's stranding people and maybe it isn't. I'm enjoying not knowing and our shared suspension of reality. It's cozy in here, even if it's too early for the evening's usual live music.

Ben and I have had just enough to drink to take the edge off, and we've started rounds of questions, like a speed date, or something equally ridiculous. Like I know anything about dating, other than I have a ban on the damn thing.

These are just ordinary, run of the mill questions. Nothing to get fussed about. It doesn't mean anything. We're just passing the time.

"Since we didn't meet online, I have no vital stats on you." Ben leans toward me, ever so slightly. His pint is between his hands. "No intel. Though you've given me more info than Grindr. I already know firsthand that you're top shelf."

I laugh, heat rising in my face. "Well, cheers for that. Spoiler alert: I'm not on social media. You can't stalk me online to find my secrets."

"What?" He clutches at his chest in shock, grinning. "Be still my beating heart. You're not on social media? What century are you from?" He leans in even more, arms on the table, hand on his drink. "I've heard about people like you. Tell me everything."

"I don't need internet voyeurs picking through my digital garbage." I shrug a shoulder. "Who wants that?"

"Well, I was rather looking forward to rummaging through your virtual bins, Charlie. I'm just going to have to work harder, that's all. Now tonight I'll have to do something else. Like…"

"You're simply gonna have to ask, I'm afraid. And I may give you answers. Or I'll give you such a pack of lies you'll be marveling about it into next year. That's a promise."

Ben laughs with delight. I do my best impression of being calm, collected, and cool, though in fact I'm not one of those things. Michael's told me I have a great poker face, which is my usual uniform for getting through most family things, and convenient for other situations.

"Are you in the witness relocation program?" Ben's scarf hangs loose around his neck as he pulls the ends off from the table where it had been dangerously close to absorbing his pint. "Diplomat's son?"

"No and no. Keep going."

"You're a world-famous criminal?" he asks. "Since you seem to know so much about them."

"Nope."

"You're world-famous for something brilliant?"

"Nope again. I'm just a uni student. But I *am* keeping score that you thought I was a criminal before you thought me brilliant," I say smoothly, smiling before I work on my ale. It's delicious, but not as delicious as the sight of him. Even a cynic like me has eyes. "I'll help you out a little. I'm not online for the simple reason I'm private. I mean, I'm not a total Luddite. I have email. And a phone. But you could always impress me and write a letter. Longhand and in cursive."

Ben laughs and gives me an unexpectedly disappointed look. "I probably won't be able to quite manage a letter, but if you texted me your address, one day I could probably send you something fabulous in the post. To make up for my faux pas in assuming you've turned to a life of crime. That's my area."

My eyebrows lift. "Only digital communication for you?"

Ben shakes his blond head, fringe falling into his eyes as he brushes it away. He chuckles. "No, no. It's not about format, though predictive text can help. I'm dyslexic."

"Oh! Sorry," I say. "I didn't mean to make things awkward."

"Not at all." Ben shrugs. "It's nothing new to me and you didn't know. I find ways to work around it, but I'm horrible at letters and numbers and things. But I'm all right with images and sounds. I learned to play guitar by ear before I got lessons. And I have a devil of a time trying to read music, even guitar tabs. So I don't. I just practice and remember. Music was my escape."

"Wow." I let this all sink in. How does one navigate daily life with dyslexia? Like uni or work or anything like that? How many daily things require reading something or other? I don't want to pry, because I feel like I'd unintentionally stuck my foot in it somewhat with teasing him about social media and letters, so I ease off. "That must be tough."

"Sometimes." Ben gives a quick smile, enough to warm me from the inside out. "I've had a few epic disasters, it's true. And I was bullied in school for it because I couldn't keep up. Because I was different. But we all have our things, don't we?"

"I suppose that's true." It's hard to imagine anyone bullying Ben. He's self-assured, friendly, adventurous. He's been successful with Halfpenny Rise, an underground idol for indie musicians to aspire to. But I suppose he's a person, just like the rest of us. And not just someone to lust after. "Kids can be proper arseholes."

He laughs. "Aye. They can be. And my family helped me a lot when I was younger, through school and homework and everything else that came after. I couldn't do what I've done without my mum's help."

For a moment, I fall quiet. Even with that little hint of his private life, I can't help but feel a moment of envy for his having a supportive family. I wipe my palms against my jeans under the table. "That sounds brilliant."

"I've been lucky. My mum's amazing."

Around us, the murmur of the dark bar provides comfort. The low light makes it easier to feel safe. And with Ben, it's a lot easier to talk to him, even as a total stranger, compared to my friends. He's leaning in, listening carefully.

"It must be nice to have your family on your side," I admit. "I'm the outsider, if I'm honest. I mean, even as a kid they sent me away to school. Till I got kicked out of them for being an arse, and then I did day school."

And I've said too much. I don't talk to anyone about my family except Emily, who's a brilliant listener. Why am I telling him about my family? I'm notoriously private.

Shit. Oversharing, Charlie. Too much. Definitely too much.

But Ben's expression softens. He takes my hand across the table. I let him. The squeeze of his fingers wrapped around mine gives me a visceral thrill. Even with feeling raw in front of him. "You can tell me about that, if you want."

Drawing in a breath, I look at him, then away. The man behind the backlit bar, which has an impressive wall of spirits, works to neaten up before the evening crowd, lost in a deep clean. He methodically puts glasses away after wiping down the shelf and straightens bottles into a tidy line.

Well, he did ask.

"I know I'm lucky about some things, but my parents have never seen eye to eye with me. And I can't entirely blame them," I confess, glancing at him. "I'm not always easy to be around. I'm now trying to make up for all of my past mistakes, so I study full-time and work full-time, and I have my band too."

I can't bring up my daughter. Not over pints to a stranger, even if I've told him about my family of origin. My real family are Carys and Emily. And Michael. But it's too soon to let him know about all of that, about the people who matter more than anyone else in the world, and the past. After all, it's supposed to be a fun round of drinks. Yet somehow things got more serious. I'm not sure how that happened.

"I've had troubles with my family, a long time ago. And I feel guilty for leaving my mum alone back home." Ben chews his lip, considering me. "But that sounds tough to live with. If your family's not in your court." He squeezes my hand. "I think you're brilliant to be around, Charlie. You're funny and confident. So clever, with your uni and talk about writing letters. I could never do all of that and work too. God, sometimes I get so nervous in daily life because I think everyone's far more clever than I am. And you work so hard. I can see that even at the café the times I've been in. You're never standing around, waiting to be told what to do. You're getting things done. It takes me ages to do anything useful with reading or writing."

I gulp and squeeze his hand back, running my thumb over the calluses of his fingertips from playing the guitar. Did he really say those things about me? "I'm not actually confident, it's fake. Believe me. Inside my head's a mess. And I work because I have a lot of obligations."

He laughs with delight. "Ach, only a confident man would take me into the stockroom and have a session like that. And I can't see inside your head. Just the outside bits. Which are fab to look at, by the way. I just know whatever you tell me."

"Did you miss the rest about me continually making myself an arse in front of you?"

"I think you're amazing."

I shift, focusing on my pint for a moment to center

myself. Perhaps a slight shift in conversation is in order, to safer topics.

"Um, cheers. New question." Straightening in my chair, I do my best to gather myself after that unexpected moment of opening up to Ben. How did that happen? It's too easy to let my guard down around him. I've got to be careful. Yet some other part of me just wants to keep talking to him, to tell him everything. Which would be a guaranteed disaster, and I selfishly want to keep him here a while longer yet.

"Let's have it." He rests his chin in hand, elbow propped on the table.

Damn, he's distracting. Ben's not the usual sort I go for—not that I have a type—but he's lightly built, slim, almost graceful. He's attractive, definitely, but in a more unconventional and nonconforming way. With his hat off, I can see a few black streaks through his blond hair, his soft jumper's neckline revealing his collarbone with the scarf to the side. I'd love to chase that with my tongue. Maybe later, if I don't make things too awkward again.

His smile gets bigger and I drink hurriedly to cover my moment of gawping over him. I'm sure he knows what's just happened, but never mind. I'll cover.

"Who are your musical influences?" I ask. An absolutely sensible, stand-up question to ask a musician. Nothing overly personal about it. Safe.

Ben tilts his head, considering. "Probably Bowie was the first one. Love him."

"I suspected. Confirms my Bowie hypothesis."

"Probably the others might surprise you a little. I love guitar, but singers…wow. I'm a huge fan of Florence and the Machine—she has such a big voice. And Nina Simone."

"Interesting." It's not what I'd expected him to say. The more he gives me, the more curious I become about him. This could very easily become addictive. I've got to make sure that doesn't happen. One night. That's my cutoff. One night of indulgence and no more. That's all I can afford to spare. Too many things need tending.

"How about you, Charlie?" His expression is open and soft as he listens.

Oh fuck.

He's getting to me, even with my resolutions, like he really does want to know about me. And that makes me feel a little flutter in my gut, if I'm honest with myself. The way he says my name in that Scottish accent… But keeping to epic sexual encounters, which I'm totally down for, I could take him over this table here and now and put on an early performance for the Crobar crowd that's gathering. Instead of making a public spectacle, I keep my trousers on, thinking of my answer.

"It's so hard to choose. There's loads." I fidget with my pint glass. "I love anything sounding a little bittersweet. The Doves, Joy Division, Hozier. It's more about how it feels, you know?"

"Oh, Hozier, aye. I hear all that," Ben enthuses, nodding emphatically like he couldn't agree more. "Absolutely. Music is pure emotion. And I love emotion, deep into my guts. All of them. It's a great show when I can tell the audience is picking up what I'm feeling."

I nod. "I know what you mean. Those are the best gigs. It's amazing when the crowd's totally into it. I mean, I've just played tiny hole-in-the-wall places. I still can't believe you've seen me play."

"Oh, aye. I catch loads of music. As much as I can, around work. And gigs and rehearsals."

"What's work, then? I guess that's a regular job on top of music?"

"Regular enough, I suppose. Nothing fancy. I'm a bar man at a pub not far from here when I'm not playing," Ben explains over his ale. "It's not a posh office job or anything important like that, but I know how to mix drinks and serve pints and that suits me. Plus, I'm already up late playing with the band and going to gigs, so I figured the hours worked."

"You're smarter than I am. My job at the café is great because I can have all the hours and coffee I want—and it's not bad around uni classes. Usually flexible," I offer. "But shit, Saturday mornings are the worst part after being out on Fridays. Except…"

"Except?" Ben asks, his blue eyes rapt.

My breath catches. He's distracting again. Still. Something.

Stop it.

"Except for you. That was worth all the rough Saturday mornings," I say, sheepish.

Wow, why the hell did I just say that? Charlie, you're only making this worse for yourself. You can't actually afford to start to…actually like him.

He laughs, and it's a rich reward that warms me from the inside out, here in our private corner of the bar. "Well, listen, I've had enough rough Saturday mornings myself after gigs, so. Occasionally, I do have to pull the lunch shift on Saturdays at the pub, and the rest of the time I have rehearsal, which is why I've been stopping by your café on the way in after I caught sight of you. Then, I just had to keep coming back." Ben grins. "Even with the dodgy service that first time. There was just too much there to pass up, I ken."

"Oh hell. I'm not gonna live that one down, am I?"

"Afraid not, mate." He cracks up again, shaking his head. "Irresistible. And refreshing. I don't ever get that, and I like it. I'm not letting you forget."

Does that mean he thinks there will be more than this one day? Another day with Ben and me? That can't be, though. But hell, the banter and the tease of Ben, so close that I can feel the burn of him on my skin from here… What does he look like minus the layers he's wearing now, without that scarf with all the colors?

He shifts, and under the table he takes my hand where it rests on my thigh, and I can't breathe with the warmth of his fingers. I can't even make words and by the way that arsehole's grinning he obviously knows what he's doing to me.

"Two more questions," he says, holding my gaze. His eyes are like the sea. Waves could break in them. I could drown. I have. And I could write all sorts of terrible poetry or songs about their depths without any regrets. Something's wrong with me.

"'Kay," I say, reeling. The fewer words, the less of a chance to sound like a fool.

"Since you're not online to stalk—and that's fine—I'm just curious...how old are you?"

I laugh. "Is that all? Easy. Twenty-one. Does that meet with your approval?"

"Aye, it does."

"Do you think any differently about me now?" I ask.

"No. I was just curious."

"And how old are you, then?" I counter.

"Twenty-five. That makes me an older man." He laughs, momentarily sitting back in his chair. "You'll need to respect your elders."

"Ha."

I'm not sure how old I expected Ben to be. I'm surprised and not. He looks younger, but knowing that he's had some success in music, I'm guessing it's not his first band out of the gate. Later, I'm going to have to do an internet search on him out of politeness' sake and get a band history, at least. I lift my pint and take a drink.

"And your second question?" I ask.

"It has two parts," Ben says. "First part is, are you having fun with me?"

"Yes," I say immediately. No further thought needed on that one. That episode in the stockroom will be seared in my memory for all time. Shit, it must be the drinks making me say these things. Like someone else is in charge of my mouth.

He beams. "I'm having a great time with you."

I fear I'm grinning inanely at him in response.

"Then…ready for part two of the question?"

"Uh-huh."

"Would you come home with me now?"

My eyebrows lift and I say yes, or make some sort of noises to that effect, and next thing we're kissing again—like we'd kissed in the street, like there's no one around in London but us. And I can't help but notice it feels like something important after our session in the bar.

Sex is easy. Being vulnerable isn't.

I've let my guard down just a little, something I rarely do. We leave the bar and I give myself over to his lingering kisses and his hands on my hips, leaning in the shadows of Manette Street together, ankle deep in snow.

Chapter Nine

After a walk in darkness, we arrive to a quiet lane of mews houses located not far from Soho, tucked away in the city's core, which were once stables for carriage horses. The day's long gone, but the snow blanketing London has created a bright sort of evening with the city lights reflected on white. We've escaped into some other London, a sort of magical city where things like this can happen, rather than the usual tired routine I live between work and uni. Ordinarily, I'm waiting for real life to begin a couple of years from now when I'm done. Instead, I'm living right now in this moment, with my arms around Ben, tasting the nape of his neck and the salt of his skin as he tries to navigate the lock to his place in the dark amid distraction.

As soon as the heavy front door shuts and latches, we're inside leaning against it, kissing something fierce, my hands up under that pink jumper of his with the leaping rabbit appliquéd on the front. He gasps out at my icy hands and catches my face between his as our kisses continue, urgent and hungry.

God, oh God. I can't think. I don't want to think.

Forget me. Forget my life.

I'm helping Ben out of his coat and tossing it to the floor, and we pause long enough to kick off boots and tease and gasp before he grabs my hand and takes me to his bedroom. I have no idea where we are exactly, here in the dark together, and quite frankly, I don't care.

Does he live with anyone? Who knows? Invisible housemates are the best kind, though. And there's none to be seen. Or heard.

He lightly bites my bottom lip and breaks away long enough to turn on a small lamp, casting a soft glow. It's enough to see him and bits of the double room we stand in. It's full of things that I can't quite make out, odd shapes in the dark. There's a shine of glass from a tall sash window.

Ben reaches to pull the curtain mostly closed as I catch him and kiss him hard again, our mouths bumping in our haste. He moans and I push him down firmly by his shoulders to sit on the bed.

I strip him of his jumper and throw it on the floor, rewarded with the sight of his pale skin and a scatter of freckles visible in the low light along the tops of his shoulders. With a rough kiss, I press him onto the bed, burning a trail down his chest with eager lips and a wicked scrape of teeth to get his attention. In response, he slides his hands along my back, beneath my shirt, skimming the burn of my skin.

"You're so fucking hot." And Ben's glorious beneath me, golden and bright even in the low light, like darkness couldn't subdue him.

My hand teases his stiff cock through his jeans, and he's trying—and failing—to unbutton my shirt as he gasps and squirms with pleasure beneath me.

Moving further south, I loosen his belt. I unbutton his fly and shove clothing down off his hips, revealing his hard-on. Magnificent. With a lick around the head, my mouth and hand work in unison. His back arches.

"Yeah…" I'm breathless at the sight of him like that.

"God…don't stop…" Ben gasps.

"Oh, I won't."

There's no plan to stop.

Instead, the rhythm of my hand only escalates, till he jerks and groans. His breathing is uneven.

And then I pause—not stop—long enough to yank my shirt off overhead, throwing it across the room somewhere in the vicinity of his jumper. The cold air is a shock to my skin.

Clumsily, I find my wallet in my jeans to retrieve a condom, cursing the foil in the low light and what way does this damn thing go on anyway and I shred the packet in my urgency and I figure it out in the half dark and hastily roll the condom on. Then I suck his rigid cock till he's crying out, his fingers rough in my hair, and he shoves lube at me.

"You want me?" I breathe against his ear.

My brain threatens to start thinking about how much I told him about my family, more than I've told anyone else, and yet Ben still wants me, but then he's demanding, pressing at me. And my brain fucks right off.

"God—yes—right now—"

I squirt lube in my hand. The cool liquid is abrupt, but it doesn't matter because I'm on fire, working myself into an unbearable ache before turning my attention to teasing Ben again, pressing a finger inside, then another. And he's so tight, so desperate as he writhes beneath me.

"More," Ben begs while I continue to torment him.

He grabs my arse, the pain of his fingernails digging into my skin exhilarating.

"Yeah, like that." My rough kiss is hot against his flushed skin—his cheekbone, his shoulder—and I'm turned on by how responsive he is to me. And hell, I give him more. I want to give him everything. But everything isn't enough, not fucking enough—

And moments later, I push inside. And holy fuck, he feels incredible, warmer than I could have imagined. I thrust deep, my muscles taut. I'm a spring ready to uncoil.

His back arches sharply again. He sobs out, and I sure hope he doesn't have housemates or that they're not home or can't hear us or something merciful like that.

God, he's fucking noisy. It's glorious how he responds to me.

"Like that?" I ride Ben, intensely aroused by his obvious pleasure, fit to burst as my balls ache with want. I clutch him.

"Ohh—"

I bite his shoulder and rock and cry and then he's coming messily all over his belly and I follow, gasping, while he clutches at me and we collapse in a trembling, hyper-aroused jumble in each other's arms. We're left as nothing but a scatter of reflexes, plastered together.

Jesus.

As I come back to something closer to reality, I'm aware of several things, like the rich scent of Ben's skin and cologne, and how the house smells of baking. A streetlamp casts light through the partially drawn curtain, bathing Ben in cool light beneath me, the fan of his hair on the pillow. The chill winter air washes over our exposed skin, and I reach for the crumple of Ben's duvet pushed to the side in our frantic union and cover us.

When I lift my face from where it's pressed against his skin, he kisses me rough. We taste of sex and each other, something like the denouement after an orchestral crescendo, the curtains falling with a whisper of velvet, the lights out and a deep, profound blackness before the audience demands an encore.

His arms are tight around me. He's still shaking.

"All right?" I whisper between kisses. Quite possibly I'm shaking, too.

"More than," Ben says.

We begin all over again, urgent and raw, fucking like our lives depend on it, till we're damp against each other, his scent drowning me, and I want nothing else but the urgency of us together.

If only we could let days pass like this and time didn't have meaning, caught inside a snowy alternate London where it's him and me and nothing else exists.

It's safe to say that after tonight, I'm officially addicted to Ben. And that can't be.

Chapter Ten

In the dead of night, I awaken in a soul-wracking panic, turning onto my back as I suck in cold air. And I'm naked. Everything's unfamiliar and the bed doesn't feel right. It's a proper bed, for starters. Luxurious, which is the first sign something's wrong. Not saggy.

Where the hell am I? What's going on?

And someone's beside me.

There's *never* someone beside me.

Fuck.

Then I force a breath, then another.

There's no time to panic. I need to think.

Pick three things to focus on. The softness of the pillow. The dark of the room. The strange comfort of the bed. That's three, and oh shit—

I remember in a rush: Ben.

And do I ever remember Ben. What a night. Incredible. Talk about forbidden pleasures, and then some.

A glance over shows he's sleeping curled on his side next to me, his face in shadow and his silhouette limned in moonlight. And hell—he's beautiful.

What did I just do?

There's no time for such things. I can't have any more of Ben, because this indulgence could lead to…well, who knows what that might lead to. I can't risk it. He's a gateway drug. People as amazing as Ben aren't for me, even if I did date.

Which I don't.

Dating is something that my friends do. I hear all of their wild stories about who they've pulled or the epic disasters following big nights out. Stories over pints that happen to other people, not me these days. Just like the stories I read for uni, I'm observing life happening for other people, while my life is on hold. And for good reason. The most important reasons.

And besides, this isn't real. It's just another hookup.

Let's be honest. A proper musician wouldn't want to date me. Not one that's successful. I mean, I'm more than all right for a night out, but that's got to be it. He must have mistaken me for some other barista who has a band and goes to uni. In fact, he must leave a string of devastated baristas in his wake, because frankly he's seriously devastating.

Time for a reality check, Charlie.

If only I hadn't been such a mess-up when I was a teenager. How different would my life be now? I could do anything I wanted. Like that of my friends, carrying on in the usual carefree way at the bar and going to parties and not worrying about too much.

But I fell in with the wrong set back in school, young and fast. Over-the-top living. I got kicked out of a couple of boarding schools and nearly kicked out of home too. In that blur of drug-induced highs and lows, Emily was my confidante, and one thing led to another one night, and along came our daughter. Carys is the best thing in my life, but I've got a high price to pay for the shit I've pulled. I fought hard to get to this point. The stakes are too high if I fail—not for me, but for Emily and Carys.

I can't let them down. They need me.

My stomach knots. I grip the edge of the covers, staring up at the blackness of the ceiling in the low light.

The best thing to do—the most sensible thing—is to pretend this didn't happen. That way, when Ben's just a stockroom memory, I won't miss him. He'll find some real rocker to be with who's his equal, who actually goes and plays regular gigs and tours and records. Not some sop of a barista slogging through his wreck of a life in Soho, trying to support his small daughter.

This is way too risky. Opening up more to Ben, no matter how tempting it is, or how interested he seems—it's too dangerous. No matter how much I want him. Wanting just leads to trouble.

Shifting, I ease upright, careful to not disturb Ben, who I swear looks like a naughty angel in his sleep, minus the wings.

I peel the blankets back. Better slip out now, just get home to think. It'd be better for everyone before this goes any further.

But oh, he's so tempting, lying in bed like that. I'd love to curl up around him and stay in bed and not worry about anything for a long while. Till dawn. But seeing dawn together would mean this indulgence has carried on a second day, and that can't be. I shake my head, hoping to clear it of my confusion and want.

Swinging my legs over the side of the bed, I press the balls of my feet onto cool hardwood and rise. I find my boxers and jeans and try not to curse when my belt buckle jangles.

"Charlie?"

There's a rustle of cotton sheets as Ben sits up, tousled and sleepy, disoriented and uncertain.

"I should go," I say quietly, caught.

I can't even sneak out properly.

Ben frowns and rubs his eyes before reaching out a hand to me. "Don't go. You can stay."

So tempting. I hesitate. So damn tempting. He's glorious in the moonlight. "I…I've got work."

The lie feels terrible on my tongue.

"In the middle of the night? Please stay," he entreats, shifting amid the soft nest of the blankets. "I hope I didn't say or do anything that upset you—"

"Oh no. Far from it. I've had the best time."

"Then?" he tries. He rubs his eyes again.

"Then…" What can I say that doesn't sound lame? That there's ghosts in my past, that things I once did came with a cost more than the pills I have to take each day to help me cope with daily living. To help me get out of bed each day. To help me not fall apart.

Lovely people and things aren't meant for me—at least not now. Maybe when I'm thirty. Forty, even. Or even next year. That would be the mature thing to do, right? But if I say that, he'll think I'm even more weird than I am for trying to sneak out like a cad. Like he meant nothing, which is far from the truth.

I want to blurt out how much I like him already. Even if that's too much to say. Or tell him how much I'd like to repeat last night. And all of yesterday, if I'm honest. Even all the way back to that first time we met in the café—where I don't call him a wanker right off the bat.

"Come to bed, Charlie," he says, his voice husky with sleep. "Please. There's a snowstorm out there and it'll be a nightmare getting anywhere at this hour."

All very true. All very reasonable.

With a breath and a stab of fear, I relent and crawl back into bed, drawing Ben close in my arms. He wriggles against me, arranging pillows and blankets to cocoon together. And it feels amazing just to lie here together, skin to skin, in the blissful warmth of this new thing between us that's happened over one intense day. His smile is visible even in the low light and my breath catches. He's gorgeous. Curling up together right now is only going to make things harder when I have to go tomorrow, but he looks so damned happy. What's it like to feel that way? I settle against the pillows, his head tucked against me, and we drowse. Sublime.

Curled close, I sleep again.

Chapter Eleven

The soft sky overhead shows the first brightening of day, gray snow clouds lingering as I leave Ben's, crunching through ankle-deep snow. If this keeps up, London will be glaciated. Which might not be a bad thing, if nature reclaims the place and saves me from myself. Because last night was a major slip. It wasn't even a Friday night, which is when I go out, and I felt way too much. So many fantastic things.

Yes, I'm escaping like a thief into the—well, not quite night. Pre-dawn, maybe. And yes, I'm an arse, after he brought me back to bed a couple of hours ago.

How inconvenient. And tempting.

And, most of all, confusing. That was the most fantastic twenty-four hours of sex that I've had in my life. But Ben doesn't fit into my plan of what I need to do, no matter how much I want him.

To be honest, I'm disappointed too. There's some kind of lump in my throat and a murky feeling in the pit of my stomach. Feelings are for other people. Not me. I have to think of my little girl and her mum and what they need.

Even so, when I glance back over my shoulder, it's so tempting to turn around and go back to him. Go back to the most fun I've had. But there's too much to do. I can't get distracted.

While he was mostly asleep, I slid out of bed a second time, saying I had to go to work, and left very quickly before he woke up for real and we had to have a conversation about trading numbers or worse, making future plans. I didn't tell Ben that I'm not actually scheduled to work today, but I'm not going to let something silly like the usual café scheduling stop me. And besides, going to Richmond for lunch with my parents is definitely work. And really, I've got no end of things to do, like those essays I was given the extension for. I just pray he doesn't come looking for me today.

As I grapple with the sinking feeling in my gut, I text Emily.

Might have done something I shouldn't.

My phone pings a minute later with Emily's response. She should be asleep, but probably Carys has her up early too. *Are you high? Or in jail? x*

Neither.

On the run for murder? she asks.

Nope.

Then whatever it is, I bet you can sort it out. I have nothing but faith in you.

Thanks, George Michael. You're a swell pal. I sigh as I stop on the snowy path, holding my phone in my hands. I'm only being a little bit facetious—Emily's brilliant. And probably her perspective is better than mine. What if she's right? *Talk later?*

Absolutely. Talk then. x

I give my head a shake, as if that'll sort me out. Like it'll shake off the memories of Ben and how incredible he is. It was just a one-time thing.

But it doesn't make me feel any better, knowing that.
Keep walking, Charlie. One foot in front of the other.

I get to the café before Jasmine arrives to open. Even though my bed is tempting, never mind the greater appeal of returning to Ben's bed with Ben in it, I continue with my plan to work. I mean, I said I would. I'm keeping my word...even if I'm not scheduled. There's comfort in the familiar routine. And the extra few quid won't hurt my bank account either. Christmas is looming.

The sky has brightened to proper day. Honestly, though, what's wrong with me that the only place I can think of going to when I'm upset is here? Working harder will help distract me from the memory of Ben, I'm sure of it. Totally sensible, in fact. I'm sure Jasmine won't mind the help. I chew my lip.

Things are well underway when Jasmine arrives at half past eight. She stares at me as she walks into the café, removing her red scarf.

"What are you doing here?" She eyes me, appraising. "You think it's Saturday again or something?"

I stare back. "No."

Jasmine's quiet. "You like to come here for fun?"

"Something like that." I go around and start taking down overturned wooden chairs from darkly varnished tables. Jasmine helps. "I figure if I work the other six days of the week, why not work Sunday and make it a perfect set? God will understand."

She shakes her head. "What's happened?"

"What makes you think something's happened?"

"I've got ears. I heard you and Ben Campbell in the back yesterday—"

My eyebrows shoot up in alarm as I gawp, face hot. So

she had recognized Ben, too. The brick wall between the stockroom and the rest of the café was solid. I would have wagered a million quid on it. This is worse than I thought.

Words spill out. "You didn't hear from out here—"

"No, no—"

"Jesus, thank you."

"I went to take out the rubbish, and, um, *then* I heard..."

Mortified, I look anywhere but at her. My face is on fire.

"I figured after that you'd be having a brilliant time and that you'd be carrying on. And definitely not turning up to open on Sunday morning. So, it's a reasonable question: what's happened? Was he a total prick?"

"Oh no. No. Definitely not. That's my domain, thanks." I sigh. "Nailing. It."

So true.

Is Ben sleeping in now? It's a brilliant thing to do on a Sunday morning, a day of rest for most people. Except me. Arseholes should work harder on Sundays.

"What happened?" Jasmine purses cherry red lips, frowning as she looks at me.

We're not exactly close—I'm not close with anyone, not even my bandmates, except for Emily—but Jasmine's a friend as much as the ones I go out with usually on Friday nights. Probably more so. They're good for pints and laughs, and that's where we leave things. Jasmine's used to seeing me in all manner of conditions, but mortified is not usually on the spectrum. No wonder she's looking at me like I've turned into a serial killer.

If I race back now and reverse time, I could go directly to Ben's, get back into bed with him, and pick up where we left off, and Jasmine would be none the wiser. Spare us this awkward conversation that we're having. And me from trying to explain what's wrong when I'm caught between wanting Ben and wanting to hide under a rock.

"Charlie?"

"Sorry. I, um, had a great time. And then I left to come here."

"I gather you left, because you're standing in front of me, genius." Jasmine shakes her head, half smiling. She adjusts her hair, which is caught up in a bun. "Keep going."

"I…you know me. Not good with feelings and all that. It was just sex. One night of sex."

"You pick people up regularly enough and don't turn up here on Sunday mornings having some sort of meltdown. Why are you acting like you've just been with the vicar's son and the vicar himself just caught you in the act?" Her eyes widen. "Don't tell me he is actually the son of a vicar—I suppose it *is* Sunday."

"No! I mean, I don't know if he's the son of a vicar or the holy ghost or anything at all about him. Other than his name's Ben and he's fucking hot and a brilliant musician. And the sex was equally brilliant, for the record."

I scowl and loudly drag a table back into place, nearly jumping out of my skin when Jasmine puts a hand on my arm. When I dare look at her, she's gazing at me with wide blue eyes and a bemused expression.

"With my luck I did fuck the vicar's son," I say. "But even if his father is a vicar, presumably he's in Scotland. I don't have any other information to go on to tell me otherwise."

"Well…I suppose you'd know if you hadn't left."

"Ouch, Jas. Go easy."

She tilts her head. "You know it's all right to let yourself have some fun, right? Everyone deserves a bit of that now and again. You just met him. It's nothing serious. And yet the way you're acting…"

I'm more overwhelmed than usual, thanks to having missed my meds last night. I can visualize the vial from the chemist sitting on top of my bureau. In my room. Where

I'm not. In the pit of my stomach, anxiety rises in waves, and I could suffocate here and now, which would at least be merciful, but no.

Instead, I look at Jasmine, and Jasmine looks at me in stalemate.

I relent, gripping the back of a wooden chair. "I mean, it's nothing serious. Just sex and all that. It won't happen again."

"Just sex and all that…which got to you." She shakes her head. "Like I said, fun is allowed. I don't think Emily would mind you having a life, right?"

My knuckles are white. How can I risk someone like Ben if I can't even have a normal conversation with Jasmine?

"You don't even need to say I was here. I won't put today on my timecard, then." I stare at my hands. "I'll go soon, I promise."

"Charles Renfrew."

"Jasmine White."

"Out with it," she says. "But…for the record, I do think you're a lovely man under the grump, and maybe Ben saw that?"

My head snaps up. Stung, I don't know what to say. I gulp back air. "Maybe…"

"Maybe," she agrees. "Did you have fun, at least?"

"Fuck, yes."

"You deserve to have fun too, you know. For the record."

"Oh God. Please. Let's not talk about this anymore. We went out. We had fun. But you know I don't date."

"I do know that—but consider at least another date. Especially if you like him. It's okay. More than okay. And he *is* cute."

I look away from her and wipe down the coffee machine. I *do* like Ben. Would it be so terrible to think of going out for a drink again? It was brilliant hanging out with him. And whenever I close my eyes, I'm back with Ben again, his mouth on mine and—

Stop. I can't. It really was just a one-time thing.

Except it feels awful dismissing Ben like that. Like he didn't matter.

"Let's just continue getting ready before the first customers come. Please," I beg, desperate to leave this conversation as a memory too, to get Jasmine off the subject. "And—I'll think about it, all right?"

Jasmine's face lights up. "Excellent news. I'll make you a latte if you do the float. You're faster than me."

"Deal. And to be honest, I can't stay all day because I have to head to my parents' for lunch and then to band rehearsal."

Not even the temptation to bail on my family's Sunday lunch with a fabricated bona fide barista emergency isn't enough to chase any thoughts of Ben right out of my head.

Chapter Twelve

After helping Jasmine with the opening of the café for the Sunday morning crowd, I head back home to Finsbury Park for a shower, change of clothes—and, most importantly, my meds—in an effort to reset to a more calm state of being.

Whether that's possible after a night with Ben and impending family time remains to be seen.

When I finally arrive home to my Victorian terrace house, I kick off my trainers into the heap of shoes by the entry near the radiator and grunt a hello to my two housemates who're watching TV in the lounge. It's actually quite a handsome house, with red brick and white trim and an arch providing an alcove at the top of the front steps.

When I get to my room, the weight of the world is temporarily lifted and I can breathe again.

There are three bedrooms, two of which are proper double rooms. I've got the third bedroom, the smallest one, which is more like a single-and-a-half, because only an estate agent could call this a double with a straight face. I can move around the bed to the desk and around to the other side to get to the wardrobe and drawers, but it's a tight fit. The benefit is that it's the cheapest room. I'm also the one who cleans the house, to save on a cleaner, and Paul and Mikey cover the supplies.

To make my crowded room worse, I've jammed a small second-hand bureau beneath the sash window and a bookcase beside it in the corner. On the wall, I've got a whiteboard full of the million things I need to do, and a marked-up calendar beside it with my schedule. Fucking my brains out with Ben Campbell is nowhere on that long list. Neither is thinking about Ben's reaction when he woke to an empty bed, even with the excuse about going to work, and the inevitable twist that brings to my guts.

I wanted to wake up with him. And start another day together.

You can't think like that.

Once freshly showered and dressed for lunch and suitably medicated with the appropriate options, I'm more grounded. More in control again. After a run-through of a quick breathing exercise, I take a moment to sit on the edge of my bed.

Compared to murder, jail, or drugs, Ben is, to be fair, a much safer bet. And as much as I might want him, my stomach knots, because logically there's no way this could work. No matter what I feel. And…apparently, I'm strangely feeling a lot for someone I've banged in a stockroom and got too personal with over drinks.

Not this lifetime, Charlie.

But…

Nothing bad's happened. Emily's right. Aside from me attempting to run off like an arsehole in the middle of the night and being terribly embarrassed about bolting. My actual departure was slightly more dignified, but still curt due to my inner turmoil. Maybe I can apologize.

And maybe I can enjoy the blissful thought of Ben a little longer. I could use something to keep my spirits up, especially with what I've still got to do today. But this weakness I have for him has to stop soon. Like, pre-Christmas sort of soon. Because no matter how euphoric he makes me feel, there's everything else that's waiting for me.

Without further delay, I make a beeline for the tube, clinging to the bits of happiness I felt falling asleep in Ben's arms.

In the late afternoon, after surviving lunch by keeping my head down and letting Michael do most of the talking, I roll into the Shoreditch studio that Briar's arranged for us this week, arriving only a few minutes late. I would have been on time for rehearsal if there hadn't been a delay on the tube. I forgot about the rail replacements happening today, which happen more weekends than not.

I've entertained myself on the journey with some rather vivid daydreams about Ben. And also with more than some intrigue about the conversation that we had, his dyslexia and life in Scotland before coming to London. I shouldn't think about that, because it's only going to make things worse for me down the road, but listen: *Ben Campbell went for drinks with me.* If I told my bandmates, no one would believe me. It's about as unlikely as going for pints with Alex Turner from the Arctic Monkeys or Tom Chaplin of Keane or even Brandon Flowers.

I float my way into the rehearsal room, smothering a smile at the memory of jumping Ben in the stockroom. How can it have been just a day ago? Not even twenty-four hours.

In the rehearsal room, everyone else has arrived. Briar's tuning her guitar, her long blonde hair in a loose plait over her shoulder. She's talking with Jackson, her boyfriend, and our unofficial manager. Unofficial because we don't really have any money to pay him in anything other than pints and gratitude.

Gillian's already at her keyboards. Her dark hair is up, an orange scarf tucked around her neck. She grins. "You're late, Charles."

I roll my eyes at the formality. Echoes of my parents, right now. But a smile tugs my lips before I can stop it.

Jackson settles behind the drums. "Five minutes, mate. You owe us a round. You know the usual terms and conditions."

Buying drinks for the band is the penalty if anyone's late. Even as skint as I am, I don't care. A rule is a rule. But it was totally worth it. If I close my eyes, I can imagine Ben is still beneath me, our bodies locked in unison—

"Ooh, Charlie. You didn't even ream me out for that," Gillian says, peering at me. "And—you're smiling. Is everything okay?"

I gulp. Nobody here can know what happened. Especially not that it was Ben Campbell. Jesus, that would be gossip I'd never live down and would lead to loads of questions I definitely don't want to answer.

Briar turns to face me, adjusting her guitar strap. Today she's in long flowing white and silver layers over her jeans. She gives me an appraising look. "It's to do with a man, isn't it?"

My face burns like a wildfire. "Absolutely not."

Gillian and Briar exchange knowing looks, like they've got the Charlie Renfrew playbook down to an exact science. But they hardly know what's what, let's be real.

"Right on, Charlie." Jackson laughs and hits a cymbal.

"Fuck off, all of you," I say, opening my guitar case and retrieving my guitar. "We're never ever talking about this again."

"He'll spill eventually," announces Briar.

"Nope. You've got me confused with some other weekend gossip." I shake my head, adjusting a tuning key, then another. "You know the old saying: loose lips sink ships, and all of that."

"We'll buy him a pint later and he'll give us all of the hot gossip," Matt tells them with confidence as he picks up his bass guitar.

I clear my throat and tap loudly on the body of my guitar. The resonating hollow sound gets their attention, right back to the point. "In case you've all forgotten, we're here to rehearse. We've got a big gig in just over a week, and we don't want to squander Briar's gift to us by heckling me, an innocent here. Let's go. From the top of the set list." I thump my guitar again for emphasis.

Jackson and Briar share a grin, totally unfussed by my grumble, which is basically the usual noise coming from my direction.

Finally, everyone settles in, and we get to work. And later, when we go for pints and I buy them all the promised round, I don't utter a word about Ben. Or let out any more wayward smiles or hints of daydreaming. I've got to shove that away. Pretend it never happened. It'll be easier like that, for everyone. That's another sort of rehearsal right there. Right now, it's back to the default Renfrew poker face.

Chapter Thirteen

After returning home from rehearsal, I set down the bag of takeaway and flop into my desk chair with a sigh, bone-tired. The takeaway's a rare treat, and I got the special because it was the cheapest and fastest option. It's indulgent, especially after the pub. I'm wrecked, though. Not enough sleep, too much action, literal and evasive and otherwise.

Wearily, I rub my eyes. All that sex had been fun, and the resulting adrenaline and angst got me through the afternoon. But now that the sun has gone again, I'm ready for bed and it's not even 6:00 p.m.

A scatter of notes and textbooks lie on the desk beside my old laptop. So does *Pride and Prejudice* for an essay I still need to write over the break when I missed the deadline. However, if I start reading now, I'll fall asleep three pages in. Plus, there's an exam the first week back and two tutorials and I haven't done enough to get ready for any of it.

With a sigh, I retrieve the takeaway box with noodles and veg. The spice helps wake me up a little. But as I sit there, I can't miss the mountain of dirty laundry in the corner. There's another clean pile in need of folding. I've been getting by the last few days by scavenging from that pile because I don't have time to deal with it properly. I figure I'm only going to wear the clothes again anyway.

I'm too tired for all of it, and it's getting on. Time to call Carys and Emily before it gets too late. I text Emily and set up the call on my laptop for the video. Poor Carys thinks her daddy is her mum's laptop computer, Emily told me last week. Carys has taken to tapping the laptop to wake it up, asking, "Daddy?"

"Hey, Em."

"Hey," Emily says cheerfully. "Good timing. We've just finished dinner. Did you make things worse for yourself since this morning?"

"No—"

There's a commotion in the background.

"Daaaaaaaddy!" Carys climbs up onto her mother's lap. Emily scoops her up, giving her a snuggle while she makes a face, then plonks her onto her booster seat at the table, moving the laptop safely out of toddler range.

"Hi, darling." I grin at the sight of Carys staring intently at me on the screen. No matter how exhausted I am, I'm always thrilled to see her.

"Daddy!" She crows with laughter, as if I'm the funniest thing she's ever seen, and it's the sound of pure joy.

"It's me," I confirm, waving at her. "See?"

"Come play!"

"I wish I could, but I can't. Not yet. I'm all the way in London."

She scowls, an expression she's clearly inherited from me. She doesn't know what London is, but she recognizes a *no* when she hears one. God, I wish I could see her every day, and never tell her no.

"Why?"

"Because that's where I live. And you live in Wales. Remember the long train ride?"

"Want train!"

I laugh. It's amazing how seeing Carys even for a few minutes can lift my spirits so much. "You do. And I'll come very soon to visit for Christmas. On the train. And I'll see you and your mum and your gran."

She peers at me, restless in her chair. Em's got her buckled in, ready for the inevitable squirms.

"When I come to see you, we'll play trains, I promise."

Carys looks satisfied with that. "Now?"

"I wish I could, darling. In a few days."

Emily comes into view to save a brewing storm as Carys looks tearfully at me. "Bath time. Say good night to Daddy."

"Good night, Carys."

"Night, Daddy," Carys says mournfully, as though saying good night is causing my two-year-old profound suffering. Fair. I have it too, that same profound suffering deep in my heart from missing her. I hate being so far away.

My guts twist. If only I was closer to give her a bath, help with the nighttime routine, help with the washing up or anything to give Emily a hand. And, of course, play trains with my baby girl.

After the call, I flop on the bed. For some time, I lie there, staring at the ceiling.

Priorities, Charlie. Carys is what matters. You and Em made a choice.

It's terrible being so far from them. It won't be forever. It can't be. After this weekend, they're an excellent reminder of what I need to focus on.

The rest of Sunday evening passes in a blur of emo misery, another diagnosis that should be in the *Diagnostic and Statistical Manual of Mental Disorders*. It sounds far better than depression and generalized anxiety disorder, with bonus panic attacks for the win. At least the hallucinations stopped when I quit shoving drugs and things into my system. Binge-drinking, inappropriate men, chasing highs... If it had been toxic, I'd been all in.

By ten o'clock, I've worn myself out, paced over the creaky hardwood of my room till even the floor was tired of me, sick of thinking, sick of myself.

Give me a different life, universe. I'd like a do-over. And a brain that's not a champion arsehole.

I carefully avoid thinking of how disappointed Ben looked when he awoke to find me sneaking away the first time in the night. A shiver runs through me at the memory. I hate that I disappointed him.

We never actually exchanged phone numbers, so there're no messages today. And I'm not on social media, so that's out. I'm left with the overwhelming urge to drown myself in liquor but I keep it together, staying up late watching shit online to keep from thinking of Ben. It works—mostly. Right now, there's a carefully carved Ben-void in my memory.

Besides, there's Carys and the upcoming holidays. There're essays to write and books to read and the reading list to start on for next term. There's a load of things to think about other than Ben. I just don't have time in my life for him, like it or not. It was a fun one-night thing. That's it.

Let it go, Charlie. Let Ben go.

That all works till I shut off the laptop and the lights and slide beneath the covers. Alone. When I close my eyes, I can see him in front of me with his easy grin and striped scarf and leather jacket, the simple freedom of snogging in the snow in a magic moment out on Denmark Street, stolen away from our usual, very different lives, and lying skin to skin in his bed, just hours ago. And guiltily, I linger on that image of us, together in his room lit by the moon, sprawled on the bed, happily exhausted and wanting nothing else in that moment, until sleep takes me.

Chapter Fourteen

By Monday, I'm back to the usual and more settled as a result. It's a new week. I can forget the weekend's highs and lows. Christmas is coming up fast and there's loads to do once I get through these latest shifts, least of all the shopping for Wales with my latest wages.

The café's busy, and today the Soho shoppers are out to do some serious damage. Which means the café is full of them when they need a break from corporate consumerism and all of that Christmas retail cheer. A flat white is a brilliant salve for overspending, or at least a time-out. There's also a layer of students crept around the edges, planted at the wooden tables like some kind of permanent fixture.

I'm back to my typical grumbling café persona. That bout of happiness was only a lapse. Even with Jasmine's pep talk yesterday, I have the all-too-vivid reminder of my bandmates' abject glee at trying to figure out why I was doing something so banal as smile. The worst. I have a careful veneer of gruff and surliness to maintain. Any deviation will lead to questions that I don't want to answer.

And that's time wasted which would be far better spent imagining Ben naked on the bed, all temptation and vice and the way he just *looks* at me, like he's trying to remember every last scrap of me, trying to imagine what I might do next—

The latest piercing shriek of Lars abusing the steamer rips me back to the present, appalling reality in the café. The good news is that the peak of the lunch rush is over and Jasmine, Lars, and I aren't quite losing our minds up front. We're damned busy, but not desperate. It's a lull between rounds of desperation, at least. More people will hit the café soon enough.

I pause to drag the cuff of my black sleeve across my forehead, then glance at Jasmine, who's stalled out in filling the order I called to her a moment ago.

She doesn't answer me.

"Ground control to Moon Unit," I say. "One broccoli cheddar soup and a croissant. Plus one cappuccino, extra hot. I don't know if Lars heard the last bit."

Jasmine continues to look out at the floor as another rush begins. She purses her lips, seemingly in deep contemplation.

Muttering under my breath, I turn from the till once I've handed the latest customer their receipt. "Jas?"

Jasmine nods out at the crowd. "I think you've got business, Charlie."

"Of course we've got business. There's a queue nearly to the door. So, kindly hurry up. Please and thanks."

"That's not what I mean. Settle down, cowboy."

Scowling, I follow her gaze. "Oh, fucking hell."

Right in front of me, next up in the queue, is Ben.

As usual, he wears an irresistibly soft jumper, this one with alternating pale gray and charcoal stripes and a black V-neck collar that gives a peek at the hollow at the base of his throat. Something I wouldn't mind investigating with my mouth anywhere but here. He's in a moss-green wool hat, his bleached fringe brushed across his brow, and the usual colorful scarf and leather jacket.

Ben's beautiful as ever. And...unsmiling, his jaw set.

I gulp.

Shit.

So much for my twenty-four hours of careful denial. Ben's missing his usual spark. His hands are stuffed in his pockets and his shoulders are slumped as he considers me.

The man's turned up days early. If he had the sense to keep to the usual routine of when we see each other, I'd be safely away in Wales, and he'd probably be off doing whatever he did at the holidays.

"Maybe you should go on a break." Jasmine hovers by my side, hesitant. Finally, she shows signs of filling the food order. "Lars and I will cover. You're nearly done for the day anyway."

Swallowing hard, I ignore her, fixed on Ben.

He doesn't say anything, apparently caught in the same awkward moment that I'm drowning in.

"Americano?" I ask in a whisper. "I, er, hear the brioches are delicious."

Ben purses his lips slightly, searching my eyes.

"On the house."

He sighs, shakes his head, and walks away.

Fuck. I've hurt him.

So much for slipping away being the light escape for both of us. Clearly, we need to talk about this. Except I'm absolutely terrible about discussing my feelings, quite possibly the last man in England qualified to talk about them. Especially when I shouldn't have any, since it's only been a couple of encounters.

But...he's more than a couple of encounters. A lot more. Already. And...if he's upset, maybe he feels like it's something more too?

What have I done?

"Hey! Wait." Hurriedly, I pull off my apron and trail him outside into the snowy cold like we had done before, pre-stockroom shenanigans. Except that had been magic and this...this is all my fault.

"Wait. Please."

Ben stops in the middle of the pavement. It's a long moment before he turns to look at me.

"I'm sorry. I'm so sorry, Ben. I didn't know what to do. I panicked. I would've left you a note, but then I thought maybe you wouldn't be able to read it, especially with my terrible writing, and this is all definitely my fault. Not yours. I should have left my number but I thought it was a one-time thing and—"

I stop to gulp air as my eyes sting. *It's not everything. Shit, Charlie. Say something to make it better.* "Sometimes I can't think straight, and—and I just have to get away. And breathe. And I guess I'm still breathing, so that's a win? Why am I still talking?" Oh my God, I'm standing in the street rambling and making a scene. My mother would die to see my display of emotion out in public for anyone walking past to see. The words won't stop till blood rushes in my ears and my face burns and the world spins.

That much is true. I can't say to him to look me up when I'm forty instead. That's going to lead to a lot more talking and there's no way that it can work out. Not with him living large as a rocker and me as a dad, even if my little girl's in another country. I've got to put her first, even so.

Then Ben's expression softens. He's pale under his freckles, with shadows beneath his eyes. "I didn't know what I'd done wrong. Why you'd leave in the morning without saying anything. Or...even leaving a note."

He's tearing me up inside.

"It's my fault, believe me. Not yours, Ben. It wasn't

anything you did—please believe me."

Ben hesitates, then nods at last. It's obvious I'm a mess, wringing my hands and staring at him as we stand together in slush and ice.

"You're all right?" he asks, assessing. Worried now as his expression relaxes a little.

I nod hurriedly. "I'll be fine. This is normal enough for me. Which I guess isn't normal. I mean, you're not normal, you're something else, too. I mean—of *course* you're normal—oh fuck, why am I still talking? Again. Shit."

My mouth has ideas of its own, while my brain shut off around five minutes ago. Despite acting like an arse, I'm not getting the dressing down I've earned.

Tentatively, he reaches out to take my hand. I draw a slow, deep breath as I gaze at him. He's calming. I don't have any right to this calm after how I've acted, but I'm grateful.

Around us, cars pass in the sleet. It's a wintry gray day where the sun can't win the battle to shine. Overhead, the uniform cloud blankets London. Graying snow sits in heaps where it's been piled to the margins of the pavements to let pedestrians walk, salt and grit thrown down for traction.

A small smile crosses Ben's lips. "I could tell you were in a bit of a state when you woke in the night."

"Mmm," I concede, shrugging a shoulder in acknowledgment. "It's probably permanent, that state."

He goes quiet again. "Then, I thought, if you're not just off somewhere having a meltdown, you must've regretted being with me. Since you didn't leave a note or your number. You were just…gone. I mean, you said you had work, but I thought you'd wake me, so clearly you thought it was a mistake—"

"No! Oh God, no. I had a brilliant time with you, believe me. That couldn't be further from the truth—no regrets about you. At all."

His smile broadens. "Thought so."

"What?" I'm unable to suppress my smile. "You just wanted to hear me say that, didn't you? And let me do all of—well, that."

I wave my hand in a gesture intended to encompass emoting in the street but it's probably coming across as a random, though hopefully endearing, set of flails.

"Kind of." He tilts his head. "Then I thought another thing. Probably silly, since we've just met, and I suppose technically it was a hookup and all, but this feels important— but then I thought…maybe you have a boyfriend at home to get back to."

"What?" I gawp, my eyebrows lifting. "Boyfriend? Jesus, no. No. Definitely no boyfriend—I don't date. Actually—fuck it. The truth is that I have a dating ban. For the greater good. Public safety. God, what a thought, a boyfriend."

Me having a boyfriend is as likely as me turning into a unicorn. That's an idea far more foreign than feelings.

He chuckles, and I could be wrong, but I swear there's a moment where he looks disappointed when I bring up the ban, a fleeting troubled expression across his face. Probably most people our age don't have dating bans, but there we are. It's my way to stand out in the world.

"All right then. I just needed to check." He hesitates. "I once dated a married man for months before I realized he was married and then later I wondered how I'd missed all the clues. Max. That's another story for another time, maybe."

"Fucking hell." I shake my head. "Well, rest assured, no boyfriend. Not even close."

Ben squeezes my fingers and I shiver, from cold or who knows what. But we're standing out here and he's the only thing to register in my consciousness at this moment.

And then I know I'm going to say something else rather out there, especially for a one-night hookup. "I'm sorry, Ben.

The last thing I want to do is hurt you. Taking off like I did wasn't brilliant, and I should have woken you up properly or left a note or my number. Something."

People continue to go up and down the pavement around us with bags of Christmas shopping. And it's also still freezing out here, and I shudder with cold. The day's dull and the streetlamps have come on. The neighboring shops have their Christmas lights on.

"You're forgiven."

And we stare intently at each other. Probably neither one of us is breathing. Quite possibly, we may suffocate and need some serious mouth-to-mouth to recover.

"I missed you, Charlie. Even after one night."

Did he actually just say that? So simply, like it didn't cost him his spleen to say it?

"You did?" I ask. Something in me melts. I make myself take in a deep breath, make my shoulders relax.

"Aye. I did." Ben gives me a wry look. "But I don't want to interfere with your policy. I don't expect an exemption from the ban. You probably have good reasons."

I squeeze his fingers, warm in mine. "It's a bit complicated," I admit. "To be honest, it's a lot complicated. But—it doesn't have to do with any boyfriends, husbands, or lovers on the side. I swear."

Ben nods, then dares to lift my hand to press against his lips. I push a finger into his warm mouth as he sucks. Heaven. Pedestrians skirt around us with grumbles and complaints, but neither of us move, caught up in each other.

"Huh." Eventually, I reclaim my hand.

"I wish...well, never mind what I wish. But I had a grand time with you, and I wouldn't be sorry for more. We'll call it meaningless sex if you want. No strings."

I trace his lips. They sear against my frozen fingers.

"Don't say anything right now." Ben looks intently at me,

like his eyes can keep me quiet through sheer force of will. And I stay silent while he continues. "Think about it. I'll give you my number and you can call me if you want anything like that. And if you don't call, I get it's policy, and not personal." He smiles.

Gulping, I nod. And, at last, we exchange our numbers. "Maybe...we can keep doing this while the snow sticks around."

That's a few days, tops. No harm in that, right? An exemption to the dating ban when there's snow.

Ben beams at me. "Let's do that."

"'Kay." I give a tentative smile, my heart careening around.

"I know you need to get back to work, but I want to say that I feel better for having talked with you. Cheers for that," Ben confesses.

"I'm sorry for doing such a shit thing, especially with your history with other men. I feel terrible."

We gaze at each other. Hesitate. Do we hug? Kiss?

He turns to leave, to walk down the pavement, away from me, but it's tearing me up inside.

"Wait!" I blurt, unable to let him go quite yet. There's nothing chill about the desperation in my voice.

Ben turns back, looking worried. "What?"

"I can't let you go without—well, without telling you more. Something...something important."

He catches my hand, squeezing it. Our gazes lock. "Tell me. Whatever it is," Ben whispers. "If it's important to you, it's important to me."

"I—well, the thing is, I left for a couple of reasons, but also because I didn't think I deserved you. You're brilliant and funny and successful—and fucking hot—and...it couldn't be happening to me. It couldn't be my life. I was convinced it had to be a mistake. That you made a mistake." My eyes fill with unexpected tears at being vulnerable before Ben, out here on a Soho street while London life continues as usual around us. "Wanting me. Even for a night or two or, I guess, feeling that there may be something there. Like I'm not rubbish. That you like me just the way I am. Everything else in my life seems to have…conditions. But not you. And…I'm not used to being vulnerable in front of people. Especially about someone that—well, that I care about. Already."

Ben traces my tears away, hot against the coolness of his fingers. Stricken, he catches my face between his hands. "Charlie…you deserve all of the brilliant, beautiful things. Every last one of them. No matter how complicated it is. I know I didn't make a mistake. And I can tell this isn't easy for you. And it's okay. If you want to talk more, I'm here for it. For you."

Light-headed, I can't believe what he says. Can't take it, really. How could he think those things?

But it thrills me to hear him say it, to say it like that, without a doubt in his eyes or his voice, while he holds me like I'm the most important thing in the universe in that moment. So I kiss him, and he kisses me with reverence, and some distant part of me that might give fucks notes that we're probably making a spectacle on the street, but I don't care. Not one bit. My family isn't here to complain. And Jasmine can tease me all she wants later.

"It was the best night I've had in a very long time." My arms around him, I force a steadying breath into my lungs. God. If this is what swooning feels like, no wonder the literary heroines I read about for uni had chaise longues everywhere to catch them when it came to matters of the heart. I can't take it. I tremble.

"Ach, Charlie," Ben manages. And his eyes are damp then too.

And we stand there, grinning at each other. I take his

hand.

"Well, if you like, you can come over later." Ben looks anxious, but he can't stop smiling either.

Some part of me hesitates, just for a nanosecond.

Ben shifts from foot to foot, squeezing my hand with assurances, even in that simple gesture. "No strings—"

"Of *course* I'm coming over."

And we laugh.

Fucking hell, it's not even a Friday night. The whole routine's off. I'll just have to pretend it's a weekend of Fridays. I'll ask Jasmine to cover my short shift tomorrow, for a worthy cause she might approve of.

"Can you wait fifteen minutes for me to finish my shift?"

Hell, can I wait fifteen minutes?

"Absolutely."

Let's see what happens next.

Chapter Fifteen

It's safe to say that Ben waited for me to finish out my shift. Then we found a way to work overtime together on Monday night. And on Tuesday morning, I'm still in Ben's bed. This time, I skip the 3:00 a.m. sneaking out or work excuses. While the snow falls once more over London, time suspends again, keeping us in our own private world for another day.

Beyond the old sash window snowflakes descend slowly, lazy and large, like something from a film. It's the first thing I see when I open my eyes and drift to wakefulness in Ben's bed. The snowflakes dance and whirl in a hypnotic tapestry. Maybe I'm awake in a lucid dream.

We're tangled in his bed together, warm in the cotton sheets and a duvet. There's a hand-knit blanket on top, in a range of colors fit to match that amazing striped scarf he'd caught me in for greedy kisses that first day out in the snow. Now, he's curled against my chest and I wonder what he's dreaming of, because he just gave a contented sigh in his sleep. Bloody adorable.

I trace the soft skin of his freckled shoulder.

Shifting, I stretch carefully beneath him, my back complaining after having been in bed so long. This isn't actually the first time I've woken this morning—we've already had a tryst and collapsed in quivering exhaustion, and maybe that's why he's still looking so fucking pleased in his sleep.

It's funny the quirks that make up a person. I still can't believe he put on a whole show of being a coffee aficionado just to get my attention, when it's turned out he's a chronic tea-drinker—preferring a loose-leaf Earl Grey and English Breakfast Tea blend, with a touch more Earl Grey. Two sugars to one cream. Course, I've kept him in cream as promised. And I'm the sugar, since I'm generous like that.

More quirks: daylight flooding his room reveals that he has this collection of jumpers that a teenage girl would envy. The sequined unicorn one might be my favorite. In contrast, there's a collection of bleached white crania of small creatures on the fireplace's mantle at the foot of the bed, and an array of candles in plum, midnight, and gold in the hearth. Sage and lavender are tied in bundles with strands of sky-blue yarn, hanging over it all. A bookcase on the opposite wall from the bed in the double room promises illustrated grimoires and albums and neatly folded graphic print T-shirts. His guitars sit neatly in a rack beside the shelves.

"Ohh…" Ben makes signs toward wakefulness with my movement.

"Morning. Again," I whisper before kissing him. And he's definitely awake, because he kisses back before sitting up, rubbing his eyes.

"Make me tea, coffee boy," Ben says with a sleepy grin.

"Do you always wake up so demanding?"

"This is me being most courteous, thank you very much. I don't need extra sass with my tea," Ben says lightly. He stretches his arms overhead, slender muscles over bone. Graceful, even.

In the ease of being with him, my panic over the other night is a distant memory, like it belonged to someone else. Probably helped by the fact I'd had my pills in the pocket of my coat to take when I woke in the night and went back to bed.

I reach out to tweak his titanium nipple ring and he groans slightly. "I think you demand extra sass with your tea, actually. Proof is in, I'm afraid."

He leans forward to kiss me. "Tea. Faster."

"Harder too, I bet."

At last, I get up, shivering at the cool air. I've got to be in serious like to leave the comfort of a warm bed with Ben in it. God, feelings are such a disaster. Hell. There's no time for feelings. But never mind—he's looking at me in that way he has.

"Of *course* harder." Ben laughs, and takes pity on me as I shiver. He rises and hands me his peacock feather print dressing gown from the foot of the bed, finding himself a set of black-cuffed gray woolen thermals.

"Making tea in a strange kitchen while wearing feathers. What've I come to?" I lament as we make our way through his Victorian house, pine floorboards creaking. His housemates are either still asleep or out.

The snow blanketing the garden casts cool winter light into the kitchen through tall windows as we enter. Birds scratch delicate lines out in the snow, looking for food. I should put something out for them after tea so they can have breakfast, too. Who watches out for them in winter?

Ben slaps my arse lightly. "I have faith in you. You're a professional, Charlie."

"Not a professional tea-maker," I say, and gasp slightly as he slides his arms around my waist once I put the kettle on the stove, lining the nape of my neck with teasing kisses. "Coffee only. Please."

"You'll make me a flat white later," he drawls. "Just to keep your dark barista heart happy and purposeful."

I laugh and turn to kiss him properly before setting to work again on the tea. I reach for the battered Earl Grey blend tin. "All right. Better yet, I can get Jasmine to make you one at the café. She's working this afternoon. We can stop by."

"'Kay," he says. "What are your plans today, anyway?"

Shit, he'd have to mention reality. *Well, fuck you, reality. I'm enjoying this hiatus from my regularly scheduled life.*

"Plans?" What, there's a world beyond this dreamy one, beyond this robin's-egg-blue kitchen with red mugs and teapots set out on the wood counter? Beyond Ben's equally blue eyes? Distantly, I recall I have band rehearsal later in the evening. That's an eternity away: hours and hours. A lifetime. A little longer here wouldn't hurt, would it?

"Nothing today," I say. "Not till after supper. I'll work on my essays another time."

He brightens. "Spend the day with me doing things that don't matter? Just hanging out?"

"Like you even need to ask."

We kiss again. It's kind of ridiculously soppy, but Jasmine's not here to give me a hard time about it, and he's so delicious, I'm going to be damn greedy with my kisses. And we have to do something while the tea steeps, don't we? These stolen minutes need to be taken advantage of.

As my hand slides inside Ben's boxers to tease him, he lets out a soft whimper.

Before long, I'm on my knees with his cock in my mouth. His hands clutch my hair as he sobs out, leaning back against the fridge—a brilliant way to start the day.

My mouth works in rhythm with his thrusts and then he's whimpering, pulling desperately on my hair until he cries out and erupts intensely all over my hand and floor. Then he sags against the fridge while I gaze up at him and swallow, licking my lips.

"Mmm," I say.

He's flushed under his freckles, his blond hair a mess from earlier. For once, he doesn't have any witty comebacks as his pale thighs tremble, thermals around his knees, and he tries to catch his breath.

Grinning at his stunned expression, I rise to give him a kiss. "There. And I think your tea's about ready, too."

Ben tries to pull himself together as I pour and follow the usual tea rituals, following directions that could be in his grimoire: let the tea steep for a generous five minutes, warm the mugs, pour the tea, add two spoonfuls of sugar and a splash of milk, five stirs. I serve it with a flourish, then I repeat the same for myself after letting it steep a little longer to my taste. But Ben's cream lingering on my tongue is the real secret ingredient.

He sighs his approval, blissed out. "I'll keep you."

"Naturally."

We grin at each other, transfixed, even though my guts twist.

Don't think. Don't ruin this moment.

I'll let myself have today with Ben, at least for a few more hours. What would I do at home but torture myself with the memory of last night anyway? There'll be plenty of time later for self-flagellation and the careful eradication of Scottish-related memories as needed. This kind of self-indulgence is what has gotten me in trouble before. My judgment isn't for trusting. But right now, this feels so good.

Then, Ben grabs my hand and in a haze we take our tea back to bed. To make sure the cream's fresh, of course.

Chapter Sixteen

Ben has a glint in his eye and snowflakes on his fringe when he takes my hand to crunch through snow in Islington. We skirt past his neighbor brushing snow off his car with a broom. There's a fair bit of the white stuff for London, and transport's suitably fucked today, but we're not going anywhere far that needs a tube or train. We managed a short bus ride to get this far. I'm not sure exactly where we're going, but Ben's excited.

"You still won't tell me where we're headed?" I ask, reaching out to tug the pompom of his wool fair isle hat in blues and greens that draw out his eyes.

"Nope." He swats at me lightly, grinning. "Not terribly far, though."

We keep going. He draws me into a lane of shops, stealing a kiss beneath a snowy black awning.

"So greedy," I murmur.

It's hard to think of a time before Ben, but it's only been three days. Well, three days since the third Saturday in a row when we kissed in the snow in front of the café. Damn, I have it bad already. No wonder Jasmine's been relentless.

I've become more of a space cadet at work than usual. It's impossible to concentrate on uni with someone like Ben careening into my life. There has to be a calibration period, and I think he feels the same way about me. We're practically giddy. I move in to kiss him back.

"Mmm, hold that thought. There's something I want you to see. But you can't peek. I'll guide you—shut your eyes."

"Shut my eyes?"

"Trust me?"

I hesitate.

I mean, who knows what Ben's into, exactly. How much is there to know after only a week? I know little, other than he's Scottish, rocks out like he was born on stage playing to live audiences—which I knew from before this last week—and fucks with intent, which I've learned since. He doesn't strike me as the axe-murderer sort, but then again, Ted Bundy had seemed perfectly nice at first, too. Perhaps he has a secret lair where he keeps lions and he's going to feed me to them, like some weird snuff kink.

Will Camden Passage be the last thing I ever see?

"Don't worry, it's nothing bad," he breathes against me, licking my earlobe, and I shudder. "I bet your nan would approve."

"What? Leave my nan out of this," I protest. "You sick bastard."

He gives that delighted laugh that does something odd in the core of me, and then his lips are on mine and I melt.

"You promise you're not a serial killer?" I ask.

"Charlie! You shouldn't say such things about your nan, for God's sake. Manners."

I grin, and his hands are over my eyes.

"Now we've cleared that up, we're nearly there," he says. "Who knows what you're thinking with that overactive imagination of yours, but I'm promising good things. You'll see. Now. All you have to do is keep walking. I won't steer you into walls or traffic or anything foul, I promise."

"Shit, I wasn't worried about that before, but now I am."

"Hush. C'mon, we're walking here."

And we do. One tentative step after another, and I really do hope we won't be walking like this for too long. But he's good to his word.

"Stop," he says easily. "Hang on while I get the door."

"This better not be a lion's den. Is that some weird Scottish kink? Like shortbread?"

"Aye, shortbread's an important kink to be aware of, but I'd say keeping dens is something more in line with your people, babe. Wasn't Byron English? Kept a bear at Cambridge, I think. Doubtless he'd have needed a den for that. And Byron was half Scottish, actually."

"God, what a horrible thought." I grimace, trying to imagine where one would keep a bear in that town—roaming the Backs, picking off tender first-year freshers arriving at uni? Or perhaps in some college quadrangle? Complete with *"keep off the grass—don't feed the bear"* placards for the tourists?

I hear the creak of a door and bells and figure it must be a shop from the lane, because we haven't gotten far. A music shop? But why the mystery then? Or some sort of sex shop? Opium den maybe? Hell if I know.

"Open your eyes," Ben says, a smile in his voice.

And I do, blinking against the light as I try to take stock of my surroundings. This isn't any kind of sex shop or opium den. There are colors everywhere. It takes a moment to make the connection. "You've brought me to…a wool shop?"

"Isn't it grand?" he enthuses with glee. "Welcome to my church."

"And here I thought that was the stage," I say, glancing around. It looks like a very nice wool shop, though I don't have a clue about these things. There are shoppers in here, including a couple of ladies who must be nans.

A woman comes over to us and I'm immediately thinking of desperate excuses why I'd be in a wool shop. But Ben is nonplussed. In fact, he gives her his charismatic grin.

"Ben, so good to see you," she says, and they exchange a hug and air kisses, much to my surprise. He must be a regular.

"Hiya, Eleanor. Meet my friend, Charlie."

"Hello, Charlie," she says with a warm smile, dark hair skimming her shoulders. She's at least middle-aged, not quite nan age, but definitely older than us. "Very good to meet you."

"Hi," I say. She seems nice, and I let my guard down a little.

"Can I help you find anything today?" Eleanor asks.

I look at Ben. He smiles in his open and easy way. "I'm just showing Charlie one of my favorite places."

And then I feel a bit guilty for having been taken aback at first. I'm absolutely intrigued by Ben and what he likes, and I want to know more about him.

Eleanor smiles, looking appraisingly at me, and I feel my face warming under her scrutiny before she looks at Ben again. "Well, let me know if I can help either of you find anything. Though I suspect you might've found something you've been looking for already," she says mildly with a wink before she goes off to help the other customers.

That left my face burning and I dare a glance at Ben. How could someone like him want for anything? In fact, his being single is near impossible. How could that be? And how could I actually be the answer? And who exactly is Eleanor to him, anyway?

Ben must see all the question marks in my eyes—along with my furious blush—and he gives me a quick grin. Between our coats, he takes my hand to squeeze my fingers. "She's right."

"Holy shit."

While my heart thumps to a new rhythm, my head in a daze somewhere with the whirling snowflakes beyond the shop front window, Ben leads me over to a display of yarn. Even I can see the colors are glorious: rich purple and chocolate and crimson. And when I pick up a ball of yarn, it's impossibly soft.

"I met Eleanor last year when I first came to London."

"Oh?" Curious, I glance up at him from the cloud of silver wool in my hand. "Is that right?"

"Aye. When I moved here, I didn't know anyone. I left all of my mates in Edinburgh to come down south and make a serious go with my music."

Jesus, Charlie. You really don't know much about this fabulous guy. I have so many questions.

"That's seriously brave, man. I don't know if I could have done that," I confess. My entire life's been in North London. Technically, Edinburgh isn't that far away, but Scotland is another country and about five or six hours on the train.

"For that first week, I'd thought I'd made a terrible mistake." Ben shakes his blond head. "No band, no job. Just some savings and an idea. I'll admit I was feeling a bit sorry for myself at first. I was so lonely. Early on, I would walk the streets of my neighborhood, getting to know the place, giving me something to do. And I happened to read a notice in a coffee shop like yours for knitting lessons. And I figured, why the hell not? So I came here and signed up, and Eleanor taught me the basics. Ever since, I've come to the weekly knit night. She's like having another mum."

I grin at him. "Aww, bless."

"So I've learned to make things like this." Ben takes the wool hat off his head and hands it over. It's damp from melting snowflakes on top of the knitted ones, the motifs in sage green and sky and midnight blue.

"You made this?" I ask, incredulous. Now, I don't know the first thing about knitting, but it looks damn complicated, with the needles and the yarn and everything. "It looks like something you'd get in a store. Except far nicer than H&M or Uniqlo. Shit, is there anything you can't do?"

Ben laughs with delight. He leans in to give me a teasing kiss, and I melt like those damn snowflakes, his hat crushed between us. "Oh plenty, believe me."

We spend a moment in a space that's all our own. No wool shop, no other customers, no London. In a world of our own making: population two. We gaze at each other. God, I can't wait to learn more about Ben.

"Would you make me something?" I ask at last, when I have gathered some of my senses back.

"Ach, no. You see, there's a curse."

"What? What curse? Is this another Scottish thing you haven't told me about?" I tease.

"It's a knitting thing. If you're dating someone and you make something for them, you're bound to break up after. And—well, I don't want that to happen," Ben confesses sheepishly. "Because I really do like you."

"Ah, you numpty," I murmur and kiss him again. Never mind Eleanor and anyone else watching us in here. I'm thrilled he wants to keep us safe from a knitting curse.

"I'll teach you, though, if you want," he offers, eyes dancing.

"You have a far higher estimation of my capabilities than I do, mate."

"You haven't even tried knitting yet."

"So why are we here, then? Aside from showing me your favorite places."

"I need your help to pick out some colors," he says immediately, gesturing at the display. Yarn is spread artfully on a white table, cascading from a shelf and baskets, with knitting books and patterns. "I think these bulky yarns. I have a project in mind."

"What are you making?"

"Can't say yet. It's a surprise."

"But the curse..." I manage, surprised after what he told me a moment ago. "Is it for you?"

Ben considers, smiling. God, that smile. Right, before I get lost in daydreams about chasing the freckles from his cheeks to somewhere considerably lower, I make myself focus. He's talking. I think.

"...for us," he finishes.

"Right." Flustered, I chew my lip. Shit. I missed what he was saying. *Focus, Charlie.*

We go to work selecting colors. I pick out a blue that matches Ben's eyes, beautiful and deep, a shade I could dive into.

Chapter Seventeen

We have another crunch through snow back to Ben's house, the snowflakes coming down something fierce. He empties the carrier bag full of wool on his bed: soft pink and charcoal and sea blue, burnt orange and sage green and ivory. Everything feels magical this afternoon, time suspended, like time belongs to people other than us.

The city's transformed under a fresh canopy of white—and so am I, having grinned all of the way back to Ben's, not even caring in the slightest who saw me like that. I love getting to know him, and I'm thrilled he trusted me enough to share his secret wool habit with me. When was the last time I was so curious about someone? Or, if I'm totally honest, so happy?

"Will you make another hat?" I ask curiously, admiring the wool haul. Unable to resist, I squeeze the sea-blue ball of yarn from the scatter on the bed, soft in my hand.

I'm definitely getting into the spirt of this now, after my initial hesitation. I've already been caught up in Ben's passion for making things. In addition to his hat, he'd knit the multicolored striped scarf he wore the day we met, and the throw blanket on the bed. And I have a suspicion he's knit a pullover or cardigan or two, along with the colorful socks on his feet.

Ben grins like he'd been waiting ages for me to ask that specific question. He comes close, sliding his arms around my waist, and nuzzles me, which instantly sparks a cascade of goose bumps across my body. "Nope. I have something else in mind."

I've forgotten what we were saying, and I think he has too. I slide my hands beneath his cloud soft pullover, and his skin is silk. Euphoria thrums taut in my body.

Oh God, he's way better than any drug.

Before long, I'm helping him out of his top and he's keen to return the favor. Compared to the morning, we're more leisurely in our kisses and teasing. Slowly, each piece of clothing falls away: pullovers and jeans and boxers. I leave his socks on, though, because the fuchsia, periwinkle, and dove gray is too damn appealing, and my Debenham's black socks from a plastic pack are appalling by comparison. Those come off.

We stand in front of the fireplace, fingers tracing each other's bodies, learning a new landscape. What will make him sigh, shudder, gasp? What will make him feel anything like I feel right now, my breath caught up in my chest, a tangle of anticipation and longing? I explore his body, limned by the spill of daylight from the window behind us. As he responds to me, I thrill in the luxury of him.

My fingernails lightly rake Ben's back as he groans softly. God, I want him. I want to please him. I want him to want me just as badly.

I cup his arse, press my hardness against his thigh. Meanwhile, he drifts slow kisses across my shoulders and chest, soft as the snowflakes outside. His mouth sears a promise, an answer to my questions, and I tremble in response. Somehow, it feels like we have all the time in the world, caught suspended inside a snow globe, separate from the city beyond this room, separate from reality.

Ben draws me into a deep kiss and I shudder, senses heightened after prolonged teasing. He delights in my responses to him, so raw and so eager. My heart's exposed like I haven't dared with anyone else. I'm way past pretending I still have any facade of cool, open in my longing for him.

My cock aches, hot and urgent. Eventually, he sinks to his knees, so close I can feel his breath. His tongue darts for a teasing lick along the head of my damp cock and I can't help a soft cry. He grins up at me before starting a merciless blow job that soon has me desperate for release. And he teases me to the brink and stops.

He looks up at me with serious sea-blue eyes before that grin I already love appears, wicked and impish and irresistible. "Right. So now you're going to tie me up."

What?

"Hmm?" I reel before him on unsteady legs, trying to catch my breath. God, what a state he's left me in. "'Kay."

We haven't covered this sort of territory before, but I'm certainly into it. "Like handcuffs?"

"Like in wool." Ben's grin widens, so open and all for me. He nods at the bed, the chaotic tumble of spilled yarn. "You're going to make me look brilliant. And then you can do anything you want to me."

"Holy shit, you're serious." I laugh, delighted.

Right, so if this is what crafts is all about, I'm definitely in. Except…I have absolutely no idea what I'm doing. But I'm damn eager to learn.

"Absolutely." He dives onto the bed and lobs the pink yarn at me. His cock is rigid, reaching for his belly. Freckles cover his face, shoulders and arms, paling on his torso, and reappear on his legs. "Safe word's 'nan.'"

"That's sick."

Ben laughs, a beautiful pink blush running from his face to his chest. He brushes bleached hair from his eyes as he gazes affectionately at me. "A color per limb. Go. You have bedposts. Start wrapping. Think shibari."

I lick my lips, absorbing the gorgeous sight of him, lean and pale, spread out on the crimson duvet. At least I know what he's talking about, though I'm not exactly up on Japanese bondage techniques, and I can't promise what I do will be beautiful. But if he wants to be caught in a web of color, that I can manage. With glee.

"Also...blindfold me. I want to be impressed when you let me see again." He reaches into the bedside drawer and pulls out a midnight silk sash.

"Into surprises, hmm?" I drawl teasingly, but my stomach is tight with anticipation.

"Mmm."

"Close your eyes," I command, breathing hard.

"That's the spirit." He closes his eyes. I draw the silk around his face, tying the scarf securely behind his head, careful not to catch his hair, but I don't think he's the sort to complain even if I did. I push him down on the bed.

Ben sighs happily, stretching out languidly, like he has no bones, practically feline. I kiss the inside of his wrist, and so begins my project. He's absolutely perfect, lying there all unabashed and beautiful. And the way he looks at me, so trusting, thrills me to the core. Better give the man what he wants, and then some.

I wrap and wrap and wrap, making artwork out of Ben. Around his wrists. Around the dark wooden slats of the headboard.

Left wrist—pink. Right wrist—orange.

While I work on him, I pause every so often to tease his body with a rogue kiss, nip, scratch. He groans and squirms.

"Keep going," Ben urges. Mussed up hair falls over his blindfold. The angles of his cheekbones, the line of his jaw, are highlighted by the snowy daylight. He quivers like a man unraveling.

When his breath catches as I circle and tweak a nipple, I move south to draw his seeping cock into my mouth. Shuddering with pleasure, he shifts beneath me, and I move down, past his balls, to trace the delicate skin of his inner thigh, the blue veins beneath.

Left ankle—green. Right ankle—blue.

God, Ben's a sight, trussed up and blindfolded and unmoving.

Ben's silent now, legs splayed to my specifications. I trace his warm stomach, rising and falling in response to my mouth, then the line of his rib cage, savoring the vision of him. He jumps slightly, his body taut, cock still rigid.

"Fucking hot," I say, awed.

He's a web of colors now, a tapestry caught against the dark wood bed frame, the sweep of crimson beneath him, the midnight blue of his blindfold. His blond hair is fanned out on the sky-blue pillowcase. And I reach for my phone and take a picture, because something so fucking impressive needs to be caught in time beyond my memory. After all, he's my first craft project.

And then I begin to tease my way up his inner thigh as he shudders. I reach for the lube, and soon it's the taste of Ben in my mouth and he's gasping. Then one finger's inside him and he groans with pleasure.

"Like that, huh?" I drawl, my voice low. His reward equals two fingers teasing him relentlessly.

"Oh God," he manages.

"Shh…" I tell him, intrigued to know if he can be quiet when he's so turned on. "Quiet."

I'm fit to burst myself, watching him pale against warm

sheets with the slashes of colors on his limbs, and that does something to me. Then I track a teasing, meandering path from his cock to his mouth as he practically purrs, twisting beneath me, our skin on fire as we touch.

When I kiss him hard, he gasps. After a condom, I press my cock in, unrelenting and without mercy, and his back arches as I dig my fingers into his twisting hips to keep him from bucking. And we move together, sob together, come together in a fit of urgency and longing and something that promises to be so much more, and fuck, he trusts me to do this thing to him and I'm lost in the ecstasy of Ben and me and this cascade of colors.

Eventually, we come back to our senses. Or mostly.

There's trembling and it takes me a moment—it's me that's shaking, from exertion, from the rawness of being together with Ben. For letting him mean so much to me already. Like some core part of me recognizes something brilliant in him, along with the hot and sexy part. It must be something like intuition, like instinct, more reliable than my brain. But right now, it's some other part that's taken charge, my heart hammering away. Blissed out, I hold him tight. And I can't remember a time before Ben, or ever wanting someone so much. I want to live in this moment forever.

I lift my head from where I'd buried it against his neck, brushing my mouth against his. The navy blindfold still covers his eyes. At last I shift it out of the way to restore his sight.

"Mmm…" Ben takes a moment for his eyes to adjust to the light, then he absorbs the sight of the ad hoc bindings I'd made with his colorful yarn and his mystery and vulnerability when he gave himself over entirely to me.

A slow smile curls his lips, like dawn breaking over some magnificent vista, as he takes in what I've done.

"I suppose I'll let you talk now…" I tease softly, kissing him reverently before he has a chance to respond.

"Oh, good." Ben admires the colorful yarn securing him to the bed. "If you're planning on keeping me as your prisoner, I'm going to have needs. Like shortbread, for example."

"What if I said there's a panic in your motherland 'cause there's no more shortbread to be had?" I retort.

"It's not all Walker's, mate. Shortbread from airports, pfft. We bake, you know."

"You tell yourself what you want to believe." I brush his lips with mine, feeling his smile against my mouth. This must be what a bit of heaven tastes like. "By the way, I'm entirely sold on crafts now."

"You've done an excellent job," he says proudly. "Now you'll need to untie me and wind that back into balls for next time."

My damn foolish grin is near permanent, because he said there'll be a next time. God, what is this feeling? I'm on some kind of high that I didn't know was possible. Oh, I have it bad for a certain Scot who is full of talents and mystery. The more we're together, the more I want to know. The way he looks at me makes me think he might be feeling something similar too, all soft-eyed and glorious. What other secrets does he have?

"And Charlie?"

"Yes?"

"I think it might be time for tea after all that."

We laugh with glee. Of course we'll have tea and of course we'll continue on like this again after, till it's time for my own band rehearsal later. We'll live in the quiet of the snow that continues to fall, the snowflakes beyond Ben's window dancing and bright. And like Ben had said earlier, my dark barista heart is full of something unexpected. Something overwhelming and grand.

But can I trust this feeling? Familiar worries start to creep back alongside reality as my breath steadies. Ben's not part of my scheduled plan. Like uni. Like getting ready for Christmas. I don't know what to do about it all, other than savor this fantastic afternoon with Ben in his room and ignore reality for one more day.

Chapter Eighteen

At home the next day, my primal reptilian brain is in the driver's seat. I'm up super early to make up for all of the slacking and distraction over the last few days.

After the bliss of yesterday with Ben, coming home alone to my room was disorienting. Even though I have the loom of the whiteboard's *to do* list hanging over my bed telling me exactly what I need to do and when, I'm well behind now on my planned uni work between the weekend and the last couple of days. Bliss has been replaced with stress, a sobering comedown after my escapades with Ben.

When Emily calls at the usual time for me to talk to Carys, there's a moment where I'm tempted not to answer. It's already bad that I missed yesterday's call, leaving a heaviness in my chest.

"Hey," I say. "Gotta keep this short. I'm in mid-thought on my essay and I'm gonna literally lose the plot if this is more than five minutes."

"No problem," Emily agrees easily and puts Carys on straight away.

But I'm distracted, and Carys picks up on my vibes, and she's unsettled too. "Play wif dawg," she instructs, squirming. Emily's holding the phone steady but Carys careens in and out of the video call.

"Wish I could, baby. I can't."

"No?"

"No," I confirm, feeling heavy. "Sorry."

"No! Bad Daddy!" She grabs at the phone and the image of her blurs with her hand over the camera.

She bursts into tears, and I feel horrible. "I'm really sorry..."

But she drops the phone or Emily does and the call's cut off. It's just as well. Seems I'm failing at being a dad as well as my uni work. Ugh.

I've made a right mess of things.

So far, Emily hasn't asked what's up. Even if she did, I'm not sure what I could say by way of explanation.

Torrid fling with an indie rocker that I couldn't say no to instead of thinking about our daughter.

Shit, now I feel even worse.

I stare at the crooked curtain rail over the window, which becomes the target of my anxiety. Instead of the lectures, or arranging a call with Emily, I become laser focused on taking down the rod and installing it properly, now taking on vital importance. The curtains are dusty, though. I drag out our motley assortment of tools from the cupboard under the stairs that heaves with the hoover and the summer barbeque equipment for our tiny garden.

And that's not nearly enough to take the edge off. So I take the hoover and vacuum everything: cushions and crevices and the darkest corners of the house best suited for cobwebs. I polish the windows to see the abundant snow outside like a guilty reminder, and then the mirrors till my reflection gleams.

My laundry pile's only grown bigger, and I haven't done the Christmas shopping yet for Carys or my family.

One last rational scrap of me remains. The rest of me has given over to a spiral of gloomy thoughts as I neaten my room for the third time: I'm down to dusting invisible dust. Not that I'm a clean freak or anything, but cleaning and organizing makes me think I've some control in my life, according to my therapist. By the time I head out the door for my noon shift, there's been laundry and tidying and even dusting of the walls and windowsills. I was already behind on house cleaning duties after a weekend spent mostly with Ben.

All of this, of course, is my effort to process what's happened with Ben, who is some kind of ecstasy I haven't earned. Perhaps he's a hallucinogen. Perhaps I'm having a relapse. I've cleaned for hours to keep from rushing to my phone to text him something lame and rambling, like I've been kidnapped by spies and can't see him again, or the more to the point "I'm far too weird to date" text every guy wants to see, especially after connecting for real, as well as having fantastic sex. And, well, meeting someone like Ben doesn't happen to someone like me.

A message like that has to be better than ghosting someone, right? At least it's a confirmation that I disappeared. Not that I really want to disappear. I want to be here. Or there, with Ben. Just...not so overwhelmed with everything.

Speaking of overwhelmed, there's yet another scheduled rehearsal. Jackson went wild booking us into studios ahead of the break since there won't be much time once we're all back after Christmas to get ready for our gig.

Still feeling wretched, I call him as soon as I get on the bus.

"It's got to be serious if you're actually calling me straight out."

"I can't make it tonight. I'm screwed on this essay, man."

"I thought term was out for you?"

I shift out of the way as a passenger clomps past me with an armful of colorful bags. Christmas shopping, I bet. "Nah, especially not for me. I get to make up shit that I missed last month 'cause of working too much and Carys. My lecturer was sympathetic 'cause he's a dad too, but I still gotta do stuff before I go to Wales. So…I hope you don't hate me for canceling again."

"You do what you need to do, Charlie. We'll make do."

When we hang up, it's no comfort knowing he wasn't exactly mad, but not enthusiastic either.

Work passes uneventfully, and when I return home after picking up a couple of gifts on the way, I get back to my schoolwork with renewed vigor. It's satisfying to check off a couple of things on that too-long whiteboard list. All that's left is the big essay.

I pull out my suitcase as a reward for getting at least some of what needed doing done. My freshly washed clothes from the earlier round of laundry are folded on the desk. Beside the clothes are a couple of small stocking stuffers for Carys that I've picked up in recent weeks. I may as well close the loop and start to place things in a suitcase. I find gift wrap for the presents and start in on that too.

The day has been rough, but I'm starting to feel like I'm back to the comfort of my usual routines. I always feel better when I do. No more upheavals. No more spinning thoughts. No more feeling too much, like there's an expanding universe inside me, vast and uncomfortable. Just wrapping presents and packing.

When I check my phone an hour or so later, there's a text from Ben.

How's your day? Want to come over? x

That's when I die about a million times because fuck yes, I want to go over. Like, right now. More than anything. But that's impossible, because I need to finish my essay before I leave. And this is getting dangerous. Way too dangerous. Too fast, too much, too intense.

I mean, I have a schedule. A plan. No dating. And I might be able to fool myself into a weekend of Fridays, but it's the middle of the week—a Wednesday. A day entirely meant to be sensible, and very far from the weekend.

Standing back, I look critically at the curtains over the kitchen sink. Too much dust. Clearly the way to deal with this dilemma is to wash them along with the bedroom curtains, because no man can fall in serious like with another man who has dusty curtains, and I swear that's no kind of euphemism. I bet Ben's curtains are perfect. To be honest, I didn't get a chance to look around much when we were together, because we could have been on the moon for all I noticed. Everything was Ben and fucking incredible.

With a sigh, I climb onto the counter to take down the curtains.

All I want is Ben. And it's impossible. With a gulp, I send a text back.

I can't. I'm leaving in a couple of days and I've got a lot on for Christmas. You're brilliant. I just think you and me, I don't think this can happen. I'm sorry. x

Staring at the phone, I don't know what to say to make it better. It'll probably just make it worse. And yeah, it's gonna suck, but I have a whole set of reasonable, responsible Wednesday activities that'll keep me busy. Busy and safe. Because routines are safe and obsessions with gorgeous guitar players are not.

To be honest, I want Wednesday to fuck off and die, but it doesn't.

I feel like complete hell when I hit send.

Chapter Nineteen

Later that evening, I sit, sick to my stomach. Seriously, something's wrong with me. Well, obviously—and officially—there is. Anyone else, say Lars from the café or Briar from the band, would probably say I need to live now and go for it, but they don't have the responsibilities I do. But it doesn't change what I want right now—Ben. Geography will have to help me get back on track: Ben will be a distant memory by the time I reach Wales for Christmas.

Reaching for the phone again, I call Emily as planned at 7:00 p.m.

"Hiya, Charlie." She smiles as we do our usual video call, sitting in her gran's bright and modern front room.

"Hey."

She's quiet for a moment, wise in the million silences of one Charles Renfrew, so I'm not surprised it takes her a nanosecond to figure out I'm more out of sorts than usual.

"How are you? You look a bit rough. Is everything all right?" she asks with a slight frown.

I shrug a shoulder. Where even to begin? Or, more

appropriately, what to say and what to leave out. "It will be. I think."

"Well, I know you've been more scarce than usual the last few days," she says. "And…I don't know what, exactly. Preoccupied when I have heard from you."

"Mm."

"Mm?" She gives me an encouraging smile.

I groan, rubbing my face with my hand. "Don't worry, I'm still clean."

"Should I be worried that you're struggling?" Emily asks.

"No, no. I'm not near that, thank God. No. It's…well, it's going to sound silly."

She chuckles. "Try me."

"I…" How to explain Ben? Words don't do him justice. "There's…"

"It's okay. Whatever it is."

"Oh no, it isn't. I violated the ban. Well, not that I quite dated anyone, mind—"

She looks startled. Emily's well-versed on my dating ban. "Go on."

"There's a man. Ben." I try again. Second time lucky? Let's find out. "Who I was…having sex with. Except…it feels like more than that. And it can't be."

Emily's expression softens. "I think that sounds lovely, if you've found someone that you want to see more than once."

Panic rises. "You missed the whole part about the ban and how this can't be. What the hell did I do?"

"What *did* you do?"

"Well, he started it," I say accusingly, like that'll absolve me of all responsibility in our brief union since I wasn't the instigator. "You said I found someone but actually he found me, just in the café. Working. Like I do. Repeat customer."

She laughs.

"It's not funny."

"I'm not laughing at you, lovely. I just think there must be something special about him to catch your attention for more than a night," she says. "I'm curious to know more."

I hop up to pace my room's creaky hardwood floor. "He's a musician. A proper one. He's funny and filthy and beautiful. A dream, if I'm honest. I swear my subconscious mind's made him up and he can't be real."

"He sounds wonderful."

"Don't get excited," I warn darkly. Em's positively buoyant at the prospect of an unexpected spike in my shuttered romantic life. "I just basically told him to fuck off after a few days of sex. Fantastic sex. That I'm too busy to see him. Because of—well, everything." I wave my hands around, very much unlike a man in control. "You know—you and Carys, uni, work, the band—"

"You didn't." She stares.

I don't know if she's more startled that I admitted to being with someone over multiple days, or that I told him to fuck off. In any case, she's looking at me—rightfully—as though I've entirely lost my mind. Which, clearly, I have.

"Of course I did. How could I not? You know the situation, Em."

"You deserve to have a life too." She pauses, considering. "You know I date. Do you judge me for that?"

"Of course not."

"Then?"

"It's different," I protest. How can she not see that?

"I still think you're addicted to beating yourself up." Emily sighs. "So, you actually told him to fuck off?"

"Well, I was slightly more polite about it, but basically, yes."

She shakes her head.

"What did you say, exactly?"

"Oh, I don't know. I stopped short of saying something

about me being busy washing curtains while writing an essay and packing for Wales, because, if anything, that might sound even worse..."

Emily groans. "Charlie. Is this the gay equivalent of saying you're staying in to wash your hair?"

"Ha. It's true! Go on, ream me out. I can tell you're dying to say something."

"No, I'm not."

I'm quiet for a long moment, wary as we contemplate each other across the video call. "I worried maybe he wouldn't understand because he's got bad dyslexia. But then I haven't heard a peep since then. He's obviously gotten the message that I'm busy."

Emily runs her fingers through her long hair as she frowns. "You're avoiding someone who's into you? That you like?"

"Well, yes—just because I'm into something doesn't mean it's a good idea." I look at Emily, defiant. I could rattle off a long list without even trying. "There's plenty of evidence to back that up, remember?"

"*Charles.*"

"Emily." I sit up straight, giving her my best *take me seriously* face. It's the next face after the Renfrew poker face. If she's gonna *Charles* me like my mother, she's getting the face. Even if she does have a point, I'm not ready to concede. I could totally die on this hill.

"I know you, remember? This doesn't sound like your usual hookup. You don't ever tell me about those."

I screw up my face. Putting Emily off isn't an easy thing. "Believe me, he's got plenty of admirers out there. He doesn't need to be single if he doesn't want to be."

"Do you want to be single?" she challenges.

Startled, I make some kind of undignified sound. I suck on my bottom lip before I reply more properly like I actually have an answer. I mean, I kind of do. It's just the answer to a different question. "I don't know. I mean, it doesn't matter what I want, does it? I have things to do that are more important, like helping you. And Carys."

She's quiet. In the background, Carys plays and sing-songs to herself.

"You know you deserve happiness, don't you?" Emily says. "A chance to live? You get to do that, even with Carys."

Heat rises in my face. Caught. Emily went straight for the jugular. She may look nice, but behold—apex predator. I open my mouth but no sound comes out.

"Happy doesn't factor into it," I say finally. "That's a luxury."

She ignores that. "Does Ben make you happy?"

I hesitate. A million times yes. "Well, of course—"

"Then you better tell him. Before it's too late. And give yourselves a chance to explore whatever's between you, whether it works out or it doesn't. You just need to let yourself live. Not stuck in things behind you or waiting for future you. Obviously, Ben sees something in you that exists *right now*."

Of course she's right. And I'm overwhelmed, so I just nod, letting this sink in.

Emily shifts. "How about a glimpse of Carys? She's playing."

"I can hear her."

"She's talking to the dinosaur you sent." Emily smiles. So do I.

After a smallish sort of commotion, with the net result of seeing Carys plonked on the floor in her mum's lap, Em holding the phone so Carys can see me, I smile at my daughter.

Carys is cute in her goat pajamas, with dark hair and green eyes like me. Spitting image, Emily insists, but Carys is far more adorable. No matter how miserable I feel, whenever I see my daughter, I wonder at this small, magnificent person we made. Everything seems more hopeful when I see her.

Leaning in to peer at the phone, Carys gives a death-grip to the tyrannosaurus in her fist.

"Say hi to Daddy, darling," Emily encourages, her blond hair falling over her shoulder as she gives Carys a kiss on the cheek.

She tolerates this with only a minor squirm, which means she's mostly distracted, attention rapt on me for at least a few seconds. I'll take the window.

"Daddy!"

"Hi, Carys." A smile stretches across my lips, which is fairly inevitable whenever I see our incredible girl.

"Dino," she declares with authority, smiling back at me with glee. The toy is shoved against the phone and they've been blocked out by a T-Rex and I can't stop laughing, while Emily tries to sort the dinosaur and Carys out. The phone tumbles on the rug, catching sight of Carys tearing past, laughing.

"Her favorite," Emily informs me as she picks up the phone, Carys beside her, climbing Emily's arm. "Say thanks for the dinosaurs."

"T'ANKS." Carys grins at me, peering down at the screen.

The phone shifts back to Emily. "Call him. Tell him about the things that've happened, if you want a chance at this working out. If he's what you want."

Of course he's what I want, but how do I find the courage?

Chapter Twenty

The problem with getting involved—either peripherally with the vigorous sexing or, God help me, full-on dating, or whatever's going on—with an up-and-coming rock singer is that his gigs sell out.

At the box office the next day, I beg like a man with nothing left to lose, because Ben's silence is deafening. I haven't heard anything all day. Not a peep. Not even an accidental pocket dial. Nothing. It's a complete disaster. It's all my fault. Emily's right.

I'm a jerk.

"Please." I stare with intent, pleading shamelessly. "I'll do anything. I mean it. It's really important. I just need one ticket, man."

The man shakes his head. He's in an old Oasis T-shirt, silver-haired. His earlobes are full of metal. "Sorry, mate. Sold out. Halfpenny Rise is the hot ticket tonight."

"I really need to talk to Ben," I say.

We both hear the desperation in my voice. Hopefully the sort of desperation that's appealing enough to manifest tickets out of nowhere from sheer force of will. Or better yet, the sort of desperation that can manifest Ben right here, right now.

He laughs, shaking his head regretfully. "Oh yeah? Who doesn't want to talk to Ben Campbell? Are you press?"

"Well...yes." I stand tall, running a hand through my hair to neaten it in an effort to look like a reporter and not like a frantic wild man who's been slogging through snow and slush.

"Credentials?" he asks patiently, sticking out a hand to take them.

"I left them at home?"

He shakes his head, resolute. "C'mon, mate. I told you the gig's sold out. Your best bet's the scalpers tonight."

I groan, not surprised but disappointed anyway. "All right. Cheers."

It'll serve me right to pay through the nose to grovel. Maybe he should be charging for tickets to that upcoming spectacle, a side-show to the gig.

Meanwhile, another snowfall warning's gone out for London.

When I arrive at The Underground rock club—and pay more than double for a ticket from my café income—the show's already well underway. Snow's hit the city again. The wait for the bus was useless, with no hope of the damn things running. I walked two miles in the snow, my leather boots and socks soaked through for my troubles. There was no way I'd miss the gig, though. It's standing room only, shoulder to shoulder. I get a beer and make my way closer to the stage.

The opening act has already played. Ben's band tears up the stage like they were born to it. No wonder they've been successful—their album is incredible, but seeing them perform is a whole other level. Their sound and presence can't be captured in a studio recording. Ben's magic up there.

Lights dazzle and flash with the music: electric yellow and blues and purples vibrate. On stage, Ben stands front and center, blazing on his guitar and his voice soars, otherworldly and strong, leaving me with goose bumps. He's in head-to-toe black, with a lavender scarf looped loosely around his neck. I can't help but think of him the other night splayed nude in a riot of colors, bound and immobile, and the hottest thing I'd ever seen. Tonight, it's that same surrender, where he gives himself over to the music and the performance, like nothing else matters in the universe. There's nothing held back.

There's a big voice in his slight body. Every molecule of him is devoted to music when he performs. He's so present that there's no way I could look away, even if I wanted to.

Snaking through the crowd, I slip closer and closer, till I'm off to the side of the dance floor in the club. He has such an ease on stage. Everyone in the room buzzes with energy.

I can't stop grinning. I'm still stunned that somehow our orbits have collided in the last few days. It's too much to hope for anything more, for the spell to continue. For now, I'll bask in the ecstasy of Ben.

The show eventually ends with cries for an encore. The band obliges with great finesse. I swear at one point Ben sees me, but that must have been a trick of the lights and my desperate imagination. I know from my own small gigs how dazzling the stage lights are. The crowd becomes a dark mass, and the only thing visible are the faces of the people who stand at the very front.

When the lights come up again, it takes me a long moment to come back from the magic of the show, letting the din and jostle of the crowd ground me to the present again.

Reaching into my pocket, I retrieve my phone and text.

I'm sorry—I've been an arse. I'll be outside if you want

to talk. C xx
    But will Ben come?

Chapter Twenty-One

After the rock club's cleared out, I stand out front on Camden High Street. It's very late. The rock crowd's left, the sensible gone home. But I'm out in the snow again, and the chill air stings my face as the wind blusters. I'm left with my somewhat less than sparkling thoughts for company. And some rapidly fading desperate hope.

Ben hasn't responded to my text. Again.

There's prolonged panic courtesy of my brain—what if he doesn't show up?

Be real, Charlie. If he was coming out, he would've been out half an hour ago. Go home.

Yet I can't leave.

It's a long wait. A cold wait. A wait long enough to take stock a million times over about the foolish thing I said via text. Basically telling Ben that I didn't have space for him in my life.

Shit, I've fucked this up. Bad.

But against all odds, Ben eventually appears. He's still wearing his lavender scarf that he wore onstage, looped loosely around his neck, the ends tucked into his leather jacket.

Oh God. He's here. He's actually here. I can't believe it, after what I did.

"Ben." My mouth's gone totally dry at the sight of him. It takes real effort to speak. "That was...incredible. I bought a ticket to see you tonight, hoping we could talk. And I'm... so lame. Incredibly lame. That was so fucking inexcusable of me. I don't know what's wrong with me sometimes. I'm so sorry."

Ben studies me, frowning. He's quiet long enough that I might have a panic attack standing here as his frown deepens.

"Charlie," he says in his lilt. A crisp acknowledgment with bite like the winter air against my face.

Breathe. *One-two-three* in, *four-five-six* out. Again. Till oxygen hits my brain.

"Ben—"

He holds up his hands. "You just sent a text, like I didn't matter at all to you, even after the last few days together. I thought I was starting to mean something to you. When I got your message tonight, I wasn't sure if I would come out to see you after the show. I'm still not sure I'm doing the right thing by seeing you, to be honest. You were very clear about your priorities. You have other, more important things happening in your life."

"Let me try to explain." My voice is low and strained. The desperation creeps back. It's a gut blow. My chest is tight, and despite the chill air, my face burns. "I wasn't lying to you when I said it's complicated."

At this hour and with the snow, the pavement's deserted out here. Snow continues to fall. The world is white. We're the only two people left in it.

Ben folds his arms across his chest.

And I totally deserve the standoffish pose he's giving me.

"I'm so sorry. You're right. That *was* shit of me to send a text like that. And not talk properly. Sometimes I do things that don't make sense. I often do things that don't make sense, let's be real. What the hell is communication? I just…panicked. It's an anxiety thing. We should've talked."

He eyes me, relenting slightly. "Panicked?"

I nod and shuffle in the snow that reaches to our ankles.

"Panicked," I confirm. "It's not an excuse. But…the truth is, I have a dating ban because I don't trust myself because of my past. And you—you could have just about anyone. You're so talented. You'll just get disappointed in me, along with the other stuff I've got going on. You'll find someone better, I know it."

"Isn't that something for me to figure out?" Ben counters, lifting his jaw. "I like you and so far you've snuck off twice, then blown me off in a text. What am I supposed to think?"

"See, disappointment. Exactly." I nod glumly, gazing at Ben. He looks brilliant, even when he's upset with me.

Ben makes a sound. He folds his arms across his chest. "No, mate. That's a cop-out. That's what that is."

"I have an…anxiety disorder," I blurt. Words tumble out, a slick of them like an oil spill. "I have an actual letter that says I'm mad. I take meds and go to therapy and try to keep to a routine because it's less likely I'll fuck up again like I've done in the past. Like getting kicked out of school or getting into drugs and…disappointing my family all over again. Supposedly routines help."

I haven't told him my family includes my daughter and best friend, Emily. How could I even begin to explain that?

Ben blinks. He stares at me for a long moment, letting my words sink in. "Shit, Charlie. I didn't know. And you didn't tell me. Why wouldn't you tell me?"

I gulp. "Because I figured you wouldn't want to be with someone like that. That this would only last for a day or two and that'd be it. And then you'd find someone else instead who's a proper adult and has their shit together. Unlike me. I don't feel like I've got anything under control, to be honest."

"And what did I just tell you?"

"That's something for you to figure out?"

"Aye. You're learning." Ben looks satisfied. A hint of a smile is on his lips. "We all have things, Charlie. Every last one of us."

I swallow hard. "I've...I've never met anyone like you before. Who sees things like you do."

Ben gives a wry smile. "I say you need to be open-minded to what you don't know."

He's right. I think of Ben wrapped in wool, of being pulled tight in my scarf as we kissed that first day in the snow at the café. I think of all the million ways he's shown kindness and interest.

And then I ran off like a coward.

I fumble in my pockets. "I'm so sorry."

"Ach."

But he still stands with his arms across his chest.

I fumble in my pockets, embarrassed, but I'm all in now. God help me. I'll make myself silly several times over for Ben. "I made this for you. Because I couldn't find words. When I couldn't sleep. When I was up all night thinking of what a mess I was and how brilliant you'd been."

Ben's eyebrows lift.

"Don't worry," I say quickly. "It's not fancy. It's a bit silly, honestly."

"I love silly," Ben assures me.

Screwing up my face and sucking back air, I present him with a USB stick. More like shoved it into his hand. Reflexively, he grabs the small plastic case.

"It's admittedly a rather shit presentation for a mixtape, but we're not in the eighties and I didn't have a cassette player kicking about. Plus we're not in *Say Anything* and I'm not John Cusack blasting tunes to win you back. But I could do that, if it helps." I look hopefully at him.

Ben gawps for a moment, then recovers. His face softens as he studies the USB stick. My chest thumps a beat.

"It's a bit random. Some Smiths. Some Joy Division. A little bit of Tears for Fears. And, um, Peter Gabriel, which is really proof of how much I'm into you. Just don't let me give you *The Best of Sting.*"

Ben steps up to me, delighted. He takes my face between his hands and gives me such a thorough kiss that we could melt the snow right where we stand.

And that's more than okay.

Chapter Twenty-Two

After more snogging, we gaze at each other on the street. I'm a bit dizzy from the combination of his kisses and letting my emotions come to the surface. Ben's fresh-faced, also trying to catch his breath. Cars hiss past as we stand on the snow-packed pavement. The dark night is soft overhead and clouds reflect the city's glow.

"I'm amazed you came tonight, to be honest." Ben's face is soft. Vulnerable in a way I haven't seen before. "I thought I wouldn't see you again."

"No snowfall would stop me. I ended up walking. Because I needed to see you. To talk. To apologize for being a complete and utter arsehole."

"I'm always happy to talk to you." Ben smiles, tilting his head. "No matter what it is, Charlie. You should know that by now."

"Message received." I reach out and take his hand. He squeezes my fingers. "I guess we can try talking. Gotta admit that's not my area of expertise."

"Let's go to my house and get out of the cold. And

practice talking." Ben reaches out to adjust my scarf.

"We might need to walk." I look around us. The street's virtually deserted. And I haven't seen any buses go by. "Public transport's a disaster with all the snow. Believe me."

"Maybe a taxi tonight, if there's one to be had."

I hesitate over the cost, but I don't want to say anything. We could try to walk to find a stop for the night bus, which is a debacle at the best of times in snow-free conditions, with the drunks and everyone else.

"Where's your gear?" I ask.

"Billy's taking our kit tonight in the van. He's one of my bandmates. And housemates," Ben says. "Don't worry, I'll get the taxi."

"Oh no…"

"It's no bother, honestly. I insist."

Before long, he's flagged down a taxi, which is some sort of miracle on its own that there was a free one to be found, given the snow. We hold hands in the back. When we arrive at Ben's house, his street is silent and bright with the freshly fallen snow.

He kisses me impulsively before we go up the steps to the entry. "I'll admit I was thinking of you all night. Before you sent that text. I needed to talk to you too to figure out what was going on. Even with your strange behavior. I missed you."

My face warms. I slide my arms around him as he unlocks the door, leaning my head against his shoulder. It's a comfortable gesture. He puts his arms around me and draws me into another, more leisurely kiss. I've missed this too. So much.

"Ben," I whisper like a promise, despite it all.

"Let's get inside, it's freezing out here," says Ben softly.

"I thought you Scots are used to winter. Unlike us soft Londoners down south."

"Oh, aye. But I'm becoming a soft Londoner after a

couple of years here."

We laugh, and I'm more at ease again.

Once inside, we take off our coats. I'm thrilled to get out of my soaked boots and socks. My boots are squelching wet.

Beside me, Ben gasps. "Your feet!"

I peer down at them after putting my waterlogged socks on the radiator by the door and my boots on the doormat. My feet are red with cold. They ache.

"They got wet. The bus took too long, and I didn't want to wait any longer in the cold, so I walked to Camden from the café."

"Let me put the kettle on. And we'll sit by the fire for a bit to help you warm up."

I smile, thinking of various ways he could warm me up as I trail him to the kitchen, curious to see what he'll do. Being taken care of is an unusual feeling. There's nothing but demands on my time, things to do for others, schoolwork, rehearsals. Sleep, and the cycle only repeats.

"You're running the risk of spoiling me if you do that," I tell him. "What can I do to help?"

Ben waves my comment off. "You'll let me do something for you, that's what you can do."

Weird idea, that. Something I'm not used to, not at all. But something I bet I could grow to like—too much. Way too much.

He wraps his arms around me, holding me close. I bury my face in his shoulder, and the scent of him is already so familiar. Being held like this is also unfamiliar. Imagine having Ben to myself like this. "I should be doing things for you. After what I did. Much more than a mixtape."

He just laughs. "I'm getting the idea you don't get much spoiling. I'd like to fix that. You can do things for me another time when you're not half frozen."

I lean against him, comforted by his embrace.

Ben rubs my back, then breaks away to ready the tea. Watching him go through the familiar rituals of tea-making is soothing. Ben sets everything on a tray, including a bottle of whiskey, and leads us to the living room. He sets the tray down on the leather ottoman before turning on the gas fire. Taking me by the hand, he sits me on the sofa and wraps a blanket around my shoulders.

He gives me another appraising gaze. "Tea first. Then whiskey."

"Spoken like a man who knows his priorities."

Picking up the teapot, Ben pours and fixes the tea the way I like before passing a mug over, and then tends to his own. When he settles in beside me, he puts my feet in his lap, his hands over them for a long moment. Warm.

"Jesus, these are ice blocks, not feet." He kneads them gently.

I laugh. "I have to deal with what nature gave me. I wasn't missing your gig. Not for any reason. I had to come see you. To try to explain and to apologize for being a mess. Again. For that terrible text, for starters."

He shakes his head, eyes crinkling with a smile. What does he see when he looks at me like that?

"Charlie," Ben murmurs in his lilt.

"I love how you say that." I shiver as he continues to massage my bare feet.

What do I need to do for Ben to keep saying my name like that? What if I become accustomed to this sort of thing? Or what if it all falls apart? I'll be left haunted by the memories of Ben's foot massages and so much more when this all ends—fucking hell, he's good.

"It's the least I can do, after turning you to ice on my account, literally leaving you out in the cold." Ben shakes his head, his lip ring catching the light from the fire. "I should've thought about the weather more. But...I'm so glad you came out tonight. And you're forgiven, for the record. I can tell you're not used to having someone close."

That's undeniably true. I gulp. Nerves take over.

"Are you sure you didn't want to be out tonight with your mates instead?" A flutter of anxiety cuts to the quick, and my mouth takes off before my brain can catch up.

"There's no place I'd rather be right now than here with you." Ben pretends to consider. There's mischief in his eyes. "Well, it was either that or getting all my teeth pulled, so—"

I squawk my protest and swat at him, and he cracks up and so do I and we're lost in gales of laughter. Eventually, we calm down and drink tea again. I wipe tears of mirth with the cuff of my shirt.

"Way to sell it, Mr. Campbell," I say at last when I can speak again.

He grins. "We were in danger of getting too soppy. But I don't mind that, actually. There're worse things than telling someone you're into that you're into them. And I'm into you, Charlie. You're fab."

My breath catches. "Oh, don't mess me about—"

"I'm not." Ben provides assurances through a teasing kiss that, as usual, leaves me having an out of body experience. "Why do you think I'd mess you about?"

"Oh, I don't know. Because I've messed you about?"

"I won't mess you about," Ben assures me. "I promise."

"I just don't want...I guess I don't want to tell you too much about me. In case it's too much. And because...well, I thought I'd just see you once or twice, and that would be it. Because my life's complicated. But it's been a few days now, and we've seen each other more than twice, and...I can't forget you. I suppose I've got to come clean sooner or later at this point. And well, I...I like you too. I'm scared that if I tell you about me, about the things I've done, this will end. That you'll change your mind when you know what my real life is like."

He shifts and takes my hand, resting his other hand on my ankle. I peer at him over my tea, hands wrapped around the top of the mug. There's kindness and curiosity in his smile. And those ever steady sea-blue eyes, dark and dramatic against the shock of bleached blond hair that falls over his forehead as he considers me.

"Charlie?"

"Yes?"

"You're already more than enough."

"How can you say that, not knowing about me?" My face warms. Something inside me twists, tangled between excitement and terror.

"Oh, I know a few things. That you make a mean latte. That you're hilarious. That you fuck like a beast and have an unholy way with yarn. And I'm so curious about you. You're wicked clever, for starters. And I know you're a fab musician yourself. But I don't want to push. I get the idea you're holding things back. You said your life's complicated. We'll work it out, if that's what you want. I mean, it's what I want. I've been around long enough and have seen and heard some things."

I fidget with my mug. "I have it in my head that after tonight you'll be off visiting your family and mates in Scotland for Christmas, and then we'll be back to our ordinary lives. You'll be busy doing all the many things that you do. And you'll forget about me. And I'll be back to my usual, and whatever this is going on between us will just be a memory."

He squeezes my hand, then lifts it to kiss the inside of my wrist. Distracting, curse him. I shiver.

"I won't disappear on you. I have a short trip home for a few days but I'll be back before you know it. And we can see each other again if you want. I do. Just…talk to me. What are you thinking?"

My face is on fire. May as well let him know everything and then we'll see what he makes of me. "You'll be off having a great time in Edinburgh. I'm going home to my parents' house briefly for what promises to be another awkward Christmas Eve gathering with my family. I'm the black sheep of the family, by the way. 'Cause of my screwups. And then I need to go to Wales for actual Christmas."

His focus is so intent on me, I wonder if he even remembers to breathe. It's unnerving.

"What screwups?" Ben asks gently.

And there's a landslide of memories jumbled all at once. Disappointing people. Hurting people. Hurting myself too.

Out with it. You've stalled long enough.

"You truly want to know?"

"Yes."

I sigh. Confession time, at last.

And out with the rest.

"I had a long spell with drink and drugs that started in school and got really out of hand. When people went off galivanting for their gap year, I did rehab and therapy. A lot of it."

Ben squeezes my hand again.

"I can have drinks now and again. Casual. I'll smoke a joint on occasion. But that's it. Nothing more than that. I lost people I cared about 'cause of it. And I know it sounds silly, because I'm young…"

"Not at all. Addiction happens to people of all ages."

I could nearly weep with relief to hear Ben say that.

"It's been hard." Tentative, I fidget. "There's been fuck-ups along the way. Relapses. But…in that year, the year where I was out of control, some bad things happened. I nearly died. And I experimented with a lot of things…and…one thing led to another, and I had sex with a friend, and she got pregnant. And so…I'm a father." I hold his gaze, unwavering. Through all the struggles of the last few years, the best thing to happen to me was Carys. She gave me something to focus on when I couldn't see the way. "I have a little girl. She's two. I don't see her often enough, not nearly as much as I'd like. It's terrible having her so far away. So I have to go see her for Christmas. I mean, I want to. I need to."

"Aww, bless, Charlie." Ben shifts to hold me tight.

And it's silly, but I cry into his shoulder, letting out the tension caught in my body. He hasn't run away. Or kicked me out. In fact, I sense no kind of judgment from him. I don't understand why not. "I wish I could be there more with my daughter, but I can't be there often enough, and I hate it. Everything I do—well, she has to come first."

"What's her name?" Shifting, Ben carefully wipes tears from my face.

I straighten, trying to gather my composure. "Carys. I'll show you a photo in a while, if you want."

"I would love that. When you're ready."

Feeling unsteady, I sip on my tea. I can just hear my therapist congratulating me on being vulnerable, about sharing things with someone I care about. I'm only starting to know Ben, but there's something calming about him. Something I can trust. Where does his strength come from?

"And that's all right?" I ask, searching his eyes.

"Of course it's all right. It's all part of your history. Who you are. And I love knowing who you are, Charlie."

"Oh God, cheers. Because some people still just see me as a screwup. Including myself."

Ben shakes his head. "No. From what I've seen, you're anything but. You work hard. You're in uni?"

I nod. "Full-time…"

"Aye. And you work."

"True…"

"How many hours?"

"Depends on the week, but usually a lot. Right now, nearly full-time, before I go to Wales."

His eyebrows climb. "And you have a band on top of all that?"

"Yes. But we don't rehearse as much as we should, though we're doing more than usual because we have a big gig coming up. We're trying to do a demo, but it's hard. I'm working all these hours so I can send money to Emily—Carys's mum—and there's not a lot of time or money left over between that and tuition and rent and bills and everything."

"I feel like a slacker compared to you."

I laugh and shake my head. "Oh no. This is my doing. I want to do everything I can for Carys. And for Emily. I feel so bad for Emily. She was due to go to uni too, but it was too much with a new baby. And her family didn't deal well with things either, so she went to stay with her gran in Swansea. At any rate, we're still very close. Plus, my band's got a gig soon after I'm back and I'm planning to send my share of that money to her and Carys."

Ben is silent, considering me for a long moment. "You've got to be one of the hardest working people I know. That's a lot to deal with on your own."

"Yeah. I suppose."

Ben pulls me close against his chest. "Like you said, Emily and Carys are the people that count. And yourself, of course."

I smile at him, reaching out to touch his face, pale stubble against his jaw. Comfortingly rough. "And…what you think matters to me too. Already. You count."

Despite the dating ban.

He kisses me then, light at first, then deep and lingering. "Likewise. What you think is important to me too."

Closing my eyes, I make myself relax in his arms.

"Where did you come from?" I lean into him and the

radiating warmth of his body. "To see things this way?"

"I see things as they are. And..." His voice lowers to a conspiratorial whisper as he affectionately nips my ear. "You already know where I come from. Edinburgh. Stockbridge, if you want to be specific."

I laugh. "Okay, I know that much. Is this a secret baked into shortbread or kept inside Scottish teas? Is this why you don't drink coffee?"

Ben laughs too. "I'd tell you, but I'd have to kill you. Can't have all my cultural secrets so easily."

"I swear you're some kind of genius, though."

"Oh, far from it. Time for my confession, before you go far down that road: I didn't even finish school. Damn thing, this dyslexia. I hated it. I hated school. I hated words on pages. Instead, I worked and lived and got myself into scrapes and out of them again. So, maybe I have some common sense from all this, learning the hard way for almost a decade."

I let this sink in. "How old were you when you left school?"

"Fifteen," says Ben. "And to be honest, I think it's shocking I made it that far. That's due to my mum and a couple of good teachers. But I was a terrible student, and I was too different to fit in at school. All I wanted was music. So, I left school for music. I needed to make it work. I worked a lot of shit jobs, played in bands, did whatever it took to get by. And I finally made the move down south after the latest band in Glasgow fell apart."

"And met people like Eleanor in the wool shop and your current band?" I ask.

"Aye, just so." He reaches out to brush hair from my eyes. "It's a bit of an unconventional life, but I'm happy with it, and that's all I can really ask for. The only thing missing, really, is someone to share things with. Have fun with. Have a life with."

My eyebrows climb as I take another moment to let that all sink in too. "I find it very hard to believe you don't already have a boyfriend."

He laughs with delight. "Oh, believe me, boyfriends don't just grow on trees. Especially in London. There's not too many trees here to grow them. Not like in the country or up in the Highlands. I mean, I've been down to Hyde Park, looking to harvest boyfriends from trees, but frankly, they're quite picked over."

I laugh and lose myself to the release. "If I find out you keep a harem of men in your loft..."

"Cleared them out last week, as soon as I met you. I told them it was time to move on. New year, new me, new man, and all that," Ben says. His eyes dance.

My face hurts from smiling so much. "Oh yeah?"

"Aye. Well, mostly. It's been tough, though. I might meet someone fun for a night or two, or for drinks, or just for sex. And I have friends for different things. But finding someone who has all the elements together? Now, that's not easy. I think you've got some fine combinations worth exploring. If you feel the same way about me, that is."

"Oh..." Air rushes out of my lungs. What's he saying, exactly?

"Only if you want," he says. "We don't need to be exclusive if you're not into that, but I think...I think going on another date with you would be grand, Charlie. Get to know each other more. What do you think?"

I squeeze his hand.

Maybe Emily's right. Maybe I need to let go of the dating ban and take a chance. At least for a little while.

"Believe me, I don't have time for dating a harem with my schedule. Just you. I mean...maybe a little longer? Till the snow melts?"

He grins. "Fair enough. I've cut back on my harem. And

I hear you about your schedule. I definitely don't want to interfere with time spent with your daughter. Plus, I've got my tour coming up after Christmas. It's going to be busy, and I want it to be big, you know?"

"I don't want to hold you back if you want to see other people. I get it. I'm also really busy and all that—"

"But listen. There's no one else I want to date right now. My ex is old news." Ben pauses, as though to clear his head of memories, a flicker of something across his face. "I want to get to know *you*. When you have time. I'll wait. And do whatever I can to help you."

An ex? Interesting.

I want to know more about that, but tonight we've covered more than plenty. I don't want to wreck the mood after getting to this point after the mess I made of things. I'll leave the subject for another day. But it's silly that it didn't occur to me before that he has histories and hurts of his own. I guess I was just thinking it was a weekend fling and what does Ben's history matter? And I didn't expect the weird twist of my guts at that flicker of *something* across Ben's face at the mention of his ex.

What if I'm the rebound diversion? Then again, what does it matter? This can't last beyond the snow melt, can it? And yet it feels like so much more, even in a handful of days. Because he sees me. *As I am, not as I should be or how other people want me to be.*

Heat rises in my face again. "I'm not used to this sort of attention."

Ben lightly bites my fingers. "I can tell. You'll need to start getting used to it, I'm afraid. Beginning now."

I laugh, relaxing at last between his touch and his interest. "All right."

"Good?"

"Good. More than great. Fantastic."

Ben's gone and done something funny to me, leaving me all soft inside. We kiss then and once more it's electric between us.

His kisses burn my lips, his hands roaming and hot, and I'm whimpering and hungering for more. I want him—all of him—most greedily and soon we're sliding urgent fingers inside each other's clothes by the fire. Soft sounds escape us and dear God this would be a terrible time for his housemate to walk in. He must have had the same thought, and we pause long enough to fumble our way down the hall to his room and resume.

We kiss in the doorway. I press him inside the room.

Ben beams at me, his lips against my ear. "I'd rather like it if you tied me up again."

"Mmm." Excellent news: tying him the other day had been rather spectacular. I could grow used to trussing Ben into art, sculpting him into new forms.

He leads me over to a wooden box—a mid-sized oak chest—sat on a table and he opens it, revealing all manner of things. Sex toys. Floggers. Restraints.

"Very educational," I say, grasping his arse while I rummage through the box, taking stock. As far as I can make out, there's two sets of cuffs, one in black leather and the other in gold. I think he'd look spectacular in gold, like a naughty angel in gilt, bound to the bed so I can commit all manner of sins to him. I shudder in anticipation.

"These." I retrieve the gold set of restraints.

"Mmm," he says with approval, satisfied. "What else? You'll need to tie me down, probably. I mean, I hate to interfere with your vision."

I shiver at the thought, running my fingers over the items in the box, trying to figure out what's what. There are lengths of rope in different shades: oxblood, black, green. Tape, even. Colorful strapping catches my eye. My fingers hesitate over dark purple leather. Like the yarn, I'm drawn to the color.

I take the items over to the bed, setting them down on the crimson bedspread.

"A fine vintage," he says lightly, kissing me as we continue to help each other out of our clothes. I strip him down. I still wear my boxers while I admire the sight of him. In the low light, he's all lean muscle, arms toned from all that guitar playing or bar work, or who knows what. But he's a vision to look at and after our revelations not long ago, all our emotions are on the surface, at least for me. I'm not used to feeling like this, and it's another sort of euphoria.

I see him like this and I'm filled with all kinds of urges. Like the discovery of another me beneath the surface, dormant, that comes to life when I touch Ben. And the desire to do filthy things, to have him beg and release at my bidding, already has me dancing on the edge of euphoria. Combined with some angst that I'm not entirely sure of what I'm doing. But judging by the way he looks at me, he's well up for anything. His body's already taut with anticipation. His breath catches just so, the movement of his stomach barely visible beneath his graceful ribs.

We stand face to face, my hand tracing his pecs. They're warm and sleek, covered in fine hair, and when I tease his nipples, he shivers, watching me.

"Down," I say. I flick his titanium nipple piercing.

Obediently, he sinks to his knees in one fluid movement as though he has no bones.

"Wrists behind your back."

His smile broadens. Already, his cock is stiff, straining skyward from the prelude of my teasing.

I cuff him, then pause to admire the lines of his body from behind: the planes of soft skin, the curves of his buttocks, the angles of his shoulder blades. His blond hair is disheveled as always. Freckles cascade down the length of him, fading along his back and arse, lit by the lamp's warm glow.

I run a hand across Ben's shoulder blades. He shivers. I rake my fingers between them, along his spine and into his hair, tugging his head back slightly.

Ben moans softly. "Yeah…"

"Like that, huh." My fingers tighten.

His breath catches.

"No talking," I say.

I catch him by the elbow and help him up onto the bed, bending him over to display his arse, a pale vision. God. I'm hard in my boxers as I watch him like this. To improve the sight, I put the ankle cuffs on him, and after a false start, I secure each foot to a post of the bed. Definitely better. His legs are splayed tight, and he's on his stomach. With light fingers, I tease his balls and his arse. He groans.

"Shh," I say.

He presses his face into the covers to muffle himself as my fingers continue to torment. It's learning a new language, learning Ben's body, each quiver and reaction. I work him as I rub myself against his arse. He's all gold and dark purple leather, caught under firm restraint, and I take in the sight of him. Beautiful.

Two more things to make this perfect.

I find his navy blindfold and take his sight. He trembles. When I place a pillow under his hips, his cock's already seeping. Mine is too. We're both worked up after our conversation.

And he trusts me. God, he trusts me.

Stepping out of my boxers, I reach for a condom and lube, pausing to prepare myself and him, teasing relentlessly with demanding fingers as he sobs out until I stop just as suddenly and he cries out with the absence of me. And then I press and press till I'm fully inside, deep until he gasps. I bite the nape of his neck and grasp his hips.

"You want this?" I ask.

Ben groans with desire. I bite his shoulder for good measure and hold him tight against me, working him as I work myself, and I know we won't last long like this and he's shaking so hard, biting down on his own lip to keep from calling out, crying out, giving over everything he has and everything he is to me, and I ride him without mercy, a union of language, and he's gasping, on the cusp of coming.

"Say it," I demand. I grasp him tight against me, riding him, and oh it's pure ecstasy having him like this, unable to move even if he wanted to, but I know he's getting off on the restraint, the deprivation of movement, the weight of my body. Beneath me, he bucks and writhes and shudders.

"Fuck. God. Charlie, please. Oh please."

"You can't come yet," I declare.

He sobs out.

I tease and let up, tease and let up, tease again and then it's hard to say who's going more wild—him or me—with the damn relentless teasing and then I finally give him what he wants, a proper fucking and he's pinned beneath the weight of me, splayed, and we press together and I stroke him mercilessly till he spurts all over my hand and the bed and the cushions and I follow and collapse on him as we both shudder and shake.

"Holy shit," I gasp.

Ben groans.

My arms are tight around his waist, my face against his shoulder blade. His legs tremble. I stay like this as long as I dare, till I withdraw to deal with the condom. I pause to admire the sight of him again.

"I could leave you like this till next time." I just might, too.

"You could." Ben tries to catch his breath. "But you'll still need to bring me shortbread and tea."

And we laugh as I release his ankle restraints and wrists, falling into bed together in a tumble of limbs and leather, caught in each other's embrace.

"Ooh, what'd you do to me." Gazing across the pillow, he's all smiles, drowsy. "Some sort of Londoner spell, I ken."

"I don't know. I think it's you. Or it's the snow." I hesitate, fidgeting with the edge of the blanket. "I worry when it melts, you'll disappear, too."

"Aww, lovely. I'm going nowhere, I promise. We can keep seeing each other after the snow melts, you know. I'll be back soon from Edinburgh, and we can catch up when you're back from Wales."

"Promise?"

"Promise." Ben kisses me deeply and I soar somewhere over the sprawling city, like I'm looking down at us in Ben's artful room of sage and skulls, taxidermy and graphic posters. It's a secret haven in here, just us, the world outside kept away for another day.

"And Charlie?"

"Yes?"

"Would you like to go on our first official date? When you're back from your trip?"

"Like…like an almost boyfriend?" I dare ask.

It could be too much to hope for, but I'm feeling recklessly bold after our tryst, in the promise of a deepening intimacy.

"Exactly so. Starter pack," Ben encourages, brushing his lips against mine.

I'm starting to see things from his perspective. I kiss back, pulling him so close for a moment his eyelashes tickle my cheek, till we settle back comfortably against the bed.

"When do you get back? Are you in London for New Year's Eve?"

"I'm back by then, yeah."

"Date night, then." Ben's terribly pleased with the idea.

"We can do whatever we want. Or not."

"Brilliant."

We laugh, gazing at each other, our limbs entwined. Such a simple, fantastic thing.

Blood rushes in my ears, like I've come again, lying skin to skin. Some part of me coasts on sheer euphoria. The rest of my brain tries to absorb this magnificent idea of Ben—*Ben*—also wanting me like I want him so badly.

"I'd be thrilled. Like...that's the best thing I could hope for..."

"You're grand," Ben murmurs affectionately. "For all the days."

"You're brilliant too. And then some."

What strange new euphoria is this? I'm in some upside-down universe, where I have something good happen just for me. For us.

Ben grins and so do I. We lose ourselves in a kiss, amid the crinkle of cotton. Snow continues to fall beyond his window. I can't wait for our first date, with Ben beside me and the world at our feet on New Year's Eve.

Chapter Twenty-Three

The magic of Ben is soon dashed in the gray melt of slush on Christmas Eve. I've come to my parents' home in Richmond, to the realm of well-heeled posh commuters. At least it's beautiful here in the day. Dusk shelters the scrape of branches blown against the window, tap-tapping on the glass. The room darkens with the fading light. My novel's set aside.

Everything's muted here. Colors, unlike Ben's world, are carefully managed, in case they do something dangerous. No fuchsia jumpers or multicolored scarves here. There are certainly no visible piercings or anything bold to challenge the norms of upper middle class respectability. The house is muffled in shades of beige and browns, from the wood floors to the tonal landscape painting hung over the sofa.

It's like color knows better than to come here.

It would be so easy to drink something from the display of liquor bottles and decanters sparkling on the sideboard and keep going. Ordinarily, I'd have a pint, but here, everything I do is under scrutiny. I don't want to give them any material to use against me.

"Want a whiskey?" Michael asks.

We occasionally find common ground on how frustrating our parents can be. But we've got that stereotypical birth order thing going on—Michael's the first-born high-achiever, I'm the wild kid brother. Or I was. Now I'm a reformed Charlie.

When I'm here, I become beige, too.

"No thanks. Don't let me stop you, though." I nod at the drinks.

Michael's come tonight fresh from work in his suit and tie. His suitcase is doubtless packed with military precision. He's not military, but a solicitor, which is close enough. The man likes orders and rules. He's not all bad, though. Michael's come through for me when I've needed backup dealing with our parents.

While Michael pours Talisker into a tumbler, I flop into a leather armchair.

"How's uni?" he asks, taking a seat opposite me on the three-seater sofa. Naturally, it's brown too. Mum would call it dark chocolate.

"All right. Busy, I guess." Uni feels like a million years ago since Ben. Another lifetime. Like some other Charlie goes about his classes.

"You're not sure?"

"Busy," I confirm, more certainty in my voice this time. That part's true. "Working a lot. How about you?"

"Busy. Working a lot." Michael gives me a wry look as he sips on his drink.

Checkmate.

I lift my eyebrows at Michael.

"Everything's fine. Jenna's fine too. We're going skiing for a weekend getaway. Swiss Alps."

"Oh yeah?" The idea of visiting the Alps is about as foreign as taking a quick weekend getaway to the moon. I should find a rocket to take Ben sometime, maybe for our New Year's date.

"Yeah. Special occasion and all that. I'm planning to propose."

Maybe I should have had that whiskey after all. I blink. It takes me a moment to recover from his news. "That's serious."

Michael laughs. "Well, we do love each other. And we have been dating for over two years."

"Shit, really?" Time's snuck up on me when I wasn't looking. When I was busy staying sober and trying to do right by Emily and Carys. "Well, congrats."

"Don't congratulate me yet. She hasn't said yes."

"You think she won't?"

"I don't want to get cocky. The universe has a way of throwing that back in one's face." Michael tilts his head slightly, swirling his whiskey.

"Fair point." About then, my phone buzzes a notification. I fish it out of my pocket. Tomorrow, I'm due to go to Wales to see Carys and Emily.

But it's not Emily texting. It's Ben.

A smile crosses my lips.

Miss you already. Making a new scarf with our wool. B xx

The smile gets bigger.

"That's the first time I've seen you smile in ages," says Michael. "Who was that?"

"Oh, nobody." It's a reflex response when my family asks about my personal life. Aside from staying clean, I try to keep them separate. Not that I have much of a life between uni, work, and Carys.

"You're sure?"

"Well…" A pang of guilt hits me then, because Ben is far from nobody to me. "Somebody. A friend."

"A friend?" Michael looks curiously at me.

"Dammit, Michael. You and your lawyer line of interrogation." The smile's back now. Irrepressible. The Ben effect, even from a distance. "More than a friend. There. I said it."

Michael looks terribly pleased. Unlike our parents, he has no delusions that I will become all hetero through their force of will. "What's his name?"

I gulp. If I say his name, put it out there, it will make everything more real. Like maybe it wasn't all fanciful wishes and daydreams spurred by hangovers and latte withdrawal.

"Ben. His name is Ben."

Michael grins. "Well, he must be someone important for you to reveal his name."

"I know better than to resist the legal profession. With my luck I'll end up in some third-rate penitentiary with your connections."

"Well, that's true," Michael concedes. "That was a downer last Christmas."

I snort. The silly smile, I fear, might be permanent. Ben has a lot of explaining to do. He didn't warn me that might happen if we agreed on a date. Scottish trick.

"Boys," calls Mum from the other room as the doorbell rings. "Time for dinner."

Chapter Twenty-Four

Dinner is in the formal dining room. Mum calls the paint color in here aubergine, but no self-respecting aubergine would tolerate that insult or that much brown in good conscience. It's plain brown. Imagine my family's expressions if I painted the room oxblood or emerald in the night. If I called it brown, would they be any the wiser?

At the table, we're elbow-deep in relatives, including Jenna. We've poured wine for toasts, served the first course, taken the first mouthfuls. My aunt and uncle from Mum's side have joined us. They've traveled from Croydon. To listen to them, you'd think they traveled from outer Mongolia and fought off highwaymen on the way in, facing mortal peril. My dad's brother, my Uncle Johnnie, and his partner Kirsten have somehow given the beige-paint-loving gene a miss. They're off on a road trip across America. In New Orleans, specifically, when they rang my parents earlier. Whatever genes Johnnie has, I must have them too, a throwback to some early Renfrew relation.

There's talk of investments, led by my father, with

sensible advice from my brother. Everyone looks interested, except me. I'm dying inside.

I gaze at the remains of my meal. At this point, all that's left are the traces of gravy I used to drown the overcooked roast as I calculated how long I needed to sit here to be polite before I could start clearing dishes and do the washing up.

"Charles," says Great Aunt May, a cloud of silvery hair floating around her head, "will you join us tomorrow? Your mother said you'll be joining us for lunch, but I thought you were off to Wales."

I scowl, not at Aunt May but at Mum's obvious interference, then try to neutralize my expression as my father shoots me a dark look. Storm warning. I make myself look more neutral.

"Sorry, Aunt May. I won't be able to join. I'm off to see Carys."

Mum frowns at me. "Now, Charles. You should come to your Aunt May's for lunch and spend time with your family—"

"I have to catch a train tonight to Wales." I stare at my mother. "You knew that already. I told you before."

"You need to spend time with your real family," says my mother coolly. "All of us will be there tomorrow. Even Jenna will join us for lunch. We scheduled lunch instead of dinner to include her. And you and a plus one." She sighs, pained. "You never bring your girlfriends to meet us. At Christmas or otherwise."

"Charles," says my father. "Don't disappoint your mother."

"Oh, fucking hell." It spills out before I can smother the words. "Mum, you know I'm off to see Carys. You'd think you'd be happy that I'm going to see my daughter. Your granddaughter, by the way—"

"Charles!" Dad scowls.

"—and as for girlfriends, Mum, you know perfectly well that I don't bring them because there aren't any. I'm gay. Or queer. Take your pick."

My mother presses a thin hand against her forehead. "It's Christmas, Charles. Don't ruin it. Think of your Great Aunt May."

"I don't know, but I don't think Aunt May's shocked about me. It's not a secret. You and Dad are the only ones in denial about my sexuality. And the reason I don't bring people home is because you're always miserable to me, on Christmas or any other day of the year. So no, Mum, I'm not bringing over a girlfriend. Or a boyfriend, because I don't have one, not really. And if I did, I wouldn't want you to put them through a fraction of what you put me through. Not ever."

Michael catches my eye. My lips tighten. Of course he knows that there's someone, but I trust him to keep his mouth shut right now.

I don't dare mention Ben in front of everyone, not when we're on the fringe of nebulous new boyfriend territory. He's too new in my life and too important to risk in the standing family warfare. And confirming they'd never accept any of my boyfriends is a gut blow. My eyes sting with unwanted hot tears.

Mum looks scandalized, her eyes suspiciously wet too. My father's face has shifted from pink to purple to some color found in no home decor magazine.

"*Charles!*" my father bellows. "Don't raise your voice to your mother. Apologize at once."

"Sorry, Aunt May. I promise to visit another time." My voice is unsteady. "Excuse me."

And without further hesitation, I flee the table for the study. I grab my suitcase and unload the gifts I brought for my family. Alone, tears burn hot down my face.

To my mother, Carys is nothing but a living reminder of my past mistakes rather than something good, a highlight of my life so far. If they have no time for anything or anyone I care about, imagine what they would make of Ben too. It would be a lot worse.

Blinking through tears, I struggle to close my suitcase. I shove on my jacket and shoes. With the full-size suitcase and my guitar, I head out. I don't care if I have to walk to the station. I don't care if they think I'm overreacting. For once, I wish my parents were on my side—Carys's side.

Outside, rain falls. I'm not far down the lane when a car pulls up beside me, headlights casting a misty glow along the forested route. Trees are strange shadows in the dark. The tires crunch over gravel.

"Come on," says Michael, window rolled down. "I'll give you a lift to the station."

Because it's Michael, I agree. He knows better than to try to change my mind, to turn the car around to return to the Christmas nightmare back at the house. He also knows better than to apologize for them.

We're quiet on the dark ride to the station. It's not far by car. Rain drums on the roof.

When we arrive, Michael pulls up to the curb. He shuts off the car and looks at me. "I'm sorry," he says simply. "That was unfair."

A sound of acknowledgment escapes me.

"Since you skipped out on the gifts portion of the evening, I thought to give this to you now." He pulls out an envelope from his coat pocket. "For your trip. For Carys."

He knows how to cut off my protest before it begins. My mouth opens. Shuts. "Thanks. That means a lot."

Michael squeezes my shoulder. "I know Mum and Dad aren't easy, but you can always call me, all right? I hope you know that."

A lump forms in my throat, caught rough when I try to clear it. "Cheers."

"And I hope you get to spend some time together with Ben. He sounds like he's someone worth spending time with."

I gulp. "He's brilliant. And so are you. Thanks. For this. For the lift."

"You better go. Train departs in five minutes if you're taking the Overground back to London."

It's a good point, because who knows what the trains and Underground are doing tonight. If it gets too late, I'm not getting anywhere. And God knows what the connections are like to Emily's at this hour.

Something to figure out on the train into London.

Chapter Twenty-Five

By the time I pull myself into some fucking semblance of composure, on edge from the blow-out at dinner, my hard-fought calm dissolves when I go to buy a train ticket. At Victoria Station, I'm in full-blown panic attack mode. Standing on the concourse, I slam the heel of my hand against a defenseless ticket machine, because there're no direct trains to Wales at this hour. Or tomorrow. The best I can get are three changes and being stuck out in some Bristol station overnight, if I can get that far.

Impossible.

I'll miss Christmas and that can't be. A promise is a promise, and I promised Em and Carys I'd be there. I should've checked the schedule days ago. I shouldn't have gone to Richmond at all, like I did last year, and headed out earlier. Obviously no good comes of trying to please everyone. Sacrificing sleep to travel late to Wales seemed like a fine compromise at the time. Now, I hate myself for fucking everything up.

Caught between shouting or vomiting, I shake.

Oh my God, Charlie, why didn't you think this through? Shit. Fuck. Fuck again.

As I gulp back air that's nearly a sob, a passing couple look at me oddly, walking hand in hand.

Reeling away from the machine, I pace aimlessly around the concourse, past shuttered shops and a newsagent's that's open, with packaged snacks and tabloids and glossy magazines brimming with Christmas glamour and decor that Mum would be all over.

Some headline catches my eye despite my despair. ROCKER MAXIMUS ST. PIERRE CHRISTMAS SPECIAL HEARTACHE: SPLITSVILLE WITH SIENNA RUMORED. It's a big charity fundraiser on Channel 4, I think, for underprivileged kids or endangered species or another worthy cause, something I remember hearing about before, but fuck knows about the heartache part. I'm glad to know someone else is having a shit Christmas, that fame and fortune is no insulation from hurt.

Get it together. Don't make a scene. The last thing I need is the police in my business.

The problem should have been blindingly obvious, but I was too caught up in my urgency to flee my parents' house. Now, all of the rage and panic won't make the rail service run to Swansea tonight.

Fighting back tears, a desperate search on my phone for flights tomorrow morning to Wales leads to no results. Everything's sold out or horribly expensive.

Then hot tears come at last, leaving salt tracks down my face as I grip my phone. This can't be.

I promised Carys and Emily I would be there for Christmas. I must look some sight, because an older lady stops to check in on me. There's something about her that reminds me of Great Aunt May.

"Can I help?" she asks kindly.

I gulp air. Breathe. Try to remember how to breathe. Going to pieces helps nobody and solves nothing. Some part of me wants to run home, dive under the duvet, and not come out till spring.

Mortified, I shake my head, staring at my phone in disbelief. The woman must know I'm full of shit and doesn't leave.

About then, my phone comes to life, buzzing and chiming. Through the blur of unwanted tears, I make out Ben's name.

"I'm okay," I assure the woman who remains beside me.

"Hello?" I answer, sounding damnably pathetic.

"Charlie? What's wrong?" His voice is soft and familiar in my ear.

A shuddering breath shakes me. One in. Another out. Repeat.

"Charlie? Are you there?"

"I'm here," I gasp. "I'm sorry."

"Did I catch you at a bad time?" Ben's voice is full of concern. His voice is thin on the line. The announcements at the station nearly drown him out as I strain to hear his voice, soak up any comfort that I might steal. "Silly question. Clearly, I have. I can ring back—"

"No!" I say with more force than I intended. "Please don't go."

Then, embarrassingly, I burst into tears like a six-year-old. Because that will round out my public humiliation, bawling on the phone to the man I want to be my almost boyfriend that I could never bring home to my family, because my small universe would implode if I did. And my parents would never accept me having a boyfriend, just like they barely acknowledge my daughter. Imagine what they would do if they met Ben.

I shudder at the thought.

Never.

"I can't get to Wales. I had a fight with my parents and I left and now I won't get to see Carys and Emily." I shiver as I run out of air.

It's freezing out here. Even the pigeons look cold, the poor arseholes. Nobody's knit them a pullover. Do they have to worry about knitting curses too?

"Oh no. Shite. What's happened?"

"I'm a disaster. That's what's happened."

"Where are you? Are you safe?"

"I'm safe, I promise." Ben's voice helps ground me. The woman, who lingered, at last seems satisfied that she won't need to stage an intervention with a stranger.

God, after what I've told Ben about my past, he must think the worst. That I'm off my face. "I'm clean," I blurt. "Don't worry about that."

"All right, lovely. But where are you?" Ben asks. Worry's still plain in his voice. "If I wasn't in Edinburgh, I'd come get you."

"You don't even know where I am." I'm torn between laughter and tears that Ben would come to me without question, save for the small issue of several hundred kilometers between us. Which is ridiculous and fantastic and then, right then, I feel something unfamiliar, something I haven't felt in a long time: Cared for. Wanted. Worth worrying about.

Unlike going home, which ends up leaving me feeling as insignificant as dirt.

My voice wavers. "I'm still in London, at Victoria Station. I've just come in from Richmond."

Shifting, I look around. The evening traffic is winding down, since the sensible will be already at their destinations for the night. "I forgot about the trains not running late or tomorrow. There are no more trains to Wales tonight or even close. I thought maybe if I could get to Cardiff, Emily might pick me up. But nothing's running that will get me there in time. There's some problem with the National Express too—I thought the coaches always ran. I can't even get past Bristol!"

A tinge of hysteria colors my voice, caught between laughter and sucking back air to smother my desperation. So much for trying to keep it together for Ben. He's going to think me completely off my head and there goes any hope for our first date together at the end of it.

"Ach. I'm sorry," says Ben comfortingly in my ear. "The coaches aren't running tonight because of a snowstorm out that way."

"How do you know?" I blink away tears. Tears! My body's betraying me out in public. It's like one of those dreams where I wake up naked in school and everyone's staring. The rational part of me says nobody's paying attention to me out here, but that part's packed it in for the night.

"Because I checked," says Ben simply. "I was thinking of you."

"You…you did that?"

"Of course. I wondered how it'd be for you traveling to Wales tomorrow."

I gulp, tears caught up on my eyelashes. God, the things he's doing to my insides. Even a little thing like that, I feel cared for, even at a distance.

"And then I tried looking up a hire car, and it's hundreds of pounds, never mind the petrol and all of that." My voice falters.

Shit, I'm definitely, regrettably back to tears again. Perfect. I sniffle.

"And I'm breaking my promise to Carys that I'll be there to open gifts together on Christmas. I mean, I know she doesn't even understand what Christmas is, exactly. But I know. And so does Emily and Katherine, Emily's gran. How could I fuck this up so badly?"

"It'll be all right," Ben assures me. I could almost believe him. "What was your plan to get to Wales?"

"I was going to take the train. Now I remember that last year I went a day ahead instead and I've been so busy I didn't think properly and didn't book an advance ticket."

Ben's gone quiet. That's it. He'll tell me thanks but no thanks now, thinking better of getting involved or having strings-free sex with a man who can't even remember public transport doesn't run properly over Christmas.

I take in a shaky breath, bracing myself.

"Charlie?"

"Yes?"

"I've got an idea."

"What's that? Are you dumping me? Can you dump someone when you haven't been on a proper first date together?" I ask desperately, unwanted anxiety taking over my mouth again. What's the record for being pre-dumped before a proper pre-date? God, I'm going to find out. "Wait. Don't answer that. Shit. You're going to answer that, aren't you?"

Ben laughs, but it's not an unkind laugh. "Far from it. Do you want to hear my idea? I'm definitely not dumping you, by the way."

I gulp. And make myself take a steadying breath.

"What's that?" I ask finally.

"Well, I don't have the power to make trains start or planes fly or coaches run at will..." Ben begins.

So far, his idea isn't helping. My stomach sinks to the impressive depths of the Northern Line.

"But—you're welcome to borrow my car. It's just parked right now over the holidays."

Startled out of threatening tears, I blink them away. The shuttered shops blur in the station, along with the bright departures and arrivals board overhead. "You have a car?"

Parking's incredibly difficult to come by in London.

How'd Ben swing that?

"Aye. Well, shared custody of a car. Technically I own it," Ben explains. "It's a van, actually. Better for moving kit and people around. But you're welcome to borrow it. It's just sitting parked at home in London. I took the train to Edinburgh."

"Oh!" It takes a full moment for this to sink into my overwrought brain. "Seriously?"

"Aye. 'Tis no problem. My housemate is home in Boston right now. So he's not borrowing it. Molly, our other housemate, is going to stay with her family in London. I'll ring her to let her know you'll be by for the keys. If she's not there, she can hide them outside."

"You're sure it's safe?"

"It's fine. I've done it before and I'll do it again. Now. How does that sound?"

"It sounds—it sounds like a fucking miracle."

A literal Christmas miracle.

He laughs with delight. "I'm so glad I can do this much at least, so you get to see your daughter. Besides, borrowing my van's a far sight cheaper than a rental car. All you need to do is pay for the petrol. We replaced the brakes and tires not long ago, so you'll be set for winter driving."

"This is fucking incredible. You're incredible. I can't believe it. I mean, I can believe you're incredible. God, I'm going on again, aren't I?" I dare smile.

"Panicked Charlie is just as fab as non-panicked Charlie." His voice is reassuring, like he hasn't spent the last few minutes talking me out of a breakneck spiral. "If I was there, I'd make you tea. Instead, go find some. I'll ring Molly and let you know when she'll have the keys for you. Then you can head out first thing tomorrow and arrive in time for the Christmas celebrations."

"Holy shit, I could kiss you."

"Hold that thought for our date," says Ben solemnly. "I'll collect then."

Now I'm standing in the concourse grinning widely, gripping the handle of my wheelie suitcase. "You might be my hero. In fact, I know you are."

"Ach. This is something I can do. Now go find that tea."

And I go find that tea, before the café closes in the concourse, grounding myself.

True to his word, Ben texts ten minutes later with instructions to pick up the keys and van. By the time I go to bed that night in my house, I'm full of anticipation for my trip to Wales—and for seeing Ben again on New Year's.

Chapter Twenty-Six

It's well before dawn by the time I reach Ben's house, delivered via taxi. I give the driver a good tip for his troubles, which I can do because Michael's given me a generous cash gift for Christmas. It's more than enough to cover the petrol for the trip and to give the rest to Emily for Carys. Lawyering clearly is working out.

Standing in the slush, I carefully lift my suitcases over to the steps by the front door. Despite the unholy hour of 6:00 a.m., I text Molly to let her know I've arrived. It's quite the way to make introductions, pre-sun-up. I already owe her and we haven't met yet.

Without the distraction of Ben, I can take this all in better, even with the dark. I'm standing on a cobbled street in front of a mews house in Marylebone. Snow's pushed up in piles along the edges of the lane. We're not far from Soho. Not far from Chinatown too.

What I am noticing, however, is the distinct lack of a van.

Lights switch on at the top of the stairs, flanking the door, and a dark-haired woman pokes her head out. She brightens when she sees me, like I'm some find she's discovered after searching for some time, and trots down in her parka, which she's thrown on over floral pajamas and boots.

"I'm so sorry," I begin, but Molly shakes her head to stop me. "I just... I'm not sure where the van is or the keys? I didn't mean to bother you—"

"Not at all," says Molly in a Scottish accent like Ben's.

Is Ben running a safe house for Scots in London? There's so much I don't know about him. It could be entirely possible. I mean, we're two for two in this house of Scots. Before I can fret about not knowing about this, she laughs.

"Don't look so worried. I've not been to bed yet, so don't feel bad about getting me up. Or keeping me up, either. Ben's warned me about your apologies," she teases.

We walk over to dark wooden doors beside the stairs. She uses a key to open the double doors, swinging them wide. When she switches the light on, a shiny black Mercedes van is parked inside the compact garage. The van fills the space.

"Voila." Molly grins. "This is where we hide the van."

"Holy shit."

I'm dead impressed. Not only does Ben have a van and parking in central London, but it's a great van too. A reliable-looking van. A svelte van. A van that other, lesser vans would aspire to be when they become fully grown vans one day. Seriously, though, it's mint. Even from here, I can see the gloss of the paint, premium van detailing, excellent tires. And it's big enough for a band with kit, never mind me with a single suitcase and a guitar.

"Are you sure this is okay?" Hesitant, I give Molly a sidelong glance. There must be some mistake. Ben says he works as a barman when he's not playing gigs. Halfpenny Rise may literally be on the rise in London and the UK, but I didn't think he was pulling in dosh like the Arctic Monkeys. Far from it. Very far. Perhaps he's leading a Scottish crime ring. Shit. What if he's a king pin? Or running drugs? Or... God knows what. What if this garage is where he hides the bodies?

Before my brain takes off at a hundred miles per hour, I nip that in the bud. Instead, I focus on Molly.

"This is absolutely okay," Molly assures me. "Billy—my partner—is off in Boston. And Ben's away in Scotland. I'm only a short taxi ride away to my parents' later before I'm off to join Billy tomorrow. No one will be using the van in the meantime, so you may as well take advantage. The tank's full and it's been serviced not long ago. You should be fine. The lads have toured with this van, and it hasn't let them down. It has a computer that's smarter than I am, and your phone should sort out the rest. There's an emergency kit in the back, plus a spare tire and jack. Here's the keys. This one's for the van, this one's for the garage doors. And this is for the house. Feel free to make yourself at home if you're back early. Ben's back in a few days."

My head spins.

This probably isn't a good time to tell her Ben and I haven't been on an official first date yet. Hooking up doesn't count. At best, we've had an unofficial date after that, and then me being woeful a couple of times after that. Hardly a sterling recommendation of me. And—fucking hell, they're trusting me with a most excellent, mint-condition van. Aren't musicians expected to have shitty vans? I'm not sure where in the dating hierarchy between first kiss and first date van-borrowing comes in.

I start to sweat.

"You'll have a great time," Molly says cheerfully. She passes me a bag.

"What's this?"

"Baking for the road. Some chocolates too. I hear you have a thing for shortbread."

I cough, blushing. What else has Ben said about me? "Er, cheers. This is very kind."

"Smart to head out early before the traffic kicks in. I'll let you get settled in and don't worry about the doors. I'll come close them after you leave."

"Thanks. You've been so kind. You don't, um, want a copy of my driver's license or something? How do you know I won't run off with the van?"

She laughs with delight. "Ben trusts you. You can send your license to him if you're fussed."

"Well, it's a highly unflattering photo. I'm still trying to make a good impression, right? I mean, the photo's not that recent." I stop myself. This isn't the way to thank someone for getting up—or staying up, as the case might be—at all hours so I can get the keys. All of this raises more questions about Ben. "What I'm trying to say is thank you."

"You're welcome. Have a good trip. It'll be good to see you and Ben once we're all back."

"Sounds good," I say gamely, the sort of answer someone without an anxiety disorder might say. Rather than *"Oh my God, don't leave me alone and responsible for this bling van."*

And at last I'm left to familiarize myself with the van and plug in my phone. As Molly said, the van's smarter than most humans, it turns out. Judging by the kilometers, it's not totally brand new, as in freshly driven off the sales lot, but new enough. New enough that it has under 10,000 miles. Enough to make my palms sweat on the leather-wrapped steering wheel.

After a private pep talk, I carefully drive the van out of the mews, down the cobble lane past picturesque sleeping mews houses, and at last navigate London to head west to Wales.

Chapter Twenty-Seven

Ben's premium van has a kicking sound system, which shouldn't be a surprise, since it's owned by a musician. Because I have no chill, I play some Halfpenny Rise in honor of the van and Ben. Hearing his voice on the track makes my body sing too. It's so easy to think back to that last night together, pressed skin to skin in Ben's bed as he did his earnest best to warm me up after freezing my arse off in Camden.

Don't get distracted. Focus on the M4, a straight drive west from London to Swansea.

I'm tentative with the van at first, but I ease into driving it soon enough. Molly's right that it was a good idea to get out of London early. Even so, by 7:00 a.m. there are signs of building traffic, because London. Everything within the M25 is always busy. Sometimes, it's worse.

By the time I hit the countryside, tension drains from my body. I'm practically euphoric by the time I've reached the North Wessex Downs, beautiful and open. Rolling snow-covered hills soon appear. For once, I can get a real breath in, deep into my lungs. Out here, anxiety doesn't exist. Nobody cares who I am or what I've done. Even last night's fight with my parents melts away.

Molly's baking is delicious. I make myself have some self-restraint and not devour the whole thing in one go, saving some for Emily. I stop for a break outside of Bristol before crossing into Wales. By the time I pass Cardiff for the last leg of the trip before Swansea, excitement rises, and anxiety returns.

Will Carys remember me? What if Emily's gran thinks I'm not doing enough for Emily and Carys? What if Emily resents me for staying in London to finish uni and leaving her full-time with our daughter?

Emily's gran's house is west of Swansea, in the village of Llanmadoc. Her gran, Katherine, has a small but beautifully restored stone cottage with views of the sea from the Gower Peninsula. Emily works part-time at a restaurant in the village. When I feel down about Carys and Emily being so far away, it's comforting to think of them out here in this beautiful place that's barely holding on to Britain. It's the opposite of London, all fresh air and wind and sea.

When I pull up the drive to the farmhouse at lunchtime, there's even a skiff of snow on the ground here, despite it being close to the moderating water. In other parts of Wales, like the mountains, there's a fair sight more snow suitable for sledging and winter sports. But there's plenty here for snowballs, and I bet we can get at least a smallish snowman built out of the snow that's on the ground. It's nothing compared to snow in rugged north Wales, or wild Scottish munros.

I retrieve my phone from its perch on the console, plugged in to charge. Taking the cord, I slip it away in my bag. I scroll through my texts, which chimed their arrival while I drove the last stretch to Emily's. When I spot the latest from Ben, a sigh of contentment escapes me, even if we are so far apart. He's thinking of me. And I'm already missing him.

Drive safe. Let me know when you get in. B xx

I wonder what he's up to today, what it's like for him to be home in Edinburgh. Is he out with his mates? Would he tell any of them about me? It sounds a far sight better than me going to my parents' in Richmond.

Made it, lovely. Cheers again for saving the day with your brilliant van. Talk tonight? C xx

There's a thrill of anticipation in my stomach to hear his soft voice in my ear, even if it's over a phone and hundreds of kilometers. A man does what he needs to get his daily dose of Ben.

Once I get out of the van, the front door opens, Carys held in Emily's arms. She sets Carys down and my little girl comes running like a rocket toward me. Any worries I had about Carys not remembering me—or worse, being scared of me as a stranger—are forgotten when she comes running, the ends of her hair poking from beneath her hat. Scooping her up, I give her a swing around and a big kiss and snuggle.

"Daddy!" Carys chortles with glee as I hold her in my arms, against my hip.

"Who keeps feeding you?" I demand. "How come you're getting so big each time I see you? Are you eating dinosaurs for breakfast?"

Carys just laughs.

When Emily joins me, not sprinting up the path from the cottage to the parking area, I hug her with my arm that's free of a wriggling toddler and lean to kiss her cheek. She's in a oversize cream wool cardigan and sky-blue blouse, her green wellies a stand-in for snow boots.

"Great to see you." Emily's smile is warm. Her golden hair is pinned up.

"Brilliant to see you too." Already, I feel a million times lighter than I had only twenty-four hours ago when I had arrived at my parents'. Emily's my best friend, the person who gets me the most. If I dare count Ben, that makes two people. She's the one who stood by me even through my worst times.

When I set Carys down, she plays with the snow beside us.

Emily returns the hug and kiss, then gestures at the van. It gleams with obvious beauty, a bespoke car commercial on her doorstep, gloss black dazzling against the white snow. She grins, giving it a thorough once-over. "That's some hire car, Charlie. Is the café giving out Christmas bonuses this year?"

"It's an upgrade from the car hire place," I deadpan. "They were out of economy cars."

"Seriously?"

"No. Pack of lies, I'm afraid. I borrowed it from a friend."

"Which friend is that?" Curiosity is plain on her face.

I blush. "The man I told you about."

"Ooh, this is so juicy. I can't wait for the details." Emily laughs, her eyes bright. "But before I ask you a stack of questions, you must be tired after all of that driving. Come in and have a rest before dinner. There's plenty of time for questions over the next few days."

"Any odds of you forgetting your questions? Between now and, say, me leaving?" I try hopefully. A man can dream after all, even if it's a fleeting chance.

"Definitely not." She pats my arm.

We all go inside after playing with Carys in the snow for a few minutes. After kicking off snow against the front step and abandoning my boots and coat in the entry, I make my way through the timber-beamed cottage to find Katherine hard at work in the kitchen.

Emily's gran looks like a sprite with her white pixie cut. She's small in stature, but she's a force of nature. Luckily, she likes me. This is confirmed a moment later.

"Hi. Sorry to take Emily away," I say. "And it smells delicious in here."

"Charlie! Oh good, you've made it." She gives me a big hug, a genuine hug by someone who is truly glad to see me. Unlike my own family. It's an uncharitable thought. I'll call them later today to apologize for walking out last night.

Emily's gran's an artist. Her red earrings dangle and she's in head-to-toe black. "Did you have any trouble getting in?"

"Not today." I neatly sidestep last night's drama.

"Well, you're just in time. You can take the roast out of the oven. And then you and Emily can decide who carves. How's that for a plan?"

"Brilliant."

"Also—have wine. Red or white?"

I laugh. "Whatever you have going."

A few minutes later, the three of us have toasted Carys with white wine for the adults and juice for her. When the roast is out to rest before carving, I briefly call my parents to wish them a happy Christmas. To my amazement, it's not a complete disaster. We don't talk about yesterday, as if by silent agreement. They talk to Carys, they wish everyone well. Another miracle. The phone gets passed around to Great Aunt May and to Michael and Jenna too. Then after the call, we feast, greedy, till we laze around and summon the strength later for gifts and pudding. I've promised to do the washing up to make myself useful as the afternoon sun pools on hardwood.

After our meal, I play for them on my semi-acoustic hollowbody guitar that I've brought along for the trip, plugging into a mini amp, tapping on the guitar for a faux percussion section. Carys shrieks and dances with Emily and her gran in turn while I go through tunes from The Stone Roses, a classic favorite of mine and Katherine's, and we all laugh till it hurts as we try to teach Carys the words to "I Wanna Be Adored" and jam with Katherine with her guitar on "Fools Gold," then dance with unabashed enthusiasm all the way through Modest Mouse.

Sun fills the warm room, and it's joyful as we have our own Christmas concert. I can't stop smiling while I watch Carys. Here, right now, anything feels possible. Forget Maximus St. Pierre's Christmas special playing muted on the television, live from London. Earlier, the newsfeed on my phone told me that Maximus St. Pierre's wife announced their divorce today. Shame for him, but we've got our own gig going on down here, the most important one of all.

While I sing, I can't help but wonder where Ben's at today, and I hope his family's way better to him than mine is to me. We exchange Christmas texts and promise to catch up later that evening about our day.

It's a very relaxed celebration, and a happy one. After I put Carys to bed, we all sit up late over drinks and play some of Katherine's old albums, Gang of Four and The Pogues and even Joy Division. Then, me and Em alternately play tunes from our phones on the wireless speaker while we enjoy the remainder of the evening together. And I'm grateful to Katherine for welcoming here my own small family. They mean everything.

Chapter Twenty-Eight

The next day, Emily, Carys, and I are in a café warming up after a brisk seafront walk. Carys sleeps sprawled in her pushchair beside us. It's great to be the one served in the café rather than doing the serving for a change.

Together, we demolish tea and chocolate cake. Emily's shown admirable restraint, but after the constant visitors yesterday for Carys, today is a day to recoup and finally catch up.

"So tell me more about this man who's loaned you a posh van," says Emily lightly.

"I didn't know about the posh van till yesterday. It's not one of the things that, er, drew us together."

"How did you meet again?"

"At work. He was a customer." My face burns at the memory of our stockroom tryst, and the sight of coffee beans and Ben spilled everywhere. Flustered, I attempt a description fit for public consumption. "It was a…memorable first impression. Or third impression. Whatever. He kept coming back, even if I had been a bit belligerent that first time. Maybe the second time too."

"Or maybe *because* you were belligerent."

"Ha. Maybe. I'll need to ask. We haven't been on a proper date yet. We will when I get back to London. And he's back in London. I mean, it wouldn't work to go on a date with him when he's not back yet. Obviously." I fidget with the cuff of my sleeve.

Emily laughs. "It usually goes better when both people are there for the date. This is so exciting, Charlie. Look at you, going on a date! Clearly there's something there. Ooh, I love it. What are your plans? He must be really into you if he's loaning you his van and you've not even been out properly yet together."

"We've been out. Or mostly in. Or…" Shit, none of this is coming off well. Emily's thrilled though, laughing.

"So the sex is hot." Her eyes dance. She's thoroughly irreverent, paying no heed to my suffering.

"Might be." I sip my tea, my face on fire. For the sake of distraction, I add a shocking amount of sugar to my drink. Better not think of sex with Ben right now. That's just going to lead to a whole series of inappropriate thoughts. Suppressing a smile, I catch myself adding a fourth teaspoon of sugar to my tea.

Put the spoon down. Don't think of how gorgeous and hot Ben is.

"Obviously. What else?"

"He's a musician."

"He sounds perfect for you."

"Well, he's brilliant but it's a bit mortifying. He's from Halfpenny Rise, an up-and-coming band. He's seen me play, too. I might actually die of embarrassment before our date. Plus, we have rehearsal the day before we're supposed to go out and another gig soon."

"Perfect," Emily confirms. "I've heard of Halfpenny

Rise. They came through Cardiff in the summer."

"Nobody's perfect. Least of all me."

She waves a hand. "Yes, yes, we're all brimming with flaws and secret histories. But it sounds like you're perfectly suited to each other. And you clearly have chemistry, along with common ground."

Uncomfortable, I shift. "Except he's all that and I'm just some guy."

"Charlie," Emily admonishes me. "You're fab. And don't put anyone on a pedestal. You deserve good things too. Believe it or not, you're a catch yourself."

I can't quite suppress a laugh. "Not sure about that."

She waves me off. "I'm sure enough for the both of us. Now, tell me. What's your plan for your first date, if you haven't been on one yet?"

"Plan? What plan?" A sinking feeling grips my stomach, drawing it down to the level of my toes and quite possibly that of subterranean rivers. Deeper. "Shit. Are we supposed to have a plan? We haven't said anything about one. We probably should have done by now. What if I've just hallucinated the whole thing out of some desperate and deprived corner of my subconscious?"

Emily eyes me. "Not likely. So you'll just have to roll with the evening. Maybe you'll just spend it in and order takeaway. Sounds hot." She wiggles her eyebrows lewdly at me.

Blushing, I shake my head.

"You're opposed to sex?"

"No. Oh no. Just, what if he expects a posh night out to match his posh van?" My stomach tightens like a fist. Gut punch. "I'm thinking of expensive tickets and queues and premium drinks and oh God what've I done? I should've thought of this a lot sooner. I'm supposed to go on a date with someone who's well outside my orbit."

"It's fine. Obviously he's into you too. And he knows you

work in a café, remember?" She pats my hand encouragingly. "What would you like to do on your date? You have choices, you know."

My immediate thought is to go into hiding. My second thought is to pull Ben tight, to kiss him till I'm sure that I didn't imagine him or the snow that caught us together. I would kiss him till spring arrives. Till I know he's real—and till I know we're real together.

"Um," I say.

And Emily nods sympathetically.

"I need a photo," she declares.

Obligingly, I find a photo—a decent one—of Ben grinning broadly at me, his striped scarf around his neck on a snowy London street.

"Oh!" Emily sits up abruptly. "I remember him! Rumor has it that Maximus St. Pierre left his wife because of him."

"Wait. What?" I frown. "This doesn't make any sense. Ben told me he's single." And as I think back, I remember Ben saying he dated a man for a while before finding out he was married.

My eyes widen as the pieces come together. Were the headlines back in Victoria Station because his relationship was on the rocks with his wife? Or—because he misses Ben? But I shake my head. That doesn't make sense either. Anyway, this is all speculation based on Emily's take on rumors from entertainment news, not from anything that Ben's said to me. Never mind all of this.

"It's got to be fine," Emily reassures me. "He'd have mentioned to you if something was going on, right?"

"Right," I concede, telling my anxiety to fuck off. For now, it actually does.

"Show me another photo," Emily insists. And I do and then we switch back to safer topics.

Whatever we say next is nothing compared to my

newfound angst about living up to first-date expectations with a certain Ben Campbell. And some lingering curiosity about who Maximus St. Pierre is to Ben, exactly.

Chapter Twenty-Nine

Late that night, I'm exchanging lazy texts with Ben. Maximus St. Pierre doesn't come up. It's just us, catching up on our holidays, and everything feels good. Em's right. There's nothing to worry about. Especially not any tabloid nonsense. I'm flopped on the bed in the spare room, everyone else asleep in the house but me. I've put Carys to bed myself, after three stories, tucked in with a mountain of stuffies and blankets arranged to her satisfaction.

Out here, the snow's turned to rain. Soft gray skies beyond my window look to the nighttime sea. I've left the curtains open for the view. No one's around to peer in but seagulls. In the day, the view's stunning, the opposite of my house-share in London, where my room looks out on chimney pots and red-bricked terraces, stacked row upon row.

Somewhere beneath that nighttime sky, Ben's tucked up in a Scottish bed, curled under a duvet to keep him warm. I know this because he's already sent a sleepy selfie, but he rings me anyway on a video call.

"Hey." Ben smiles at me, drowsy but happy. "Five more

sleeps."

"You counting down till caviar and champagne?" I tease him. "Or whatever it is we're doing?"

"I'd settle for a kebab and kisses, to be honest."

"Discerning palate," I say lightly. "Good to know you've got reasonable expectations for a New Year's date."

"Nothing wrong with a good kebab."

"Fair. Do you cook?" I ask.

"Only breakfasts," Ben tells me from where he's nestled against his pillows, hair fanned out. "I have brunch sorted if you stay over."

Smiling, I laze back into the pillows, imagining Ben making me food. Making me anything, really. Hopefully in his great kitchen. I'd be embarrassed to have him over to mine, woefully small, and bursting full with all of my housemates and their things, plus two heaving fridges and nowhere near enough storage. It's not nearly as charming.

"Am I invited?" I ask. "If I play my cards right?"

"Only if you're naughty."

I laugh. "Sold. For the price of a kebab. Somewhere atmospheric, though. I like ambience. Like a tube station. Or a night bus."

"I like running for the last train myself. A great way to finish the night. Especially with company."

"Where would you like to meet? And when? I'll drop your van off when I'm back to London."

"How about lunch? Two o'clock? I could have a surprise."

I perk up. "A Scottish kebab?"

"You'll have turn up at mine to find out. Could be fish and chips. Bring a wee soundtrack. You've got a knack for them."

I flush, pleased Ben thinks so. Confirmation, then, that he listened to the collection I'd made for him.

"Deal."

"Bring an overnight bag when you come," Ben instructs me with a cheeky grin.

"Oh, I'll bring more than a bag."

"Can't wait to see you."

"I can't wait to see me too," I quip back, grinning lazily at him.

"Haha, very funny."

"I know. I'm a riot. Can't wait to see you. I miss you."

"I miss you too."

We exchange good nights and I settle into bed.

It's going to be brilliant to wake up with him again. Ben's eased my nerves some about our first date. Heady talk with him about kebabs can do that to a man.

• • •

The next day on the beach, Carys and I take turns chasing each other. She's bundled into a hat that Emily's knit for her, a coat zipped to her chin, and bright red boots tracking tiny prints in gray sand before the waves wash them away.

It's hard to imagine that one day she'll no longer be a toddler. She'll grow into a little girl, then a teenager, then a fab woman like Emily. One day, I'll be old, and will she be proud of me? Or embarrassed?

Will I be alone? Will I have a partner who'll be like her dad too? For a moment, I dare imagine it's Ben, as seagulls reel and cry overhead while the sun breaks free from the clouds. An impossible thought.

I'm on Carys's heels, holding her hands as she jumps and splashes us in the waves. She's having a brilliant time. After a particularly big splash for a small person, I scoop her up in my arms as she squeals.

"Too much cold water for December," I tell her cheerfully, shifting her in my arms as she slides an arm around my neck.

She whimpers a protest. "Later?"

"Probably not later," I concede. "Because it will be dark. And the sun will be sleeping and so will you."

"Tomorrow?" Carys entreats hopefully with big eyes.

I'm not sure how up she is on the concept of time. Her "tomorrow" could be in five minutes, five hours, or five days. Probably not five months, though, with the promise of warmer spring days pushing into summer.

"Tomorrow," I agree. Tomorrow I can do, because I'm still here. But when she wants me to go play with her the next day, I'll be gone. And it's a terrible thought, twisting my stomach around in strange shapes. Leaving my little girl behind will be awful, even with the promise of Ben like his own change of seasons awaiting me in London. Getting something that I want always seems to mean leaving the people I love behind. A Charlie of divided loyalties, divided lives.

Chapter Thirty

I drive back to London in sleet and fog, grateful for the excellent tires on Ben's van. Emily kept referring to it as the Posh Van, and now it's stuck. Posh Van is safely returned to Ben's home without incident—which is not even a flat, I realize now in the full light of day, but a proper house in central London. Wanting to keep things without incident, I ever so carefully back the van into the garage under the stairs. I put the keys through the mail slot after a long waffle by the front door over whether that's the right thing to do, or if I should keep the keys until I see Ben.

There's a brief moment when I'm tempted to go into the flat, but it feels too much like a violation of Ben's privacy to go in alone. I feel bad enough about going into the garage alone without him or Molly, like I'm trespassing. After, I take my two suitcases and head for public transport back home to my room in Finsbury Park. I'm back home only long enough to drop off my suitcases and have a quick shower before I'm back on the tube again, guitar in hand for tonight's rehearsal out in Stoke Newington. It's only twenty minutes away by bus, which is nothing by London standards.

It's nice to have a little time on my own in the city to help come back to myself, reacclimatize myself with London. After Wales, everything's brighter, louder, and far more hectic. Headlights dazzle in the rain. Cars slosh on. Colors are spotlit and striking: the red of the bus, traffic lights turning green, reflective signs sharp in the dark.

At the rehearsal studios, the gang trickles in for our 6:00 p.m. session.

Gillian's setting up her keyboard. Jackson sorts out his drums. The rehearsal room comes with most of the drum kit and the amps, not as posh as the rehearsal space that Briar and Jackson had for us before Christmas, but also not as likely to sprout plant life from the rugs compared to some other places we've practiced. Everyone else packs in their own instruments and gear. None of us are fortunate to have a Posh Van.

After setting my guitar case down, I slip my damp wool coat onto the back of a chair. As I tune my guitar, Gillian comes over, black hair piled on top of her head.

"How's Papa Charlie?" she asks.

I laugh, about to look over my shoulder for that guy, whoever he might be. Can't be me, can it? It's still weird to be referenced by others—hell, even by me—as a dad. "Good."

"How's Carys?"

"She's getting big. You should see her run now. She's damn fast." Taking out my phone, I share a couple photos of Carys. There's one from her birthday where she sits in a box from a gift that Katherine gave her. Another is of me holding her, with Emily, and yet another from the Christmas Day dancing in the front room.

"Adorable," says Gillian. "Fact. She can come upstage us anytime."

"Let's fly her in for next week," I say, adjusting a guitar

string that's slightly off.

"Brilliant, let's do it. You had a good time in Wales, then?"

"Absolutely." Even thinking of Wales has me thinking of Posh Van, which brings me to Ben. And then a smile I can't fight appears and I don't explain a thing. Like Ben's a greedy secret that I can't mention. Not yet. It's too new. I don't want to jinx it. Nothing's happened other than quality time in his van—without him. Plus, we haven't had our official first date and as excited as I am to see Ben on our date, part of me is still worried about the whole thing. Of course I'm worried. I'm me, after all. And I don't want to namedrop Ben or anything like that.

Before long, everyone's arrived. After warming up together, we work through the set list for next week. It's a gig at a small bar and everyone wants to bring our A game. If we do well enough, that's money to save toward professionally recording our demo, or at least keep us in rehearsal cash for a couple of sessions. There's always the worry about things being a disaster, but it shouldn't cost us anything. At least worrying's my unpaid job. I can worry for the five of us, no problem.

Between songs and banter and catching up, the evening goes quickly. It feels a bit surreal to be doing something back in my normal routine after the last few days, and the hurricane of Ben arriving into my life. And I'm back to worrying that when the snow is gone in January and we're back to the usual London drizzle, the shift in weather will take Ben with it, even with his assurances. Like the snow brought him with its magic and can take him away just as easily when it melts, because Ben wouldn't happen into my life under normal conditions.

Chapter Thirty-One

On the day of our date, I do all of the things to keep busy while waiting for time to pass. I clean my room. I do the laundry. I go for a long run. When I steam myself in the shower, at last I feel like I can breathe again. Even in the shower, the cold air settles into my lungs, like the earlier damp of the rain as I ran on Hampstead Heath, a green expanse in North London.

Around lunchtime, I receive a text from Ben.

Flight delay.

Shit. That's no kind of good news. It's terrible news. The question is: how delayed? Ben's typing on his phone and every second that passes only serves to spike my anxiety.

4pm arrival. Meet me at Gatwick? Bring the van. And that overnight bag.

For a moment, I hesitate. What's he planning, exactly? For a moment, I wonder if he has some wild idea to hop on a flight to God knows where. That can't be right, though, if he wanted me to bring the Posh Van. I'm not sure what he's up to.

I suppose this is where trust comes in. Should someone

be trusted on a first date? But this isn't really our *first* first date. Not technically. And if he was the murdering sort, he probably could have done it that day he led me blindfolded down Camden Passage to the wool shop. No snuff kink so far. I gulp and respond.

All right. Gatwick arrivals. 4pm.

And I hit send, hoping for the best.

• • •

The sun is about to set as I arrive at Gatwick Airport, slung low in the sky. Soft clouds break over the horizon, catching the light. The train is busy with travelers, and people pull suitcases, laden with bags. Once I step off the platform at the airport, my stomach dances. No new texts have arrived warning of delays. Ben didn't send his flight number, which is probably not surprising given his dyslexia and all of the numbers involved, but there are only so many flights coming in at once from Edinburgh.

On the concourse, I stop into a shop to buy a couple of bottles of water, a necessity after any flight. I put them in my duffel bag for now and join the queue of people at the arrivals area. The arrivals board tells me there was another small delay, with the plane arriving at 4:15 p.m.

The five-minute delay's long enough to make me angst when 4:20 p.m. rolls around and there's no Ben. What if there's more delays? What if he's missed his flight and lost his phone to tell me about it? After all, there's a precedent for the phone-losing, though I can't say about missing flights.

By the time Ben appears through the gates five minutes later amid a sea of passengers, I could sob with relief. And he's fucking gorgeous in his leather jacket and that striped scarf, his blond hair tousled with fresh lavender streaks. He scans the crowd and when he sees me, his face lights up and I die about a million times, standing there.

Hurrying to the end of the arrivals causeway, I meet Ben at the end. There's no hesitation then when I pull him tight in my arms and he draws me into a lingering kiss that makes me tingle to my toes and beyond, likely sparking some kind of seismic event south of London. His mouth burns and oh I can't wait for the night to come.

Eventually, we straighten. I reel.

"I missed you," I confess, smoothing his scarf.

Ben's delighted. "I missed you too, Charlie. I told my nan about you and everything," he teases.

"Oh, let's not start with family yet." Instead, I give him another impulsive kiss, which is met with enthusiasm. Forget being in an airport. I don't care who sees us kissing.

"Mmm."

Despite the concourse being full of holiday travelers, and the stream of arrivals and people coming and going from the trains and the airport's entry doors, we stand in our own world. We spend a long moment grinning at each other before I come back to some sort of sense. He must be tired from traveling, and probably dehydrated from the flight. The thimbles of water they serve onboard are nowhere enough.

"I bought water," I blurt, retrieving the water bottles. "For you, I mean. I wasn't sure if you liked sparkling or still water, so I got both."

"Aww, now that's premium service," Ben teases affectionately, taking the still water. He uncaps it and takes a drink. "Cheers. Your barista is showing."

"I know, I know, I can't help it. I would've brought you tea, but who knows if it's up to Scottish standards. I didn't dare coffee because I would judge them shamelessly. And who knows if there would be another delay. Then I'd be standing out here with a cold cup of coffee for you. That wouldn't do. And it's too cold for iced coffee."

He laughs again. "Thank God that crisis is avoided."

"A near miss."

Banter with Ben is effortless. We could go on like this all night, in our own private territory of Gatwick Airport, but it's probably not the most romantic way to spend our first date. The sparkling water would serve as our champagne, though. Till we found a lounge with drinks in here, at least.

"Right. You've kept me in suspense long enough. I didn't bring a passport or a getaway van. Are we going on the run together?" I ask archly. "You running some kind of crime ring? I'm watching for the signs, I'll have you know."

Ben reaches out and smooths my crimson scarf. "Sounds dreamy. The running away part. Not the crime ring part. I promise no crime. Unless hanging out with you is some kind of crime."

Laughing, I shake my head. "Not in England. There's an exemption."

"Thank God for that." Ben nods, admiring my weekender bag slung over my shoulder. It's herringbone wool with leather trim. "Stylish traveler, you."

I redden. "It's a gift from my family. Not recent. But it does the job."

Ben's hard-shell suitcases, by comparison, are covered in all kinds of stickers. Band stickers. Travel stickers. Random stickers. Stickers everywhere, bursting with color.

"I like the look you're going for there," I say.

Ben gazes at the cases. "Cheers. Black bags are boring. Plus, nobody's nicking these without me noticing. It's actually an anti-theft strategy."

"A winning one." I give him a level look. "Quit stalling, Morrissey."

"*Ask*," Ben says mischievously.

"Shrewd to hit back with a Smiths song. *How Soon Is Now*?" I retort.

Ben makes a show of looking at his phone, singing the opening line, enough to make me shiver. He's not loud, but it's more than enough to send tingles up my spine as he gazes at me. A couple of people glance over but don't linger. The flow of humanity continues around us.

"I think it's time to catch a train, don't you?" Ben looks innocent. "How do you feel about the sea?"

"The sea? God, is that where you're disposing of the body? Maybe I should text your nan."

Cracking up, he gives me an impulsive kiss. "I love that you always go for the most dramatic option."

"I'm just thinking of every last possibility," I assure him as we at last head toward the entrance to the train and stop by a ticket machine. "I just thought you wanted an escort back home. Technically, London is on the sea."

"Wrong direction," says Ben as he presses the screen for tickets. When he selects Brighton, my eyebrows lift.

"Brighton?"

"It's on the sea, isn't it?"

"Well, yes. Last I checked. Unless they've moved it, of course." I look thoughtfully at him, like someone might have snuck that one past me.

"I told them to hold off on that till next week, because it didn't fit my plans."

We laugh, and before I can protest, Ben's bought both tickets. The sneaky arsehole.

"I could've got mine," I protest. "Let me get them on the way back tonight."

"Oh, we're staying over, gorgeous. Unless you object, that is." Ben grins broadly as he passes over my ticket. "Next train's in fifteen minutes."

We make our way to the platform. Night has claimed the sky. Faint streaks of color scrape the clouds.

Ben looks magnificent, I have to say. For a moment, I'm

overwhelmed by a hell of a lot of feelings that slam me like a wall.

"Ben," I say hoarsely.

"What?"

I grab him by his jacket and give him a fierce kiss. To hell with who's watching. I grasp his arse. When his warm fingers catch my jaw, I could die in this moment and be a very happy man. Except being dead would mean no more kisses and no more Ben, and that would be the biggest tragedy of all.

Breathless, we come up for air. The train station spins.

"Sorry," I whisper, still feeling surprisingly vulnerable. "Had to get that out of my system."

Ben's flushed, starry-eyed as he gazes at me. "Gorgeous, you can do that any fucking time. Anywhere."

Luckily, it's busy enough that nobody's paying any particular attention to us, though a lady that could be someone's nan smiles.

"I suppose I didn't ask you properly," says Ben.

"Ask me what?"

Sparkling, he hops up onto a bench facing the south-bound platform, hand on his heart. "Charlie Renfrew, would you go to Brighton with me for our official first date?"

I crack up, glancing around at the others on the platform. "People are watching us now."

"Never mind people. Pretend it's just us. You. Me. And our private train." Ben reaches a hand out toward me with a flourish. He beams down.

"Ha," I tell him, seizing his hand and hopping up on the bench beside him. "And of course yes."

Ben pulls me close for a kiss, wrapping an arm around my waist. "I promise an excellent time."

And I wonder what Charlie he's drawn out of me, a Charlie that's starting to give no fucks about who's watching. I'm falling—hard—for Ben's charms. Leaving inhibitions on the platform, we stand on the bench with our arms around each other's waists till the train takes us south to Brighton, to the promise of a new beginning.

Chapter Thirty-Two

It's a cozy train ride to Brighton. We sit pressed together, hand in hand, gazing out of the window at the rolling green hills of the South Downs. We're a million miles away from hectic gray London. Though it doesn't matter where I am, because every time I'm with Ben, I feel like I'm on a holiday.

When we pull into Brighton Station half an hour later at 5:15 p.m., a tempestuous rain lets up. After a short taxi ride, we arrive at the hotel Ben's booked for us near Brighton Pier in Kemptown. It's a stylish hotel, clearly a splurge, and not some dive. Not that I think Ben's cheap, but I'm poor, and dives are the only sort of hotel I could afford. It's hard to wrap my mind around the idea that Ben's trying to please me. *Me*, of all people.

The lobby is spacious and colorful, with statement designer wallpaper and modern art. Ben says we're not far from the beach, but I'll need to wait till daylight to prove that. I've been to Brighton a handful of times. It's not too far from London for a day trip. If the trains behave themselves, which is questionable, it's less than two hours out here, faster on an express. The problem is that on most of those past trips to Brighton, I was high. Now, on my own, clean and sober, I've had little occasion to visit. Till today.

Ben joins me with our bags, eyes sparkling. His leather jacket is open, striped scarf loosely looped once around his neck over his pink jumper. "Bad news. They're booked for the night. We're sleeping on the beach."

"Ha. I'm onto you, Campbell. I'm not buying that for a hot minute. Plus, I saw you put the keycard in your pocket."

He laughs. "All right, all right. Come with me, then."

We find our double room on the second floor. It's just as posh as the rest of the boutique hotel. We put our bags on the luggage racks, shut the door, take in the fab room with its plush cushions and throws, grand wallpaper, and hip decor. It really is spectacular. No sort of dive, not here.

"Sea view, but you'll need to wait till tomorrow to see that. Meanwhile, you'll just have to take my word for it," he says lightly. "So, what do you think of my surprise?"

The only appropriate response is to kiss him raw like we had done on the platform at Gatwick. This time, there truly is no one around but us. Ben gasps with the suddenness of me, of my burning mouth claiming his as mine. In my arms, he shudders, body taut.

"Mmm," I manage between kisses. I'm desperate with longing after the days apart, the tease of having Ben so close. I could do a million filthy things to him. I'd love to try, at least. In this room, my plan is to work through the list, till neither one of us is coherent.

Ben grips my jaw, just as hungry. He's stiff against my hip as he rubs himself on me, eager.

Between the greedy kisses, between the thrum of our bodies reverberating like guitar strings, our urgent fingers fumble with buckles and buttons that don't easily give way.

Both of us are so desperate that we won't last long, even

so.

"Fucking hell. What sort of belt is this?" I gasp. I stop kissing Ben long enough to release his buckle, yank his jeans and boxers down to reveal his hard-on in all of its fantastic pre-cum glory.

Ben moans as I rub his hardness, leaning his forehead on my shoulder, hanging on to me. Meanwhile, he's left me with my shirt untucked, jeans unbuttoned.

I catch his jaw to kiss him rough, to kiss him so he can feel what he's done to me. How he's gotten under my skin. How can it be like this after only a few weeks of knowing him?

It's the last real coherent thought I have.

Then, I release my cock with a groan as it reaches for my belly. God, I've been hard since forever. I swear since I saw Ben at Arrivals, teased by the vibrations of the train and Ben till Brighton.

Rubbing myself against Ben's arse, I tease him with my finger. He cries out as I press into him. Every twitch and gasp only spurs me on.

"You want me?" I work him with my fingers. Ben shakes with pleasure.

"God—yes. Fuck, yes. Fuck me. Now."

My cock takes over where my fingers left off. Spit isn't the best lube, but it'll do in a pinch. I pause long enough for a lubricated condom, retrieved from my wallet. He shudders hard and I wrap my arms around him tight. I press and press, till he's taken me, all of me, and we both sob out at our union.

I press my face into the nape of his neck for a moment, reaching to work his cock as I ride him. Ben presses back, cries out, whimpers and begs. And oh, I want him begging. I want him needy. I want him to know what he does to me.

Caught rough together, I thrust and bite while he bucks and sobs. His skin is intoxicating under my tongue, the want of him. His cock is so hard in my hand. Ruthless, I jerk him without mercy. Fuck without mercy, too.

"Fuck yeah—oh God—oh Charlie—ohhh—you'll—"

And Ben spasms in my arms. He spurts wildly, all over the gray blanket he's bent over at the foot of the bed, searing hot as his belt jangles. I keep going till he bucks and cries out, legs shaking.

So I ride him, ride till I sob out too. I come soon after Ben, while he does his best to grip the bed. My hips lock with him, ride him till I can't see straight, till the room reels, till the sea beyond our window threatens to take us in a king tide.

Fucking Ben is like fucking no other man. It's wild and impulsive. It's like he performs on stage—no holding back. He's so raw.

The best high ever.

Gasping, I collapse on him as we sag onto the bed. I thrust again. Ben groans. I entwine my fingers with his, my chest pressed into his back. I lick the sweat from the nape of his neck.

God, if anyone walked in on us right now, they'd think us a ridiculous sight, Ben still in his leather jacket, me in my wool coat. Too desperate to undress. We're left with jeans and boxers around our thighs.

When I soften a while later, at last I withdraw from Ben, wanting to stay joined with him as long as I can. We shift and roll together onto the bed. I'm behind him, my arm over him, curled together.

"Fuck, that was hot." Ben's drowsy.

"You're fucking hot."

He laughs sleepily. I kiss his neck again. Nestled together, we somehow fall asleep like that, comforted in each other.

Chapter Thirty-Three

When we wake before the evening gets on, a bit sticky, we clean up only to end up with another quick tryst, this time in the steam of the shower. Truly, we've made ourselves at home in this hotel room and claimed it as ours. But how could I resist the glorious sight of Ben naked under hot water? I did what any reasonable queer man would do and seized the moment. For his part, Ben was all too happy to reciprocate.

After opening Christmas gifts—he gave me posh cologne and I gave him a set of small rainbow skeins of yarn from his wool shop—we head out into a drizzle. Hunger strikes us hard, so we venture out to find a pub dinner. Most restaurants are serving a set menu tonight. The well-dressed are out on the town for the evening. Ben and I have neatened up to smart casual attire, with shirts and nice jeans, polished boots and belts. Neither one of us is the overly fancy sort, but I have to say Ben does clean up nicely with some eyeliner and my yellow gold scarf, which he's stolen, so I take his in return.

On the street, we share a kiss in sight of the ocean on the promenade. The icy wind is cutting, so we don't linger, but it's good to confirm there's a vast sea out there, a black ocean rippling out to forever.

We end up in a popular pub, lucky to snag a table. There's a set menu here too, but we're game to go along with it. It's one less thing to make a decision about. All that really matters is spending time with Ben. We dine and drink, enjoying the night out.

"You know, for a man with a dating ban, you're doing quite well tonight on our first date," says Ben over his pint. His grin is as vast as a forever ocean too.

"Well..." I falter. "I suppose you're addictive. In my blood, now. Not sure what you did to me, exactly."

"Just bought your train ticket out here."

"So you could have your filthy way with me."

"Naturally. Why wouldn't I do that?"

We laugh and clink pints. It's always so easy, trading quips with Ben, like we were born to it.

"To the man who challenged the ban and won." I raise my glass to him, and we drink again.

"I love stories where the underdog triumphs." Ben leans on his arm against the edge of the table, pint in hand. He's making no secret about taking me in, and I blush under the heat of his scrutiny, even after our indulgent urgency back at the hotel.

"Fair. Those are stories to cheer for," I confirm. "I know this as a literature student. But I think those kinds of stories are universal."

"And Charlie?"

"Yes?"

"I'm so glad you didn't leave me hanging out alone on the platform at Gatwick," he says lightly. "But seriously, you're an incredible man and I'd like to get to know you more. If you'll consider another date."

"I just might. Though you've set a high bar now. I'm

gonna be demanding."

"Ach. It's all downhill from here, I'm afraid. Only shit dates. I'm out of ideas." Ben's deadpan. He sips his drink. "You better lower your standards immediately."

I laugh, chin in hand as I gaze at him. God. This man. Is this what swooning is like? Is this what happened to the Victorians, falling into serious like to the point they needed chaise longues everywhere and smelling salts and a pair of strong arms to catch them when they fell? Because fuck if I'm not falling for this man. It's a stunning realization. I don't know how that can be, but something in my gut knows it's true.

"I'll take it. I'm desperate," I say. "It's my turn, though, to say cheers. For the fab surprise and the getaway. And I've wanted to say a big thanks for loaning me your van and basically saving Christmas from total disaster. I don't know how I can repay you."

Ben shakes his head. "No need, gorgeous. It was an easy thing. The van was just sitting there with everyone gone."

"It's…a really nice van. I was a bit scared to drive it at first. I thought musicians were supposed to only have shit vans, held together by duct tape and a prayer."

He gives a wry smile. "Well, you know. I wanted something reliable for touring. Something that could put up with all weather, and a lot of miles. We put it through its paces around the UK last summer, and we're off again in a few days for our winter tour."

For a moment, he's quiet. Somehow, his mood has shifted, and I'm not sure why.

"Are you all right?" I ask. "I'm sorry. I don't mean to pry."

"It's a totally fair point. You're right that most musicians don't have vans like that. We're fortunate that we do. I'm very not posh. Definitely not growing up. The only reason I have anything that I do is because of a settlement for my dad."

I don't know quite what to say to that, gazing over my pint.

Ben droops, fidgeting with the ends of the gold scarf still looped around his neck. "He died. Well, eventually, from complications. Wrongful death." He swallows. "And I need to apologize to you."

"No—I'm so sorry, Ben. That's awful. I didn't realize. I'm sorry, I didn't mean to make things heavy."

"How could you know? And...I like remembering my dad. But this time of year is hard."

I give him a wry smile. "Fair." I hesitate. "Do you want to tell me about him? If not today, another time?"

He gives a tentative smile. "He was a great dad. Always there for me. He ran a pub, which is where I got my first break in music, learned to pour pints, too. When he was in a serious car accident...it was devastating. He was made a quadriplegic. Mum and I became carers overnight. We did our best, but it wasn't always easy. He was still my same dad though. I think he tried to make the best of it for us. But we had to sell the pub. Later, there were some...complications with a hospital treatment, and he was gone." He gulps. "So I'm apologizing to you because I wasn't completely honest that day we went for a pint at the Crobar after you met me outside, about why I left school. It's true about the dyslexia. But a big part of it was to look after my dad."

His eyes well up and I take his hand between mine. "I'm so sorry."

Seeing his face crumple for a moment catches something in me.

A couple of tears escape before he wipes them away with the back of his hand. "Sorry. I don't mean to ruin the night. We're supposed to be celebrating the end of the ban."

Squeezing his hand, I shake my head. "I want to know

things about you. I just don't want you to feel pressured to tell me anything you don't want to share, out of some sense of obligation."

"I wanted to tell you. I was trying to think of a way. I didn't mean for that to be tonight, though."

Ben's vulnerable before me. Shifting, I lean over to give him a kiss. "We all have something. I guess it's my turn. I had a wild child past and it's a serious personal failing that I can't get on with my parents. Nothing I do pleases them. Even though I'm clean now, they still see the past when they look at me, you know? And they won't accept that I'm gay. Mum's especially in denial. I took off early from dinner, before they could get to the usual chatter about trying to fix me up with some friend of the family's daughter."

For a moment, it all comes back: the beige room, the standoff with my mother over Carys and the distinct lack of girlfriend in my life, and the endless failure of not living up to their expectations.

"They're always comparing me to my brother, Michael. He's a success in all of the ways that someone can be a success. He's about to propose to his girlfriend, Jenna. And I'm not like that. Quite the opposite, in fact. My parents can't forgive me for my past addictions. Or for Carys. Being gay is the offensive cherry on top."

He grimaces. "Ach, Charlie. That's all so unfair. I'm sorry."

"Yeah, it was a bit shit." Downplaying Christmas makes sense. I mean, to a point I get why my parents are angry about my past fuck-ups, in addition to creating problems for the family likely meaning some loss of social street cred in their circles. "I'm basically the family pariah for life. I, er, bailed early from Christmas dinner because Mum wouldn't stop going on about me not bringing any girlfriends home and I was all fuck that, she knows I'm gay. And I don't want to put anyone through that, even if I did take them home to meet my family. As unimaginable as that is."

"I'm sorry Christmas was so rough. And about the girlfriend business." Ben considers me, chewing his lip. "If you think it's all right, and if you want, I'd like to meet them one day."

"After all of that?" I ask, incredulous. "Why? Are you a sucker for punishment? Wait. I know the answer to that."

Laughing with delight, he shakes his head when he settles again. "No, it's not that. It's just…I want to learn more about you, Charlie. Where you come from. And to show them that someone else thinks you're absolutely brilliant."

"Cheers for the vote of confidence, but it'd be a nightmare," I warn him wryly. He has no idea about the ice storm that is my mother. "But I'll think about it. I'm sure there'll be something where you can meet them, if you still really want to."

Ben brightens at that. "'Kay. Though…I'm going to be on tour for a while. I don't know if the dates will line up, but we have breaks."

"Well, let's see how that works out. If you don't change your mind." I shake my head. "My family life's a mess, admittedly."

"What about Carys's mum?" Ben's expression is a combination of curiosity and…a trace of anxiety? He hesitates for a moment. "You spent Christmas together?"

"Not like that. It's not romantic in the slightest, believe me," I say hurriedly, in case he gets the wrong idea. "We're just good friends. Best friends since school. And I'm gay. Just…one night a couple of years back we had a *lot* to drink after a night out and I guess I was hetero curious as well as off my face, and Carys happened. And…we worked through some stuff. I did too. And we're good friends, though I wouldn't call her my ex, because we didn't ever date. It was only a one-night stand. To my mother's disappointment, we didn't get married after she learned we planned to keep the baby. I said, Mum, there's no way in this lifetime I would ever marry a woman. Not even Emily. Not at nineteen, or ever. Fuck. But Em's family, and she will always be family to me. And we both agree to put Carys first. Before anything else."

Ben nods, looking understanding.

A pang of nerves hits then.

Ben's a rocker on the up, which will mean loads of time away, like he mentioned. And the rocker lifestyle of parties and drinks and glamour, while my world is one of routines and saving and nappy changes, and always planning the next trip to Wales. It's hard to imagine how this can work out longer than a few dates. My fingers twist the beer mat around.

"My life's not like what you've been through with your dad, though."

He shakes his head. The pub lights limn his hair and shoulders like liquid gold, slightly backlit. "I think...I think we all have things, Charlie. Like I said that day. I suppose it's a matter of finding people that can live with the things that you've done or been through."

That resonates with me, in my gut, and he's right. It's not about finding the perfect person, but the one that gets you and loves you, flaws and histories and all. *Especially* because of the flaws and histories and everything else that goes along with life.

I give him another kiss for that, and his mouth lingers on mine. If only I could kiss his grief away, his loss. But I realize now it's part of him, part of what makes him live in the moment like he does. And now it makes a lot more sense about the van too.

"I know you said that Emily isn't your ex, but I should probably tell you about mine," Ben confesses over his pint.

"You're not obligated to," I assure him, squeezing his

free hand in mine as it rests on the table. He chews on his bottom lip. Bloody adorable, except for the fact he's angsting. "Only if you want."

"I want to," Ben says. "You'll probably hear about him sooner rather than later. Since…well, we're dating now?" He looks at me for confirmation, a hopeful smile on his lips.

"Yes. RIP, dating ban." I chuckle and give his hand another squeeze. "It's officially canceled. And I'm all ears."

He smiles at that, but the pensive look remains. "His name is Maximus. He's a musician too."

"Maximus St. Pierre?" I ask immediately in the silence that follows, my mouth running off again before my brain, thinking back to Christmas in Wales and Emily's comments about rumors. And…wasn't there something about a Christmas Day split or something? I hold my breath and steel myself.

Shit's about to get more real, Charlie. Whatever it is. Call it intelligence or instinct.

"Maximus St. Pierre," Ben confirms, looking startled. "You knew?"

"Well, only obliquely, maybe," I admit. "I don't exactly have time to follow the lives of celebs." But just about everyone's heard of him, like they've heard of Bon Jovi or Mick Jagger. Because Maximus St. Pierre is definitely capital-C Celeb. A-list rock royalty. Fierce guitar. Probably fierce at everything else too. Anxiety turns my stomach. My grip tightens on my pint. "Em said something at Christmas because of some news headline?"

Ben can't quite suppress a groan. Wearily, he rubs a hand over his face, as if the gesture will smooth his expression and erase the past.

"It's fine, whatever it is," I tell him. By comparison, I'm inadequate, but I tell my brain to stop it. This isn't time to feed my complex after a lifetime of comparison to Michael, but now I can add Maximus St. Pierre to my anxiety fodder too. I make myself focus.

"No, no. It's fair to ask," Ben agrees. "It's just not always so easy to talk about."

Maybe I am the rebound after all.

"The past is a bitch sometimes." I flash him a half smile. "I know that much. Though not so much about exes."

"Remember when I told you when we met up at the Crobar for drinks that I had dated a married man without my knowledge?"

I nod confirmation, a wry smile on my lips.

"I have a habit of running full tilt into things. Well, it was full tilt into Maximus. He didn't wear a ring or ever mention a wife. Or a girlfriend, for that matter. It turns out he had some secret marriage with Sienna Silvers, and they had a messy on-and-off relationship—that I knew about—while he privately struggled with his own ghosts, including his sexuality. He tried to put this on me, that I came on too strong, and maybe I did. But it takes two, you know." Ben shakes his head, squirming in his seat. "I...I fell for him. And he broke my heart, if I'm totally honest. One day, he came clean after I saw texts from Sienna on his phone that he'd left on the table. And, judging by the news headlines at Christmas, Sienna must have found out, even though it's been months. Or maybe he's taken up with someone else instead. It's all in the past now." Ben shrugs away his hurt, trying to look indifferent, but he's not fooling me.

"God, Ben. That really sucks." I take this all in.

"It wasn't my favorite time. Or something I'm proud of. The media kept saying that I was into him to advance my band, but that's not true." Ben shakes his head. "But I'm more determined than ever to make it big. To show myself and everyone else that Halfpenny Rise fought to the top as some indie band coming out of obscurity and against all odds. For me and for my dad and my mum too, who I swear is my biggest fan." His face brightens at last, more like his usual self, at the mention of his mother.

"Aww, that's brilliant about your mum," I tell Ben. His hand has been in mine all of this time, as though this simple gesture is second nature to us both. It's grounding. "She's back in Edinburgh?"

He nods. "Yeah. She's still living in the same flat I grew up in. I keep saying I'll help her get something else if she wants, but she says it'll always be home. And it is. It's a relief to have it stay the same, even with all of the changes with the band getting bigger and me getting recognized sometimes."

Our meal arrives and the mood lightens. Ben's more restored to his usual self, but there's a vulnerability in him tonight after opening up to me. It's a lot to take in for both of us.

We linger over our meal and pints as the evening goes on. Eventually, though, it's getting too hot and too crowded. Ben's the one looking overwhelmed instead of me in the din of the New Year's festivities, and I'm the one who leans in and presses my mouth against his ear.

"Wanna go?" I ask.

When he nods, I don't hesitate. Still wearing Ben's striped scarf, I tuck the ends into my coat. I take him by the hand to lead him out, back to our hotel a short walk away. In the room, Ben breaks down in my arms, having the release that was caught tight in his body. Eventually quieting down, he takes my face between his hands, kissing me so deeply, so reverently, that I swear this is what heaven feels like and Ben's my church of worship. And I'm praying for him and I'm praying for me too, because—well, because somehow I'm falling for an incredible man on our first official date. Thrilling and terrifying.

Under moonlight pooling from our window with its

tied-back velvet curtains, Ben's in my arms. Every part of him is surveyed with kisses. For restoration, for longing, for the future too. As rushed as we were earlier, we are languid together, leisurely together tonight. Ben and I are tangled beneath cotton sheets, and I trace the silk of his skin as the old year gives way to the new.

Chapter Thirty-Four

The next day is bright, with sharp blue skies. Wind blows every last scrap of cloud far away over the North Sea. Waking up with Ben is intoxicating. We have a lazy morning in bed, ordering room service for breakfast before we head out for a pub brunch. Wrapped up against the chill day, we welcome the year with a walk along the promenade and a meander through the North Laines with its shops, which are mostly shuttered for the holiday.

In a café which offers excellent coffees, we warm up. Coats still on, we're bundled as we claim the seats by the window, perched on tall industrial-style stools. We watch the steady stream of walkers going by outside.

"Any resolutions?" Ben asks, fingers wrapped around the top of his mug. His freckled cheeks have color from the wind. Today's woolen hat is a silver cable-knit affair with a bright green pompom.

"Resolutions? Nah. I mean, just the overall goals, but I don't need resolutions for that," I say.

"What sort of goals?"

I shrug. They're going to be very different than Ben's goals, that much I know. "Well, I need to finish uni this year. My degree, I mean. This is my last term. Then, if I don't succumb to utter disaster, which is a distinct possibility, I will need to find a real job. The plan is for Emily to get to London by autumn, so she can take her turn at uni too. And so that Carys is closer. Ideally, we'd live nearby to share childcare more easily. And I'll help cover the bills with a decent job. If there's such a thing for an English lit student. None of it is too glamorous, but it'll be good if it works out."

Ben looks impressed. "Aye, those are fantastic goals. Well done you. It all makes sense to me why you'd want that and to see your daughter regularly. And you'll find work, I'm sure of it. Who wouldn't want you?"

I redden. "I don't know about that. I'll send you in to negotiate on my behalf, all right?"

His laugh is easy. It's impossible not to smile back. "In a second. I'll go in as your expert negotiator anytime. Just tell me who needs to be set right. I'll do it in a second."

"I'll give you a list of names when the time comes." I work on my latte in the hand-thrown ceramic mug. Blue glaze runs down its sides. "You have any resolutions?"

Ben considers me over his drink. "The big personal goal is to not start smoking again. Bad habit. Especially with the tour coming up. It's so easy to fall into bad habits. I resolve to avoid bad habits and self-sabotage, like being too impulsive and maybe a wee bit overconfident. How's that?"

"Noble," I say, smiling. "I'll follow your lead with that. Except I don't have the overconfidence problem, I don't think."

"You've got just the right amount of confidence," Ben assures me. "A charming amount."

I have to laugh at that. "Maybe sometimes."

"Always." The way he smiles at me makes me feel warm

from the inside out. Like he's got complete faith. Like I'm special, and wanted, and cared for.

"Any other goals? You said personal goals, which makes me thing there might be more."

Ben flashes a jubilant grin. "Aye, you're right. Professionally, I want Halfpenny Rise to make it big this year. Like, awards contender big. And that our gigs will sell out and the tour will be extended. And we'll record a new album later this year, be one of the top UK bands by next year. I want to say we'll be the best, but there's some fierce competition out there."

"Wow."

"We'll see what's in the cards. Though admittedly I like them stacked in my favor." Ben chuckles.

I look at him, suitably impressed. And also daunted, because as Gillian put it, Papa Charlie versus award show galas and all of that don't go together so well. Yet I want Ben, more than I care to admit even to myself. Because the idea of not having Ben in my life is more terrible than trying to figure out a way between our different set of goals.

The scary part is—what happens now? We've met the first date challenge. I didn't die of angst over it, didn't implode. But now there's the big blank space of what happens after. And…I'm into having something with Ben after. I don't have a script for that. I wasn't sure how I'd feel after New Year's, like maybe we'd be sick of each other by January, but it's not like that at all.

"Hey, can I ask you something?" I pull out of my reverie as we watch the people pass by on the pavement outside. The café hums with patrons, but it's not as loud as my café back in Soho.

"Anything." Ben peers at me over his drink, fingers wrapped around the mug, his elbow against the oak bar as he gazes at me. It's like we're any other couple doing couple stuff. Which leads me to the next thing.

"I had a text from my brother, Michael. He got engaged to his girlfriend at Christmas, and he's invited me to their engagement dinner. And…you said before that you wanted to meet my family, despite everything. You'll be away for my mother's birthday. It's probably a bad date idea, but do you… want to come with me? As my date?"

I say these words and the universe, weirdly, doesn't implode. No lightning bolt strikes me down.

Ben brightens, obviously pleased. "Absolutely, Charlie. I'd love to. I'd be thrilled to go with you."

"It'll probably be wretchedly dull and all of that," I warn him. "Michael's cool, but…I don't get on with my parents. It's kind of an oil and water situation. No matter how much I try. If you come, maybe they'll see I have my life together more than they think. And…get the picture that I'm not straight. I'm hoping though all of the attention will be on Michael and Jenna. And it was his idea to invite you. I, er, mentioned you to him at Christmas."

He entwines his fingers with mine. "Aww, that's lovely that you did. And that someone's on your side in your family."

"Well, you're important to me. And…well, I want you to stick around, you know?"

Ben leans in to kiss me. "That'd be brilliant to keep dating you. And to meet your family."

It turns out that the day is all kisses, guaranteeing wind-chapped lips by evening. Well worth it. Nighttime finds us on the rattle of a tin can train back to London, brimming with the hungover and sleepless from the parties from the night before. We're in the quiet carriage. Our phones are dutifully on silent, and the only sounds around us are the hum of the train and the rustle of newspapers. Ben dozes on my shoulder. We share headphones to listen to the playlist I made for him. He's fucking adorable. His head bobbed off and on as he fell asleep over the course of fifteen minutes before sleep finally took him.

As we near London, nerves start to gnaw on me.

My gig's a few short nights away. I've neglected to remind Ben about that. There's no end to the vulnerabilities today, between the invite to Michael and Jenna's engagement party and the show. A not-so-secret part of me hopes he forgets about the gig. He may have seen me play before, but I didn't know he was watching then. And he's so damned good at what he does, I can't help but feel a pale comparison.

I have nerves about what happens next with Ben. I have no kind of proper dating experience. The whole idea is enough to make me break out in a cold sweat, which isn't attractive.

When we're out on the concourse at Victoria Station, it's hard to believe it was a week ago I was here in a flood of tears and a full-blown mess. Now, there's a completeness and comfort that I didn't know I was missing till now.

We gaze at each other, neither one of us wanting to break the spell as reality laps at our ankles like an incoming tide. Ben's sleepy from his evening nap against my shoulder, looking deliciously rumpled. It would be so easy to make-believe, to pick up where we left off in Brighton, all tangled limbs and urgency.

But he needs to get to Marylebone. I need to get to Finsbury Park. The real world waits for us after our holiday. Whether we want to or not, it's time to escape this snowy fantasy and rejoin regular life. And find out, for better or worse, if there's a way to make this work between us for a while longer yet.

"What does tomorrow have in store for you, then?" asks Ben as we stall before entering the Underground for different directions home.

"A shift at the café. Back to work." Hard to imagine. "And, um, a rehearsal. You?"

"I'm working, too. We have a band meeting day after next. Tour logistics and rehearsals nearly daily till we go."

I fidget with my keys in my pocket. "How long will you be away?"

"We're gone from the tenth for a few weeks. If tickets sell well, the tour will probably get extended to add more dates," Ben says. "There's an itinerary. Doesn't mean much to me since I can't read it properly, but it's a long list. I'll send it on to you." Ben tilts his head, gazing at me with a soft smile. "Am I allowed to buy another ticket to your gig?"

"Well, anybody can buy a ticket," I say gamely. My face is on fire. The arsehole didn't forget after all. Shame. I suppose posters are everywhere, including back in the café. "It's not about being allowed. But, I mean, my band's no comparison to Halfpenny Rise. We're so much smaller. Though I appreciate that you want to come to the gig."

Ben laughs. "Confidence, Charlie. You're great. I've seen you and I wouldn't tell you lies. Halfpenny Rise are full-time professionals, more or less. You and your bandmates have talent on the same level. You just don't have the fame."

"We're not professionals."

"Professional enough that you have gigs lined up. Not even at your nan's house, I bet."

I have to laugh at that. What a thought. The closest I have to a nan is Great Aunt May, who will probably outlive us all. She'd probably be down for a gig at her house. I'd hate to underestimate her. And she's hardly Katherine, Emily's gran, who was a punk back in her day. Another black sheep. "Well, I suppose you're right about that," I say, feeling more at ease. "It's a small bar."

He beams, pleased. "See? I knew that. Plus the band poster says too. I took a picture."

"Haven't lost your phone in Brighton or anything?"

"Not even once," Ben says proudly.

I scrape the toe of my boot against the ground, shifting the strap of my bag on my shoulder. He's so hopeful too. "All right. You can come."

"Brilliant." Ben beams at me. "Number one fan. I'm so excited."

"I'll get you a ticket," I promise at last, laughing at his obvious glee. Here goes everything. "It's the least I can do after Brighton, all right?"

"All right."

We share a kiss. Even with my January-related anxiety, I melt against his mouth.

Just stay in the moment, Charlie. Just him, just you.

Chapter Thirty-Five

On gig night a few evenings later, I slam back a shot of whiskey before the show. It burns pleasantly on the way down, warming my throat and chest, the sensation grounding me. I've briefly emerged from the greenroom to make a beeline for the bar. Just one drink, to steady my pre-performance nerves.

What are a bunch of book nerds from uni doing on stage in front of a live audience tonight? A terrible idea.

There're friends out there, like Aubrey and his new boyfriend, Blake, and other familiar faces from Soho and my uni classes. Talk about performance anxiety and not wanting to disappoint.

When I texted Ben and asked earlier if he got nervous before a gig, he said no. I've yet to see Ben tonight—I don't even know if he's made it. He texted earlier that he was on his way, but I needed to get to the venue early with the gang to help unload our kit and do soundcheck and all of that.

I lean against the bar for the moment, wishing it was about ten degrees cooler and the venue somehow not sold out. Small bar yes, but there's still a hundred plus people in here, and apparently they're still mostly sober enough to pay attention to what's happening on center stage.

"I hear the guitarist's hot," drawls Ben beside me, appearing out of nowhere.

I nearly jump out of my skin, turning abruptly to face him. "How—when did you get here?"

"I've been here all night," Ben says cheerfully, gesturing at the crowded bar. There's a melee for drinks, while others are out on the dance floor, having a great time. "Luckily only a couple of people recognized me so far. I'm very niche and I'm a bit out of context, not being on stage myself. Performers always seem a little less grand backstage or in the front of house."

I snort. "You wanna go up there and pretend to be me? You'll do a hell of a better job. I'm sure of it."

Ben laughs, basking under the prospect of attention. "Absolutely not. First thing, I've an excellent view of the stage from here."

Which was true, with the elevated level that the bar was on, overlooking the dance floor and the tables arranged around it in a horseshoe.

"Second thing—" Ben leans in for a kiss, and when our mouths meet, it's an instant burn, even better than the whiskey. He savors me and I shudder. "That's probably the third through fifth things as well."

"Do you do this with all of the guitarists at the gigs you go see?" I ask archly. "Distract them with pre-show snogging?"

"Only the cute ones," he teases, entirely irreverent. "I personally like them looking like Charlie Renfrew. The man's a legend."

"Oh God. I'm gonna be sick if you keep that flattery up. It'd be better if you told me that it was all a bit shit, actually. That'd take the edge off."

Ben gives me a sympathetic look. "Want a drink?"

"No, no. I just had one and one's plenty. But I appreciate the thought. Tell you what, you keep going with the drinks for both of us."

"You'll be fire, lovely." Ben squeezes my hand and gives me a more lingering kiss. This time, it's less frenetic, more leisurely. Enough to bring me back and ground me. This is just a gig. One night. That's it. Then I'm back to regular life.

There are a lot of minutes in a night.

Wow, seriously, brain. Don't start calculating the number of minutes in the night, or the percentage of those minutes spent on stage. They'll pale in comparison to the number of minutes pre-show where nerves got the better of you. Because Ben is out there, watching.

"I probably should get back." It's a shame, because I'd rather stay with Ben, pretend we're alone back in Brighton together. Instead, the bar's loud and there are a million people around laughing and drinking and being rowdy.

"I'll be here when you finish," Ben promises. "I won't leave without you."

"That's what I'm afraid of."

He laughs. "Go get 'em, tiger."

"Please." With a shake of my head and a final quick kiss, I go to rejoin my bandmates in the greenroom.

Briar's wearing a crown of roses to complement her long blond hair. Where the crown came from, I have no idea, because she was sans crown fifteen minutes ago. Gillian's tucked a flower behind her ear. As I look around, it turns out my band has been thoroughly rosed while I was gone.

Gillian flashes a broad grin, approaching with roses in hand. "Your turn."

"What exactly is happening?"

"Briar wants us all to look fresh for the New Year. And red is so your color, Charlie. You'll be stunning." I don't know how her grin could get bigger, but she presents me with a rose crown too. "Just look at this beauty."

My eyebrows lift. "We're all going for this look, I take it?"

"You're both front and center. Now, don't hurt Jackson's feelings. He brought us all of these."

Jackson is about as whimsical as Briar, who is perfectly willowy and somehow gravity has enough hold on her to keep her tethered down here on earth. Sometimes, I think she might float away, seemingly distracted all of the time. Then she nails a song and feeds the audience their pancreas on a platter with the soar of her vocals. As far as I can tell, she's not quite human.

I lower my head a little for Gillian to work with the crown. She uses a couple of hair pins to secure it. Gingerly, I shake my head. The crown stays in place.

When we go out, the dazzle of the stage lights is blinding, making the crowd invisible. And that's finally when I feel calmer. Thankfully. I'm not totally calm, which is good, because I can channel that extra energy into my performance.

Jackson counts us off and then we're blazing through our set list to a crowd that roars its approval. Briar's electric and sultry, her voice carrying through the venue in such a way that even my arms are covered with goose bumps. She has power in her lungs and her magnetic presence. I do my best to keep up with supporting vocals.

Giving myself over to the music, I forget about everyone and everything except the sounds we make together. The extra rehearsals have paid off. Briar's fantastic and I'm doing everything I can to keep up with her charisma. She's down to a camisole over her full skirt as she plays to the crowd, who goes wild for her. I catch Gillian's eye and she gives me a megawatt grin as Jackson thumps the heartbeat of the bar. The crowd dances as one, euphoric. The energy in the room is frenetic. Closing my eyes, I give over to the music and sing like I haven't before, putting it all out there, the ecstasy of Ben and the angst of Carys being so far away. All of the family hurts about not being enough are left behind, and possibilities stretch ahead.

When it's like this, the five of us playing as one, it's brilliant. Like there's no me and no Briar, no Gillian, Jackson, or Matt. We're one thudding baseline, one beat. Time disappears, the venue disappears, everything disappears. It's just us and the music and we're transcendent.

At last the lights go down on our last song, but we're roared back for an encore, the crowd revved up after our performance. I knock back water in the wings, then we're back on stage. This time, I'm swapping out my electric guitar for an amplified acoustic. Jackson brings out a hand drum.

We perform two more songs, winding the crowd down from their ecstatic high, Briar leading them to sing through the chorus. Like this, we end the night in cheers and whistles, and the thunder and roar of the hundred and fifty people in the venue.

If this is a taste of Ben's world, no wonder he lives for performing.

Chapter Thirty-Six

Back on earth, I down the rest of the water when we're in the greenroom again, everyone hugging in various combinations, occasionally dripping red rose petals amid the excitement. The room's full of leather sofas, a bank of mirrors along one exposed brick wall.

"Wasn't that great?" Gillian enthuses, slinging an arm around my shoulders.

I laugh, relaxed after the show and riding the performance high. "Gotta agree."

"Best gig yet." Jackson clinks his beer with mine, dark hair curling around his ears. He's all gangly limbs in ordinary daily life, transforming into a model of coordination when he drums. "You're fire, Charlie."

"I think that was Briar," I say. "Holy shit."

Briar just smiles, twisting her hair around her fingers to make a loose plait, which she pins up. Must be hot under all of that hair. "Oh, you know. Group effort and all of that."

Jackson is there, a giant of a man who you would ordinarily think twice about crossing by the look of him. But he's a gentle soul and well-suited to Briar. He's an artist, too.

"Sooo," says Gillian, looking impish. Like Briar, she's also down to a camisole, given the summer-like heat between the stage and the greenroom. "Are you going to introduce us to your boyfriend or what, Charlie? We saw the pre-game show out front earlier. He's hot, by the way. I'm sure you noticed."

I redden. Oh God. Why didn't I think of this? "Well, he's not quite my boyfriend. Well, I'm not sure exactly. We're, um, dating. If one official date counts."

Better not mention the unofficial ones.

Personally, I'm counting the unofficial ones too from that first tryst. Three weeks of Ben, not counting the earlier weeks where he kept turning up at the café. The other night we went to the cinema after dinner, a classic date. It was brilliant. We've both been busy and I'm back to the usual crush of uni, work, and the extra rehearsals because of the gig.

"Oh please," says Briar, looking hopeful. "Is this true? You—dating?"

"True," I concede with a smile. It's impossible not to smile when thinking of Ben. "Let me go find him and bring him here."

So, I go out to the front of house and make my way through the venue, which has now turned over to the capable hands of a DJ. People dance. As I weave my way through the crowd, people stop to clap my shoulder or to tell me that I was great up there. Totally surreal.

I'm smiling and it feels strange, but good. Some part of me still refuses to believe they're talking about me.

I find Ben in a knot of admirers at the bar. And he's laughing and doubtless charming, and obviously loving the attention. Hanging back, I give him a couple of minutes as he signs a couple of autographs and talks with fans. He's leaning in, taking photos, and exchanging hugs.

So, he's been recognized. I suppose this is the crowd for it. There's a pang in my stomach I can't quite suppress, confirmation that he's not just my Ben, but there's a public Ben out there that exists in the world. And in that world, he's got to have a million better options than picking a student barista to date.

Eventually, he glimpses me after I've signed a couple of my own autographs, and he comes over at last to give me a big hug and kiss. And some guilty part of me wonders if that's a performance too, a thought come unbidden, remembering our chat back in Brighton when he said he had a habit of coming on strong. Is he flirting with everyone or is he just happy?

"Charlie! You were brilliant," Ben declares. And his smile reaches his eyes, and I trust that. "Absolutely brilliant. Best gig of yours I've seen so far."

Oh God, what a reminder that this wasn't the first time he's seen me play.

"Thanks. My bandmates caught sight of you and want to meet you, too."

Ben brightens. "You'll introduce me to your friends?"

I gulp. So begins a collision of worlds, ready or not. It was inevitable. Keeping my life nicely compartmentalized is a coping mechanism. Don't ask me what I'm scared of, but it's unsettling. But he looks just as hopeful as my bandmates.

This is happening. It'll be fine.

I lead him back to the good cheer of the party going in the greenroom. "Hey," I say to Gillian as we enter. "This is Ben Campbell."

Gillian does a double-take at Ben. He looks great in a gray shirt, something so soft I'm already thinking about how it would feel to skim my hands under it to trace his body. There are a couple of colorful streaks in his hair. He's delicious, frankly. Check that thought for later.

"Ben Campbell? The Halfpenny Rise Ben Campbell?" Gillian tries, looking startled. "Whoa. Charlie didn't mention a thing about that." She stares at me as if I've sprouted an extra head or appendage.

"Aye, so." Ben shrugs a shoulder, smiling broadly at her reaction and the recognition. In fact, he's obviously thrilled. "Good to meet you."

He charms Gillian. Then Briar. Then the rest. Those who don't recognize him straight away are soon tuned in by Gillian, and the requisite fan-personing begins. Which is fair, because he's the frontman of Halfpenny Rise, and it's well deserved.

It's a weird twist in my guts to think others want him too, that I can't selfishly keep Ben a secret to myself, to the time where we were caught in a snowy London of our own making. And he's loving the attention, that's for sure, and I stand on the edge of the circle, watching on. I fidget with the cuff of my shirt.

How can I compete with the limelight of thousands of fans when he goes on tour? Will I be replaced by the next best thing?

Snow's given way to gray drizzle, and in a couple of days he'll be gone on tour. And I'll be left behind, alone again.

Chapter Thirty-Seven

Michael's engagement party turns out to be a formal family dinner party, because that's how my family kicks back and has a good time. As tradition has it, for every family occasion, we celebrate these milestones in my parents' aubergine-but-truly-beige dining room as our default option.

This afternoon, classical music plays over the house speakers. Everyone else is gathered out in the main reception room at the front of the house, and every so often, laughter spills out so I can hear them. My parents stopped short of hiring a quartet to play, given this long-awaited day for them, to mark Michael's full passage into legitimate adult responsibility, as if the legal life and home ownership wasn't enough already.

Sleet pelts sideways outside. It's a bitterly cold day with none of the charm of snow. Ben's delayed due to rail replacements, which are par for the course on a Sunday ride out to Richmond. He leaves tomorrow on tour, which has left my stomach in knots this weekend.

I've escaped the family festivities to set out fourteen place settings, with the generous table at full expanse for twelve along the sides and my parents at either end of the table. I've tried to set out the brightest option, which is a deep purple-blue color, and coordinating cloth napkins. I've put out all of the beige trivets to take hot platters on the table, despite the woven runner. I move decadent vases of flowers, given that it's January, to the sideboard. Poor forced hyacinths, antagonized to bloom against their nature, the sorry arseholes who just want to sleep till spring.

I continue with setting the table, laying out an abundance of china and cutlery more than plenty for thirty guests instead of the fourteen that are here. But my mother was very specific in her instructions with cutlery for the various courses, and I'm following orders to keep the peace, with only the slightest subversion on my part with place setting color choices.

Nobody mentions Christmas.

It's like it didn't happen, deleted like so many of my other indiscretions and blow-ups. Redacted from the family history. As for today, everyone knows that for once I have a plus one, and I swear I can hear them all collectively holding their breath.

Fuck that.

The doorbell rings, and I jump, checking my watch. That's got to be Ben. And I better get the door before my parents do.

Despite hurrying, my mother's closer. When I arrive in the entry, the door is open, and she's stepped back to let Ben inside quickly after cursory introductions on the front step. The door slams hard behind him due to a gust of wind, rattling the inset stained glass. I cringe. What a way to punctuate the requisite *how do you dos*.

"Sorry, Mrs. Renfrew." Ben looks suitably contrite. His explosion of color thrills me and makes me nervous at the same time, because I've brought him to a place where color doesn't ordinarily dare to exist. He's wearing a Kelly-green wool hat with a large pompom and his multicolored scarf wrapped twice around his neck over a long wool coat.

My mother nods acknowledgment, reaching out a hand for his wool coat, damp with the sleet and rain. He bends to untie his combat boots and slips out of them to reveal rainbow hand-knit socks. It looks like the wool that I gave him at Christmas. Because of fucking course he's wearing rainbows here, just as my mother has gone full-on Mrs. Renfrew to him, rather than Delores.

I turn my head slightly to hide a smile behind my hand, my mother's back to me as she hangs Ben's coat. Making myself sober immediately, I dive straight in, already knowing the answer but keen to draw the attention away from Ben.

"I take it you've already made introductions?" I ask them, my voice overbright atop a violin concerto in the background.

"Yes." My mother looks at me to Ben and back again. He's in a slightly rumpled western button-down shirt, light blue with black piping, a hand-knit burnt orange cardigan that he must have made, and black jeans, with blue and black streaks in his bleached hair to match. By comparison, I'm in a crisp white shirt, tie, and charcoal gray wool trousers. Her gaze lingers over him for a split second longer than strictly necessary, and I know she's already passed judgment, a slight downturn to the neutral line of her thin lips. "We have."

"Sorry again for being late," Ben offers. "I had problems with the train. I ended up taking a taxi the rest of the way."

"Charles should have mentioned about the train." Her gaze flickers to me. I'm already—permanently—in the doghouse. "Not a problem. We've had the caterers hold lunch by half an hour to wait for you to join us."

I hide a wince. Yep, confirmation of judgment, loud and clear. Mum doesn't ordinarily hold meals for late-arriving guests. A glance in the kitchen showed all of the warming ovens in use, and the trays that the caterers had brought.

"Let me get you a drink," I say to Ben. "And make some more introductions."

"Ten minutes till lunch," my mother says before she retreats for the kitchen.

We have a private moment together, and I kiss him, his lips frozen. Even so, it feels scandalous kissing him in this house.

"I'm glad you're here," I murmur. "And sorry about Mum."

Ben's undaunted. "I'm glad to be here. I missed you."

It's been a couple of days since we've seen each other, between my work and his getting ready for his tour. Posh Van went in for servicing, Halfpenny Rise had a rehearsal and band meeting, and I've been juggling a more-than-full week between uni courses that I'm permanently behind on, and café shifts to also cover for Lars, who has a cold. I need the extra cash anyway, so I don't mind. Though I'm sorry that there's no rehearsal today for my band, it means a rare Sunday off and the chance to spend time with Ben before he goes away. The unfortunate part is spending that time together out here at my parents', even with his insistence that he wanted to come to the engagement party. He doesn't know what they're like, and I have a lifetime of knowing.

"What would you like to drink?" I ask Ben as we join everyone gathered in the reception room with its tall ceilings and smoke gray walls. Tasteful, benign art hangs in this room: oil paintings of subdued still life arrangements and pastoral scenes.

"Whatever you're having, lovely."

"I hear the Talisker's popular here. I was going to have one before you came."

So I pour two and we clink glasses. For a moment, I catch Ben looking a little anxious. Surreptitiously, I squeeze his hand. "Ready for a couple of quick intros before the main event?"

He nods, and we're off to join Michael and Jenna, who hold court at the other side of the room by cream chintz sofas.

Jenna spots us first, white-blond hair to her shoulders, partly pinned back. Her turquoise earrings are a splash of color in this room. "Charlie, it's great to see you. And this must be Ben."

We exchange hellos and a round of two-cheek air kisses with Jenna. She looks terribly pleased to see Ben, curiosity plain on her face. "Michael said that you were seeing someone. And I'm so glad to meet you, Ben. He never brings his boyfriends home."

I bite my tongue to say that's usually with good reason, and not just my anxiety talking for once. Even so, I have a bottle of anti-anxiety pills in my coat pocket should I need them. The odds are fifty-fifty, given my usual track record. Sometimes I think I should dispense valium to everyone before our meals, in a dish to also get passed around the table.

My brother joins us, and he smiles at Ben.

"Michael, this is my—" I hesitate for a second, glancing over at Ben. Why the hell didn't I think ahead about how to introduce him? But I shouldn't have worried as Ben saves the day without missing a beat.

"Boyfriend. Ben Campbell. Pleased to meet you."

They shake hands firmly. Goose bumps cover my arms.

Holy shit. Ben called himself my boyfriend in the eye of the storm.

I'd swoon right here and now, if it was safe. But it isn't, so instead we all carry on with conventional social niceties. And so I don't collapse in heap of cushions or—better yet—Ben's arms.

"Michael Renfrew, Charlie's older brother. And welcome." Michael nods at the gathering. Clusters of people converse around the room, gathered at sofas or arrangements of chairs, or by the expansive windows.

"And only brother," I quip. "He has to get the older part in for hierarchical purposes. There's no other brother, for the record."

Michael laughs at that, clapping my shoulder. "You call me out every time."

"Congratulations on your engagement," Ben tells Michael and Jenna warmly. Michael goes back to slipping his arm around Jenna, elegant as ever in a sage green wrap dress and a long string of silver pearls. "Thanks for including me."

"It's a rare treat to meet the people in Charlie's life," Michael says. He's not pointed about it, but it's true I keep my life safely compartmentalized. Of course they've met Emily and Carys, though they see them less often than I do, given they've lived out in Wales since Carys was a baby. That's logistics for you. "Thanks for joining us."

About then, my father announces the meal, and we manage to wrangle people into the dining room. It's a bit like herding cats, even with the names at each setting, small cards with my mother's elegant calligraphy. Before long, everyone's settled, and today we have wait staff given the larger gathering. Which saves me and Mum from running back and forth from the kitchen, which is what usually happens at these events.

Time will tell if there will be running out of the family event, which also tends to happen. I take a deep breath. Here's hoping for the best.

Chapter Thirty-Eight

The cooing over the food is only surpassed by the joyful cooing over Michael and Jenna's engagement news, and they haven't even procreated yet. It's only a matter of time before babies, but I'm sure they'll have them after the wedding. With Carys, Em didn't even get a baby shower here or a dinner. Anything like that has happened with her family and not mine. And my milestones aren't celebrated like my brother's accomplishments are.

Everyone dines and marvels over the meal. And it's excellent, I have to say that about the catering, pheasant for the meatarians and a veggie pastry entrée for those who don't eat meat, which is in honor of Jenna, a vegan. My parents went all out to impress.

"Tell us, when is the wedding?" Great Aunt May enquires, leaning slightly to glimpse Michael and Jenna further down the table. Everyone quiets down to hear the response.

"We haven't set a date yet," Jenna offers into the quiet. At the end of the room, the fire's lit in the hearth, and I swear I can hear it crackle. "But it will be this summer. We're thinking of August."

"How delightful, darling." My great aunt beams as if it were her own wedding. "What a remarkable time it is."

Michael and Jenna grin at each other, blushing. People chime cutlery against wineglasses, and they kiss. And the wedding foreshadowing begins.

Under the table, Ben squeezes my hand. I squeeze back, unable to imagine August or what will be happening by then. Uni will be over, and hopefully Emily and Carys will be moving to London. And if I'm lucky, I'll have a job and work to support them. And I can only dream that Ben's still in my life by then, because this a very new, unprecedented relationship, and August is eight months away.

More questions and answers are exchanged about their plans. Everyone thrills at their excitement and Jenna shows her engagement ring, which was my grandmother's, Great Aunt May's sister, who passed away years ago.

"And I haven't met this young man yet," Great Aunt May proclaims, gazing at Ben with curiosity while my parents look at him more like a specimen for dissection with laboratory precision.

Hold steady, Charlie. It's time for your A game.

And I do hold myself steady, as well as Ben's hand under the table. I squeeze tight. If Ben was brave earlier, I can be brave too. His confidence is catching. Or maybe I'm just tired of all the pussyfooting around.

"This is my boyfriend, Ben," I introduce simply into the dead silence around the table.

Ben beams and gives Great Aunt May his best grin, which is fairly irresistible. She sits up even more in her seat and smiles back, seemingly charmed. "How do you do?"

"I'm really good," Ben enthuses. "How about you?"

I gulp. As for me, I inch ever so slightly down in my chair despite my momentary boldness. Judging by my mother's expression, that's a double-strike in her books: a grammar fail and overly familiar.

"I'm very well, darling. Thank you for asking. At my age, every day is a good day." Great Aunt May's eyes sparkle. "It's either that or pushing up daisies, and I'm not ready to become fertilizer yet."

My mother looks slightly shocked as everyone else laughs.

"How did you meet?" Jenna asks curiously. "I didn't hear that part."

Force of will is not enough to keep the color from rising in my face at the memory. "Work," I say gamely, my voice wavering only a little.

My mother arches an eyebrow. She steeples her fingers over her meal. At the far end of the table, my father mirrors her.

Better not think of the spilled coffee beans in the stockroom or trysts during snowstorms or tying Ben up in all of the lush shades of the wool shop. Or of the sweet crush of his mouth against mine on the platform outside of Gatwick, or the simple pleasure of waking up together as snow falls outside. And how can it be only a few weeks when I realize through all of that, despite my worry, I've fallen in love with the man.

I cough to cover and give Ben an opportunity to speak. "Ben's a musician."

Ben grins at that. "Aye. I'm the lead singer and guitarist for Halfpenny Rise, my band. If you haven't heard of us yet, you'll be seeing us at the Brit Awards with our next album. We're heading out on the road tomorrow to tour our current album, and we're gonna rock out across the UK. And get over to Ireland too. I expect we'll be touring Europe this summer."

I swallow hard, unable to shake the feeling of my mother looking daggers at me, burrowing into my skin. When I thought Ben would cover, I didn't expect bravado at the table. Brit Awards? My stomach sinks. Ben doesn't get the silent class coding here, but I do. A glance at my father is a warning, a sharp look in his eyes.

"Is that right?" my father asks coolly.

"We'll go in my van to keep costs down," Ben continues, unfazed. "Maybe we'll do some festivals too. I'm waiting to hear on our date for Glasto."

This time, I do slide at least two inches down in my seat. Even if my parents know what Glastonbury is, rock music has never been suitable dinner conversation.

"That's brilliant," Jenna enthuses, at least one fan at the table. "I have your album. It's amazing."

"Ah, fantastic." Ben grins at her.

Any hope of shoving the genie back in the bottle is long gone. I could kick Ben's ankle under the table, but I don't think that would stop his eruption of music-related details or delete his words from our collective memory. Or erase his easy grin and western shirt, the rebellious streaks in his hair, or his lip piercing, a dazzling ray of brightness in this dull room. Like nobody can ever dull his sparkle. I don't want them to make him fade at all.

And it's obvious by the way he's going, no one ever has. Dread sits in my stomach, the meal now sitting heavy. Because I don't want this to be his first taste of being muted, because of me and my family.

"But honestly, that's enough about me," Ben says, attempting to feign modesty in the vicious quiet at the table. "You should hear Charlie play. He's brilliant himself. Along with The Screaming Pony."

This time, there's no mistaking the snap and crackle of the fire in the hearth as a heavy silence falls in the room. Wide-eyed, I stare at Ben as if he's totally lost his mind. And I don't quite kick his ankle, but I can't keep from nudging his foot hard with mine. Rainbow socks aren't immune from clouds in this dining room.

Shit, I didn't tell Ben to not bring up my music here. Mum thinks it's the next step from devil worship.

Great Aunt May is the first to speak. She looks quite concerned. "My dear, if any ponies are screaming, they will need the urgent care of a veterinarian."

Taken aback by both my touch and her response, Ben pauses to give me a sidelong glance.

"Don't worry, Aunt May," I say hurriedly. "No ponies have been harmed by my music. Or Ben's. Or by anyone."

"Aye, Charlie's right. No animal activists are after him, to my knowledge," Ben deadpans.

No one laughs.

"How did you get into music?" Michael asks, trying to help bring the conversation back on track.

"It was either music or work in a pub full-time. I mean, I still do work as a barman on occasion. My father had a pub when I was a kid. I learned to work then. I use the same work ethic that he taught me now."

"Your father was into child labor?" my father asks, a hint of incredulity in his voice.

Oh, fuck. Not Ben's dad. No fucking way they're tearing into him about his family.

"Ach, no." At last, Ben's startled into quiet. He leans back in his chair, trying to compose himself before speaking. "Far from it. Everyone in the family helped. It was just the way it was back then. When I left school after his accident, it was more than I could manage as a teen, but God if I didn't try."

Dead silence. Someone coughs slightly. Great Aunt May purses her lips.

At the end of the table, my mother finally speaks archly, laser focused on Ben like the rest of us are invisible and of no consequence. "And how exactly do you see this so-called relationship working out with your music and Charles's duties to his young daughter?"

Fuck, cutting right to the bone.

"Mum! That's hardly fair—" My face blazes with sudden heat as I ball up my fists.

"I'll decide what's fair and what isn't." My mother fixes me with her legendary stare.

I bite down on my words for at least thirty seconds, till someone attempts to resuscitate the conversation.

Ben puts a hand on my wrist between us, a gentle grounding before I totally lose it in front of everyone in what's supposed to be a celebration for Michael and Jenna.

"How *do* you envision this relationship with Charlie?" my father asks Ben.

"We've just started dating not that long ago." Ben meets his gaze. "We'll work that out together."

Mum looks at me. "Ben should be fully aware of your situation and obligations given your formerly reckless lifestyle, Charles. I trust you told him about Carys?"

"Of course I did! What did you take me for?"

"Charlie sounds like a terrific dad," Ben offers.

"And how would you know?" my mother counters instantly. "Have you seen him with Carys?"

"Well, no, but I see how hard he works for her and Emily, how he's in touch with them daily."

"It's okay, Ben." I give him a desperate look. "You don't need to defend me."

"Quite right," says my father coolly. "Our son doesn't need defending from his own parents."

"I'm championing Charlie, not defending him." Ben looks unflappable. I envy him his composure.

My mother meets Ben's gaze over steepled fingers. "Charlie has no defense for his past behavior and the mess he's made of his life."

"Please," I beg. "Stop talking about me like I'm a write-off. Or like I'm not even sitting here in front of you."

Unwanted tears sting my eyes, and like I did last month, I flee the table for the kitchen, where I startle the caterers as I burst through the door. Ben's fast on my heels.

The last I heard was Michael chiding our parents, and next thing I know I'm shaking in the kitchen, eyes blurry with tears.

Ben catches up with me, tries to gather me into his arms, but I back up abruptly into a granite counter and clatter against an empty metal caterer's tray with a sharp clang. The kitchen is steamy and hot, even with the window open to the now darkness outside. The caterers do their best to ignore us and go back to preparing the pudding course, a series of cakes and trifles.

"Don't," I snap.

He blinks, peering at me. "Charlie. I know you're upset. What they said wasn't right."

I shake with anger. Out of sorts, I'm hot and dizzy, caught on the knife edge of a panic attack.

Ben looks at the wretched state I'm in. He gives me a tight-lipped look, more grimace than smile. "Let's get the fuck out of here."

"'Kay."

He shifts and pats his pocket, then frowns. "Fuck. I left my phone back there."

A scowl comes.

Ben just sighs and takes me by the hand back through into the dining room, where everyone stops talking as we enter. Silently, I retrieve his phone, face down and abandoned by his place setting, and hand it over. I start to go to the other door, but he catches my hand again.

I give him a warning look, but Ben turns to face my parents, first my father, and then my mother. He stands to his full height. He might not be as tall as me, but as a performer, he knows how to carry himself and use his voice to full devastating effect. He's calm yet scathing.

"Listen. I get that you're all posh and English. And I'm not posh. And also Scottish, so two strikes against me, and that's even before we get to music for the third. I can more than tell you don't think I'm good enough for your son. That's all fine—I don't give a shit what people think of me, to be honest. I learned that ages ago. And it's fucking liberating. But I want you all to know that it's not okay to treat Charlie like that. Like he's a pawn in some quiet power struggle between you lot. You—you all need to know he's brilliant and funny and brave. And believe me, he puts his daughter first in everything he does. From what I can tell, he's a brilliant dad. But you don't see him. Also, for the record, he's as talented and skilled a musician as anyone in my band, and if you can't see that or accept it, you're blind and it's a crying shame. Charlie's amazing. I'm sorry you don't see that. He's shown me what it is to live with heart. Please excuse us."

"Sorry, Michael and Jenna." I hate that my voice wavers. "I didn't want to ruin your event. Just—congratulations. And I'm so fucking sorry. Again."

Once more, I bolt, this time for the opposite doors into the hallway that leads to the entry. Half blind with tears, I stuff my feet into my boots, grab my coat and burst outside into the stinging sleet. It's dark and cold and wet, and I don't care.

"Hey! Wait!" Ben calls after me. It's a good minute before he catches up, since I'm already well down the lane to the road that ultimately leads to Richmond Station. He grabs my arm, and we stop abruptly. I stare hard at him. Ben's hair is plastered to his head, his coat open and striped scarf loose, his woolen hat in hand.

I'm hyperventilating in the pouring rain. Ben's saying

more in soothing tones, but I don't hear him. It's all just meaningless noise. Even with the driving wet, I'm too hot, too upset, too everything. Fumbling in my pocket, I find the vial of anti-anxiety pills and take two. Roughly, I wipe at my face with my hands. Ben's holding my shoulders and after who knows how long of me apparently sobbing and swearing, I come back into some semblance of my usual self.

God knows what I've said.

And I'm fucking exhausted. More than. Trembling, I hug myself in the sleet, wet and miserable both.

"Can I take you home now?" Ben asks softly, tears in his eyes.

Defeated, I nod. My shoulders slump. "Yeah."

On the long ride into London, I drowse, half asleep, my arms tight across my chest, leaning into the corner of the carriage in the back seats, frozen and miserable. Even so, I don't want Ben's arm around me. Or him to hold my hand.

All I want is to be left alone.

Eventually, I fall asleep until it's time to change trains. And Ben takes me home.

Chapter Thirty-Nine

It feels like midnight by the time we get to my home in Finsbury Park, but it's only just after five o'clock, though in January this may as well be the same thing. Ben hasn't been here before, yet I'm too wrung out from the afternoon's emotions to feel any nerves about that. Or maybe it's the meds.

"Do you want me to come in?" Ben asks me, assessing. We've said little since I woke up.

"Yes. No. Maybe." I chew my lip. "Yes."

I know he probably can't stay long, because he leaves tomorrow morning on tour, and I'm sure he needs to get ready. And I'm conflicted about wanting to talk about what happened, but I also don't want to be alone as I try to process the many feelings that drown me.

At any rate, the house is quiet when we get in. It's crowded and somewhat cluttered in the main living area, but we make a beeline for my room, which is orderly. Even the bed's made. Uni books sit neatly on the desk, waiting for attention. At least the laundry's not overflowing, and the clothes are away.

The whiteboard with my ever-present list hangs on the wall over the bed. On the opposite wall is a board with photos mainly of Carys with Emily or with me.

Ben takes it all in, finally sitting down on my desk chair after he takes his coat off and hangs it on a hook behind my door. I sink onto the end of the bed after following suit and rub my face with my hands.

"How're you feeling?" Ben tries.

"Tired. And...tired."

"Fair. That was a lot."

"Yeah," I concede. "It was."

More than a lot, and I don't know what to make of it all. My family being arses, or being arses to Ben, or the whole damn thing.

"Maybe I shouldn't have come. And said all of those things that I did. I'm sorry for upsetting you."

"No more than anyone else did." I stare at him, taking in the angles of his triangular face, his light blue eyes, the scatter of freckles across his nose and cheekbones. I adore him and am furious with my parents at the same time.

"Do you want to talk about it?"

"No. But we probably ought to."

Isn't that what mature people usually do? Talk about their problems and their feelings, and work through things?

"Do you...regret inviting me?" Ben asks softly.

I hesitate, then shake my head. "No. But...I didn't expect to call you my boyfriend in front of my family."

Ben gives a half smile. "Well, you are my boyfriend, aren't you? Or I made a terrible faux pas and have been reading you wrong all of this time."

"No, I mean...well, I guess we hadn't talked about what we are to each other at this point. You're about to go for weeks or months. And I'm gonna be back here, doing"—I gesture vaguely at the board with its deadlines and schedules and lengthy to-do list before staring down in the vicinity of my toes—"all of that."

With a nod at the board, Ben pulls up in the wheelie chair in front of me. He takes my hand gently. "Forget all of that for a minute."

Reluctantly, I look up him.

"Do you want to be my boyfriend, Charlie Renfrew?"

I can't get over—don't *want* to get over—the way he looks at me, so wanting and hopeful and open. It's incredible.

What does he see when he looks at me?

"Yeah," I whisper. "I do. I want that very much."

And Ben's smile is as golden and beautiful as ever.

"Well, I want you very much. For the record. In case you didn't hear me back in Richmond."

"I heard you say that. And a lot of other things." Glum, I take him in, letting him play with my fingers.

"Tell me what's on your mind."

Where to start? Where to end? Don't let me down now, nerves. We've come this far.

"Well, there's a lot."

"Start at the beginning," Ben encourages. The way he says it, he makes it sound easy.

I squeeze my eyes shut. As much as I dread going back to this afternoon and rehashing the whole debacle in my mind, I know I need to. "I don't know if I can go in order," I admit at last. "But I can go by what's important. And I'm so sorry my parents were complete jerks to you. I'm used to it, but it's not fair to dump on you. And...I should have warned you more about what they're like. Should have said not to bring up music—"

"Charlie, I'm with you to the point of not bringing up music." Ben frowns. "But that's a huge part of who you are. And who I am. It has to be talked about."

"If it's not Baroque, they don't care. They'll do Classical

but they start getting twitchy around the late Romantics, so you know."

"They only like music by dead musicians?" Ben asks finally.

"Something like that, yeah. I guess."

"They should love so many twentieth century rockers, then. Like Morrison and Hendrix and hell, even Kurt Cobain."

Despite my misery, I smile at the idea of my father retreating to his study to listen to *Nevermind* by Nirvana. "Not this lifetime."

"Well, their loss, then. But seriously, Charlie. Let's get back to the point. Which is: you love music. It's part of you. It's part of me. We have that in common."

I squirm. "Yeah, but rock music and me brings up bad memories for them of me being a teen and running out and sneaking into gigs and getting high. And inevitably getting into trouble."

"We all make mistakes. You think I didn't do any of those things when I was a lost fifteen-year-old, angry about my dad being in a wheelchair and the unfairness of that accident that put him there, and me working all the time to help my family? But all of these things, they don't define us."

"Yeah, but they happened," I insist. "They're part of our history."

"Aye, but—see, you and your family seem to treat the shite things as the *only* history you have. And you're so much more. I'm very sorry that they can't see that, Charlie. Because they are missing a big part of you."

I shrug helplessly. "I don't think they ever saw me how I actually am. Just the worst things I've done, or the expectations I haven't lived up to. That I didn't follow the script, like Michael did."

"You're not Michael. And things happen. But look—

you're doing incredible now," Ben points out to me. "You've got a brilliant daughter and you're working through uni. And you've got goals and discipline. I ken that's more than plenty."

We contemplate each other. He's right, but why do I still feel so hollow? I run a hand through my hair, which probably looks a mess from the rain and wind.

"I just feel like a disappointment."

"You're not. You're lovely. I wish you could see it. And... you're not a teenager looking for their approval. You're an adult and live on your own terms. I mean, are they paying for your uni and lodgings?"

I shake my head. "Not a penny. I insisted. To prove to them and myself that I can make it on my own, after everything."

"There you go. Shake off those chains, lovely. They're invisible and they're not serving you."

"But they're my family."

"Do they respect you and treat you like family? Would you treat your daughter like that?"

Startled, I snap my head up, fully alert now. "No, of course not."

"So if that's not okay, why is it okay for them to treat you like that?"

"It's not," I admit, uncomfortable. "I mean, Michael and Jenna and Great Aunt May are cool. It's just my parents."

We're quiet for a long moment. Ben still has my hand. He's considering me, grave and tired and disheveled himself from the stormy afternoon, indoors and out.

"There's the family you're born into. And then there's the family you choose, gorgeous."

I gulp. And look over at the board with Em and Carys, Katherine and me. And how is it I don't have any photos of Ben, like I'm scared he might go at any moment. Like I don't deserve a shot at happiness like anyone else. "How come you're so wise?"

"I've been through things too. And I had to grow up young," Ben admits. "So, my road's not been easy either."

"There's just another thing too."

"Anything."

"Like, you're going to go away. You're going to go to all of these fantastic new cities. And see all of these people. And you'll wow everyone, like you do. And…how do I fit in all of that?"

"There's only one Charlie Renfrew out there, in all of those cities and even countries," Ben points out. "And I want you. I love you, Charlie."

A sound passes through me. Of want and exasperation and God knows what else. I can't accept that he feels that way, even though I'm starting to feel the same way, very much.

And it's impossible.

"Feelings are one thing. Reality's another. I mean, listen. You're planning on being some big rock star. And I'm planning on being a dad. You're aiming for awards and accolades. People in my band will probably quit after uni and go on to sterling careers in accountancy and insurance and who knows what, but more than that, I'm going to be working to support Carys and Emily for many years. So how does *that* work out between us?" I protest in frustration. "It can't."

"Charlie, Charlie." He catches my shoulders and gazes seriously at me, his eye contact unwavering. "There's a way if you want us to make a way. We can find one."

"*How?*" I shake my head. "It doesn't matter what I feel. There's so much to navigate. Like, shit, I hate to agree with my parents, but we do come from different worlds. And our future worlds look different too."

"They're only different if that's what you want," Ben whispers, his voice rough with emotion. "You know what I want."

"I know, but…"

"We don't need to sort this out tonight. We can just leave it. If you want. And see how things go. I don't want to push you into something you don't want. If you want me, I need you to *want* me." Ben searches my eyes.

Unhappy, I stare at Ben, take his face between my hands in turn. His skin is soft, the hint of blond stubble rough. He's looking at me as if I'm the most important thing in the world. "It's not a matter of not wanting you, petal. And, by the way, before you go all Noel and Liam Gallagher on my arse about having the best band in the world and the best boyfriend in the world and all of that fancy stuff, I worry that I'm not going to be enough for you. That my reality's not enough for you. You want grand things, and there's nothing wrong with that. I just don't. I want a simple life, to bring up my daughter knowing she's safe and loved. And—you and me—love isn't enough. Is it?"

Of course I want him. Honestly, I don't have the answer right now. It's not a matter of wanting. But logically? How can we make this work, especially after the disaster we just escaped?

"You're more than enough. Just the way you are right now." Ben takes a hand, kisses my palm reverently. I reach out to trace his jaw. "With your little girl and everything."

"I wish I could believe you," I whisper, my voice raw, caught deep in my throat.

And so, in the end, we leave things like that, left hanging and messy and hurt too. Nobody ever said being vulnerable felt comfortable.

We sit up late in the kitchen over hot chocolates, still both chilled to our bones, far too weary for sex, and Ben still needing to do most of an all-nighter to get ready to go on his tour tomorrow. Leaving me the one behind, with all of these complicated feelings and thoughts, and uncertainty ahead, despite the feelings in my heart that I don't dare trust.

Chapter Forty

With a grimace on another Saturday morning, I wipe down the steamer machine quickly before setting to make the latest round of coffees. Last night, I headed out with Jackson and Gillian to catch a gig, trying to keep myself busy and from obsessively thinking of Ben.

A couple of weeks have passed since the week of my gig and the disastrous engagement party at my parents' home. At least Michael and Jenna were sympathetic when I called them the next day, and they apparently don't hold any ill will for the scene. Michael said it livened things up.

At any rate, the January blahs are well entrenched. Ben's been away on tour. He's texted to ask me to join him on the road for a little while, but I had to remind him again of the many reasons why I can't. Much as I would like to, how can I get away?

My online stalking of reviews, student radio interviews on YouTube, and bloggers prove that Halfpenny Rise are doing well—more than. And he's a natural showman in interviews, all charm and sparkle, with sold-out venues wherever they go. They're getting great buzz, which is fair, given that they really know how to put on a great show. So far, it looks like he's making strides toward his New Year's Day resolutions.

Halfpenny Rise first headed to Ireland to play Dublin, Cork, and Belfast, before crossing back to play their way through England, Wales, and Scotland over the next month, hitting up uni towns especially, where their fanbase is biggest. There's increasingly serious talk of touring Europe in the summer. I can't imagine that Posh Van will ever let them down, but even so, I keep thinking safe travels in their direction.

I place a caramel macchiato on the counter, calling out the order. That's the last of the rush. I sigh, apparently looking forlorn enough that Jasmine pauses in her activities to check in with me.

"Pining," she diagnoses succinctly. "If it's not for the moors, it must be for a Scot."

"Very funny."

"I'm a riot," Jasmine assures me. She tilts her head, appraising me ruthlessly. "Seriously, what's wrong."

"Nothing's wrong." I wave a hand, then set to work vigorously wiping down counters. In the café, it's steady with students.

Which is true. Nothing is *wrong*, exactly. But it's not feeling right either. We're in the deep depths of a January where's it's been raining steadily for three days. London's been taken by fog. The temperature hovers above freezing, cold enough to guarantee a miserable walk in the rain, but not cold enough to snow. My fear did come true that when the snow melted, Ben would disappear.

"So where's your boyfriend playing tonight?"

"He's not my boyfriend, exactly. I mean, I guess he is. We're kind of in an...undefined phase." It's strange to think of Ben as my boyfriend. Is he still my boyfriend? Did I have a boyfriend for only a couple of days before everything got wrecked and potentially unboyfriended?

"Undefined phase?"

"We've only been on a couple of dates." It doesn't sound convincing, even to my ears.

"Uh-huh. This has been going on for over a month. Maybe two. He's your boyfriend. Didn't you say you went to Brighton together for New Year's? You don't usually go on weekend getaways with a fuck buddy. Very romantic, by the way, a seaside holiday for two."

"A month where we've mostly been apart, because of Christmas and now his tour," I point out. Which is true. What's a few days together before I was off for Christmas, and then a few days after, following our first official date in Brighton. I'm trying hard to be very rational and mature about this.

Jasmine studies me. "You know, there were whole days in there that you were...smiling and friendly to the customers. It was serious enough for me to think that I might need to stage an intervention."

"Yeah, yeah. Keep going." I wave Jasmine off. She's relentless today.

"It's really cute the way your whole face lights up if I say Ben Campbell." She looks rather wicked as she drawls his name, and my face burns.

"It's like an invocation. Be careful," I warn. Even hearing his name still sparks a visceral response. Like my body's all *fuck you, brain*, we want what we want, and to hell with the rest. "Who knows what saying his name might spark."

"I'm not worried. I'm not the one who has it bad for him."

Feeling vulnerable, I confess. "I took him to meet my family and it was a disaster."

Jasmine stares. "Whoa. That's major."

"Yeah. Kind of," I concede, my face on fire.

"Huh. So…an undefined phase?" Jasmine prods.

"It was that bad. And I'm embarrassed. About how my parents acted. And how I reacted."

She shakes her head at me. "But you're still into him?"

"Yeah." I don't even hesitate.

Jasmine smiles. "You never answered my question."

"What question?"

She rolls her eyes. "About where Ben's playing tonight."

"Oh." I pull out my phone and bring up the itinerary Ben sent me to track him. I scroll through the list of cities and dates to late January.

We talk most days. If not, we exchange texts or photos. He'll send views from the road. Or coffees that he's had that are either particularly good or particularly bad. "Not Charlie quality," he'll say. I'll send him photos of the café, of the streets around UCL. Of the famed stockroom. I artfully pour coffee beans across the back table for a photo shoot worthy of the lifestyle stuff Emily's shown me on Instagram.

Charlie Renfrew, coffee bean influencer.

"Liverpool," I announce after a thorough scroll through their tour page to confirm the date.

"Shit, Charlie. That's only an hour away on the express train. You should go meet him."

"I can't just…show up." Dismayed, I shake my head. She makes it sound so easy. And yet some part of me's still unsettled after that last night at my house, after the party. When everything felt discordant and out of sorts.

"Of course you can. You have boyfriend rights," Jasmine declares. "*Sexy* rights."

"Oh God, please never ever say that to me again. Take that back. Scarred. For. Life."

Quickly, I get back to scrubbing the counter with renewed vigor. The damned thing doesn't clean itself, especially not while Jasmine leans against it, grinning like the Cheshire Cat.

"I only have your best interests at heart. Which is, like, romance baby. Go find your man. I mean, what else are you doing on a Saturday night?"

"Studying," I retort. "Like I always do."

"Right." She laughs, entirely too pleased with herself. "You are not. Now you're just making excuses. Why not go?"

"Plenty of reasons. Train fares. Time. And I've got responsibilities, like saving money and studying."

"Surprises are very fun." Jasmine's undaunted by the realities of my life. She wiggles her eyebrows. "Never mind explicit. Your word, not mine."

"Stop."

Mercifully, a customer arrives then, and Jasmine gets to work, saving me from further cross-examination about my fledgling love life, so tender and new that it'll puff away in a gust of January wind.

Chapter Forty-One

Which is how I find myself on an express train headed north to Liverpool not too long after my shift ends at 3:00 p.m. Halfpenny Rise are getting plenty of buzz on Liverpool event listings as a "must-see" tonight. I keep scrolling on my phone for more stories about Ben's band.

The gig's sold out, of course. I debate whether to pay through the nose for a scalper's ticket again to keep the element of surprise. But that's extra cash on top of the last-minute rail ticket money, which would be better going to Emily instead. Plus, there's the logistics of actually getting in to see Ben at the rock club. I'll give up some of the element of surprise in favor of being able to see him in person after all of this.

He's obviously busy, and I'm not wanting to complicate his night, but if I send a text from the train that I'm on my way, that would give fair warning. So I do.

Surprise. Hopefully a good one—on my way to your gig tonight. x

The sun sets on the journey over green open spaces,

giving way to shadowy night. Eventually, the dazzle of city bright follows after soft darkness. Emerging from the station to rain-slicked streets, I'm blindly trusting my phone to give me details of the venue and how to get there.

A series of sparkling emojis arrive. Along with: *Will tell security to bring you in. xxxxx*

Relieved, that's one less thing to worry about. I actually have a chance to see Ben after all of this mess, at Jasmine's encouragement. Who in their right mind does this sort of thing? This isn't some sort of rom-com but real life. After three hours of travel, I've had plenty of time to go from "*what a great idea*" to "*what a shit idea*" and end up somewhere in between. I'm uneasy, wary of this impulsiveness, the sort of thing that's led me to danger before. I'm way outside of my comfort zone, in a strange city.

I'm also half starved. I've eaten some crisps along the way and a bit of fast food, which does little to settle my rebellious stomach, but I needed more than the brioche I had for lunch. When I stopped home briefly before my dash to the station, I didn't think to eat, throwing myself in the shower instead before chucking a couple of things for overnight in my bag, including the cologne he bought me for Christmas and a small dab for the road. Food didn't make the shortlist in my rush.

Outside of the venue, I'm daunted as I stand in the cold, with the nearby queue growing for the club doors that will open soon. After letting security know at the door that I've arrived, I wait for Ben. Or for someone to take me to Ben. As I wait, I notice an article taped to the box office window.

Up-and-coming band Halfpenny Rise are stealing some of the spotlight from headliner Maximus St. Pierre. Frontman Ben Campbell's molten guitar is not to be missed. He puts on a show that people will be talking about for years to come.

*Halfpenny Rise are on NME's Essential New Artists
list and Time Out's top 50 albums of the year. They
are destined for big things. Could Grammy Award–
winning St. Pierre's gritty influence be rubbing off
on the talented Ben Campbell? Will the tour rekindle
the romance between the former lovers, reunited in
music?*

What? Aside from Ben's rock swagger appearing to be
ticking closer to manifesting, what's this nonsense about
Maximus St. Pierre and a romantic reunion?

I grimace as I stare at the article. Not Maximus St.
Pierre again. However, I personally haven't heard of any
reference to him and Ben in the media before. Just what
Emily's told me, and Ben himself. But then again, what do I
know? Apparently nothing. I don't actually pay the slightest
attention to so-called entertainment news or tabloids, to be
fair. And Ben definitely hasn't mentioned anything about
his ex-boyfriend being part of the upcoming tour, or being
double-billed tonight, or whatever the hell's going on.

All I know is that my stomach knots, the sudden rush of
air deflating my lungs. I'm drowning with the lack of oxygen
when a security guard arrives to escort me in. We make our
way through the quiet club, the house lights on as the venue
gets the once-over before the doors are opened to ticket-
holders.

We make our way down through a door and corridor,
then another set of doors and another narrower black
corridor. There's a sign on a door that says GREENROOM, but
we keep going past that to a door with Ben's name on it. It's
slightly ajar.

Inside, Ben stands with his back to me, a cascade of long-stemmed roses in the arms of one Maximus St. Pierre, who leans in presumably to give Ben a kiss. He's all smolder and intensity, and intention is written over his body.

The world creeps in sudden and dark around the edges of my vision, blood draining from the remnants of my brain. The last thing I remember is running out of there like my life depended on it.

Chapter Forty-Two

Get away. Just get away.

The cold night air is a shock.

"Oh God. Oh Shit. Fuck. Double fuck. Shit fuck."

As taut as a string about to break, I go hard into the night. Walking blindly in a strange city, it's a blur of streetlamps and streetlights, tears caught on my eyelashes. Or it could be rain. Maybe both.

Fuck. How was this a good idea? Fuck ideas.

Fuck surprises too.

"Fuck!"

My fists clench. I shove them into the pockets of my coat.

Oh God, what the hell was I thinking? What was going on in there? I mean, who's Ben really? And fuck, Maximus St. Pierre is a god and I'm a nobody.

Why didn't Ben tell me he was touring with his ex-boyfriend? Or boyfriend? Or—

About to hyperventilate, I grip an ice-cold iron rail, forcing a breath into my lungs. Blood pounds in my ears. One breath. Two breaths.

Get it together.

God. If only I could get high.

No. Terrible idea. The worst idea. Worse than whatever this is.

I'm dying. Am I dying? No.

Panic attack.

"*Fuck.*"

Later, soaked and miserable, I make my way into a pub. People around me have a great time, gathered with friends by clusters of tables and the bar. It's a happy, rowdy crowd and I'm the dark cloud in it all. A trip to the toilets only confirms that I look like something the sea spat up, wretched and sodden. I try to pat my hair dry a little with paper towel, which is a fairly hopeless exercise.

I squelch to the end of the bar, hang my water absorbent coat off the back of the chair, and reminisce about snow, which doesn't have quite the same result. God, if it was snowing, none of this would be happening, would it?

Maybe this is because of the drama at my parents' home right before Ben left. And us leaving things feeling all vulnerable and shaky. Is this my fault for saying we're too different? And he went right back to the person who has way more in common with him, like that same drive for music? Plus, it's not just anyone—it's Maximus St. Pierre.

There's no way I can compete with that. Not in this lifetime, at least.

The barman looks at me wryly. "Drink?"

"Yeah. Whatever's on special."

He slides over a glass of something in short order. I take a drink, then retrieve my phone and hope that it's not soaked too. But it's survived the insult of rain in my jeans pocket beneath my coat.

I have a collection of missed messages and voicemails. All from Ben.

A text at 6:21 p.m. *Charlie? Was that you? Security said that was you. B xx*

A voicemail at 6:25 p.m. "*Come back, Charlie. Max said he saw you with security, that you took off.*"

Another text at 6:32 p.m. *Whatever you think you saw, I can explain. B xx*

A voice message at 6:48 p.m. "*Shit, Charlie. I've got to go because we're on stage in a few minutes*"—there's talking in the background—"*aye, I'm coming—look, can we catch up tonight? Please don't go.*"

I don't know whether to laugh or cry. I rub my face, down my drink, and have another. Sick to my stomach, I want to leave. I want to catch the next train headed back south, away from whatever's happened here tonight, back all the way down to Brighton. Back before that, even. Back to the magic of the snow and Ben woven into yarn, my own craft project, transcendent.

Hanging my head, I'm torn about what to do.

8:30 p.m. *Ok. Let's talk after the gig. C.*

Chapter Forty-Three

After 11:00 p.m., Ben meets me outside of the venue, pale beneath his freckles. It's been enough time for me to come back to my senses. To reality.

Our realities are not the same.

If I ever needed a reminder, this is it. There's no way I measure up to Maximus St. Pierre.

"God, Charlie…" Ben reaches out to me.

I step back, wary. I shake my head. I've had a couple of drinks, walked enough for the start of blisters on my feet in wet boots.

"What's going on?" I ask him.

"What's going on with you?" Ben asks, searching my eyes. "Talk to me."

"I came up to surprise you. Except the universe is having a laugh at me again. You pulled the surprise instead. Just as well." Heavy, I stare at him, hands stuffed in my pockets. "Serves me right for thinking this might work."

Ben frowns. As ever, he's gorgeous, even rain-damp. Even worn. His hoodie is up beneath his leather jacket. "I'm sorry. I should've told you that Max was playing tonight with us in Liverpool."

"You think?"

"They've billed us together for a few of the bigger stops. Figure they can sell more tickets like that, cause a little bit of a media stir, I guess, with our past."

A hard lump catches at the back of my throat. It's tough to speak. "Why didn't you tell me?" My voice wavers and I hate it.

"I—I don't know," Ben manages. He's crying. "I wanted to protect you. Please don't be angry."

"I am angry. I'm hurt. I thought I mattered to you—"

"Of *course* you matter to me!"

"Then what the hell was that in there?" I burst, my own tears mixing with the rain. It's so cold that I'm beyond shivering at this point, even with the stint at the pub to attempt to warm up.

"It was nothing! Just Max being Max. Dramatic. He's not you, Charlie."

I stand there, shaking my head. "Look. I see why you'd want him. I mean, fuck. He's a legend. Hot. And I'm nobody, just fucked-up Charlie."

"That's not it at all! I mean, why would *you* want *me*? I'm not clever like you, with your uni and your books. Just a man with a guitar who can pull the odd pint. And sometimes too much swagger that gets me in trouble."

I laugh and cry. "See? Except for the run-ins with trouble, we're opposites. Plus, I have Carys to worry about. She's everything, you know. I have to work and go to uni to take care of her and Emily and do right by them. And what the hell am I doing getting on a train on a whim? It's exactly this sort of thing that had me getting shitfaced not that long ago—"

"I love that you came up. It's brilliant. I'm just so sorry

that Max—that it's just not what it looks like."

"What is it, then? What?" I stare at him, defiant. "Like I imagined all of the flowers and that look on his face when he looked at you?"

"That's all him! Not me. Please believe me. I didn't know he would do that."

"But you didn't tell me about him."

We're both crying, out here in the January wind and bracing chill.

"I didn't talk to you about Max because that's in the past. I just want you, Charlie."

And I surprise us both when I'm able to speak again.

"That's not true it's in the past. He's headlining with you tonight. And whatever he's doing, he's fucking with your head. And mine. Whether you've told him about me or not." I take a long pause to steady myself. "Sometimes... sometimes wanting someone isn't enough. Words just aren't enough, Ben. No matter how pretty. No matter how much I like hearing them. It doesn't mean anything, does it?"

"It means everything. You mean everything." Hurt is plain across Ben's face. "Don't you see?"

"I guess I don't. I can't. I'm sorry, I just can't do this." My voice breaks on the last word.

Don't look at him. Whatever you do, don't look at him.

Shaking, I turn. It takes everything I have to keep from going back to him, to the man I'm wild for, left slump-shouldered in the rain. And I make myself walk, one step after another. I turn off my phone.

It's late, but the coaches run all night from the station. And it's a miserable trip alone back to London.

Chapter Forty-Four

At work on Monday, I'm extra grumpy. Even Jasmine gives me a wide berth. Lars gives me the side-eye. Everything's terrible. The rain is terrible. The over-the-top orders are terrible. My uni assignments are terrible. And the most terrible thing is the ache where Ben should be, left like a wound in my life.

I hate it.

Part of me can believe that it wasn't Ben pulling the Saturday night drama in Liverpool. Or at least part of me wants to blame it exclusively on one Maxim St. Pierre, suave musician and heartbreaker. Naturally, I spent Sunday torturing myself with endless internet searches.

It escalated something like this:

Maximus St. Pierre

Maximus St. Pierre guitar

Maximus St. Pierre boyfriend

Maximus St. Pierre Ben Campbell

Maximus St. Pierre Ben Campbell breakup

If I'm a guppy in the music world and Ben is a tuna,

Maximus is a great white shark. It's fitting, because the man displays an unnatural amount of teeth in paparazzi photos in music magazines and tabloid rags. He's got bravado down, with good reason, and more than enough stage presence on his own for a continent of rock bands.

My compulsive googling tells me a few things. At this point, I could write my own bio of the man based on my search results, like a twisted uni paper better suited for a student news column.

Born in Cheshire and raised in East London, rocker Maximus St. Pierre exudes London hipster cool. Aged thirty-two, St. Pierre's played gigs since he was sixteen, a talented ingenue rightfully deserving of acclaim. Winner of a Grammy Award, MTV Europe Music Award, American Music Award, and three previous Brit Awards, St. Pierre most recently won Album of the Year at last year's Brit Awards, a veteran of the rock scene.

Visitors to his Wiltshire farm home studio read like a who's who of British rock of the decade. Launching his own label last year, St. Pierre continues to trail-blaze in the industry. When he's not rocking out, he spends his time working to save endangered species such as the Northern Spotted Owl from the brink of extinction and gives generously to children's charities.

St. Pierre's love life has gained nearly as much attention as his musical prowess. He's continually paired with the latest up-and-comers like a shark looking for tender chum. Do his boyfriends track to success because they're already on the up, or because of St. Pierre's connections?

Okay, so I might have embellished on the last paragraph. Still.

I shake my head and sigh as I put my phone back in my

pocket and take off my apron. Lars takes over on the coffee machine while I head off for a break. Ben's very talented, all on his own. I'll probably be fired as a rock columnist given my tangents. Plus, I don't have the connections. Or the press pass, which would have been useful when I tried to get into Ben's gig weeks ago in Camden.

Grabbing my coat, I turn up the hood and set out on a walk to clear my head, despite the rain.

No good comes of obsessing, Charlie. You're doing the right thing.

Ben's in an entirely different world. A world hopefully where he's not a snack to higher-order sea life, but really, I'm barely an amoeba on this scene. And that's not being hard on myself—that's just facts.

I don't get too far on my walk when I receive a text from Emily.

Very sorry to ask, and I wouldn't if it wasn't urgent, but could you come look after Carys? We've both come down with a bad flu. Katherine's away. Please let me know. x

Cue reality.

Chapter Forty-Five

Of course I text Emily back in short order that I'll be there tonight. And I go back to the café to let them know I have to leave for a couple of days for a family emergency. It's still early in the day, not even lunch. And this time, it's not Ben saving me when I need to get to Swansea. This means no Posh Van. No flirting over texts. Thinking of the van makes me think of my tears in Victoria Station and Ben helping me without hesitation.

God. Don't think about Ben. That's not helping anything.

It's gonna be a long train ride out to Wales today. Needing something to keep my brain busy, I pop into Barnes Books, just around the corner from the café, and see my friend Aubrey, a once grumpy and now cheerful man. Just look at what love does.

Today, it's Aubrey working alone in the shop. A couple browse in the history section. They had been by the café earlier.

"Hey," I say to him. He looks about how I feel. It's a Monday after all. "I need a couple of novels with unhappy endings."

Aubrey glances up at me from his stock notes behind the till, giving me a bit of an odd look. He's a darker strawberry blond than Ben. Attractive, but he's a man off the market with Blake. "Hi, Charlie."

"I hope my request isn't too weird."

I suppose the man's heard it all by now.

"No, but that's very niche." Aubrey gives me a ghost of a smile as he considers my specific request. Even though he's young like me, he's run the shop since forever. Since I can remember. Like Ben, he had to step up to run the family business after tragedy struck.

Why can't I stop thinking of Ben? Damn brain. Whose side is it on, anyway?

"Well, if books with happy endings like Romance are a genre, aren't books with unhappy endings a genre too?" I point out.

"That's called literary fiction." Aubrey grins. He gives an expansive gesture at the fiction section beside him. "Knock yourself out."

"I only need a couple of books. Suitable for a long train ride to Cardiff."

"Well, if you insist. I might have something to suit." He gazes over at the shelves, frowning. "There are plenty of unhappy Russians in classic literature," he points out. "Or you could go full Orwell and read *Nineteen Eighty-Four*."

"Read it. Could do with another read, though. Lit student, remember? It's the right tone, though. Could also use something I haven't read before."

Aubrey looks at me gravely. "Have you read *Little Women*?"

"No..."

Without a word, he goes to the shelf and gets me a copy of each, with *The Great Gatsby* thrown in for good measure.

"That should keep you busy till at least Cardiff."

"Cheers." I waste no time in paying for my books.

Aubrey slides them over the worn wood table. "You won't thank me. They're sad."

"'Kay. Perfect. Just what I need. Misanthropes unite," I say solemnly, earning myself a smirk from Aubrey. "Right, see you when I'm back. Not sure when that'll be."

"Safe travels," says Aubrey.

I hesitate. "Uh, do you mind if I ask you something personal?"

He looks intrigued. "Like what?"

"Like…how you made things work with Blake, given that he's famous and you're not?" I ask wryly. "Asking for a friend who's been seeing a musician."

There's something about Aubrey that tells me he sees through my thin cover, which admittedly is next to nonexistent.

"By talking about things as we go. That's it, really. Blake's a regular person despite the fame."

I nod. "Good reminder. I'll let him know."

"Good luck." Aubrey smiles.

And I head into the London chill and damp for home to pack for my trip.

I start *Little Women* on the tube to Victoria Station. The hours melt away while I read about Jo, Beth, and Amy. I have to tear myself away by the time I reach Cardiff and come back to some sort of reality. Beth's illness grips me as I worry about Carys. I've texted Emily that I'll take a taxi from the station when I get to Swansea.

When I arrive at the cottage, Emily is wan when she answers the door, a gray quilt around her shoulders. "Carys is sleeping. Just went down. I'll sleep, too."

"Don't worry, I've got this," I assure her. "Go get some rest. I'd hug you, but…"

"Better not. You need to stay upright."

Em goes to bed and I set to work making a big vat of soup after checking on Carys, who is fever-flushed while she sleeps. Not too high, but still worrying. At least making some soup will keep me busy, keep me from obsessing over how to make Carys and Emily instantly well, or whether Ben's with Maximus St. Pierre, or what will happen next in *Little Women*.

But it doesn't go like that.

What happens instead for me is that Carys is up and crying in the night with fever. When she stops crying and her fever spikes, I take her in Emily's car to the hospital. We have a sleepless night, ultimately to be assured she'll be all right. More baby paracetamol, more fluids, plenty of rest.

Of course I bring *Little Women* along for the long hours in the waiting room and I finish it. And, to be honest, I end up in tears too, with Carys dozing on my shoulder. For her. For Beth. For Jo and Laurie. And then I'm crying for me and Ben and wondering if he's with Max right now. More internet searches tell me they're billed again together tonight in Manchester.

Is Ben somewhere crying over me too? Or has he forgotten, Maximus St. Pierre's legendary charm winning him over like old times? Like the photos that an internet search for "Maximus St. Pierre Ben Campbell boyfriend" shows in results.

Rubbing my eyes on my sleeve, a nurse checks on me in the waiting room.

"I'm all right, I'm all right," I gasp. I gesture at the book beside me. "It's just sad."

Aubrey was right.

She gives me a sympathetic smile. We fuss over Carys, who sleeps in my arms. Her fever comes down. A little bit longer and we'll be back to Emily's once they're sure she's had some more fluids.

Which leaves me plenty more time to think about Ben and how much I miss him. Will there be a way to make this right again?

Chapter Forty-Six

Tuesday at Emily's is a day of plenty of naps in shifts for all of us. Carys is starting to feel better but poor Emily feels worse and has stayed mostly in bed. I spend the day taking care of them.

Late afternoon, Ben texts.

I feel awful that you're angry with me. I didn't mean to hurt you. B xxx

I shift on the sofa where I'm sprawled in the last of the afternoon sun. Carys has fallen asleep on my chest. I type into my phone around her.

I'm just not sure where we can go from here. Our lives are so different. I can't compete with Maximus St. Pierre. C xx

There's no answer for a while. Then:

Max loves drama. We can work things out and find a way, if that's what you want. It's what I want. I miss you.

I sigh. Fuck if I don't miss him too, but feelings get in the way. Should I tell him what's happening with me? Does he care? He probably cares. He's a compassionate person.

I miss you too but that doesn't help anything. I'm in

Swansea. Carys is sick. Emily needed help.

Oh no, Charlie. That's awful. Can I help?

I have to laugh at that, because it's such a Ben thing to say. Even if he has a gig tonight in… I check. Birmingham. Maximus St. Pierre is still billed with him.

Can you cure the flu? I ask.

I wish. I'm sorry. He sends a crying emoji.

I'll be here for a few days to help Emily. She's sick too.

There's a long stretch where there's no response from Ben.

Can I see you when I play Cardiff on Saturday night? Please? B xxx

I screw up my face. That'll be the worst. Or the best. No, no, the worst, I tell myself sternly. That will only torture us both. We need to be mature about this.

We'll see, I text back.

Ok. Drink orange juice. B xxx

• • •

The next couple of days pass in fevers and soups. I usually escape for a little bit each day for a walk along the beach in the gusting wind to clear my head. I don't know if I'll see Ben. I don't know what to do. I think I've come down with the flu, or my body's trying to fight it off. I feel wretched.

Then I do a search for the Birmingham show. Some pap has taken a shot of Maximus and Ben together outside of a club where the afterparty was held. Maximus grins like the cat that got the canary, his arm slung around Ben's shoulder.

Ben looks terrible, unsmiling.

Chapter Forty-Seven

By Friday afternoon, Emily's joined the realm of the living again. I've also had my share of naps when Carys would let me and manage to avoid the virus myself by some miracle, through a lot of handwashing and rest when I could get it.

"Welcome back," I tell her, serving up soup and sarnies. I've already fed Carys, who plays on the floor beside the dining room table where we sit. She runs wooden trains over the meandering tracks throughout the room, back to her usual spark.

"That was awful," says Emily wryly. "Thanks again for dropping everything to come."

"Don't mention it. It's the least I could do."

"I'm just so glad you didn't catch this like I did, all in." Emily works on her tea. "Don't take the flu as a parting gift either."

I laugh. "I'll try not to."

"What did I miss? Other than most of a week?" Emily shakes her head.

"Well…" I reflect, giving her a wry smile. "I read *Little*

Women and *Nineteen Eighty-Four* and was thoroughly upset. My own doing. I asked for books with unhappy endings."

She shakes her head at me. "Why on earth would you want that? Isn't life hard enough already?"

"Fair point," I concede. "But you know that thing about misery liking company? That was my working hypothesis. Turns out it was a shit hypothesis and only made things worse."

"Of course it did. I could have told you that."

"You," I say with dignity, "were entirely out of commission. I only take so much advice from a woman who took up camp on the bathroom floor."

"You would have done exactly the same in my position." Emily laughs.

"True. And I would have been far more complain-y about the whole thing. Anyway, I just felt like suffering."

"Why?"

I shift, uncomfortable. Confession time. "Because I ended things with Ben. Though they'd barely started."

"Wait. What? You ended things with the man who made you happy?" Emily frowns at me.

"Yeah..."

"Well, that was silly. Why would you do that?"

"Because...plenty of reasons," I say, defensive. It's not a good time to think of Ben, naked and glorious on our hotel bed in Brighton, or beneath his window in his room while snowflakes drift outside. Or lost in kisses. Or sharing a laugh on the way to the wool shop while blindfolded.

"Name them."

I groan. "I don't know."

"Charlie..."

"Okay, okay. All right. So, I had an idea. Actually, it was a coworker's idea that I go surprise Ben and go to his gig in Liverpool. I got there and security was taking me to him...

only to discover fucking Maximus St. Pierre kissing Ben after giving him an armful of the most beautiful roses I've ever seen. Probably caught him in mid-marriage proposal." I grimace. "So naturally I freaked out and ran away. Which is the only reasonable response, in my defense, when the guy you're seeing is obviously involved with Maximus St. Pierre."

Emily takes a long moment to process this, looking startled. "The musician."

"The clockmaker."

She shakes her head. "I'm trying to help you. Don't get snippy with me. Or I'll Charles you."

She knows how much I hate being called by my full name.

"Sorry." I give her an apologetic look. "So I took off. We talked later. He said it wasn't his idea but Maximus's. I said I just couldn't do whatever we're doing, that he didn't tell me about Maximus. I mean, seriously, Emily. I don't have time for romance. I need to worry about you and Carys. Just look at this last week. Case in point."

Emily sighs. "Is that what you want?"

"Want?" I waver. "Wanting never helped anything."

She laughs. "Do you like Ben?"

"Of course I like Ben." More than like Ben, if I'm honest. I've more than liked Ben since dangerously soon after we got together. So soon it scared me.

Emily gives me an appraising look. "And he treats you well? I mean, clearly he's thoughtful to loan you the van to get here last time. And every time I heard you talk about him before this you were practically glowing. You sounded… happy."

I gulp. "So?"

"Oh, Charlie. It's not often you find someone who makes you happy *and* treats you well. And you have so much in common…"

"But you and Carys…it's different than his world."

"You can have Ben and help us, you know. It's not an either-or scenario. There's plenty of people who date who are single parents. Or are coparents. Or whatever." Emily shrugs a shoulder. "Wouldn't you want me to have a partner?"

"Well, sure—"

"You wouldn't think less of me for dating, would you?"

"No!"

"Then I'm not sure what you're looking for, but he sounds very much like someone worth getting to know more. In my humble opinion."

My phone chimes then. Somehow the arsehole knows I'm talking about him. His ears must be burning somewhere out there.

Arrived early in Cardiff. B xxx

"Shit. It's Ben. He's here. Well, not Swansea-here. But in Cardiff."

Emily considers me, tapping her lips with her fingers. "Have him stop by. You can go out for a drink and talk after."

"*Here?*" I do a double-take. My voice climbs.

"Why not? I'm curious to meet this man for myself. Would that help?"

"Maybe," I relent.

"He's important to you?"

Swallowing hard, I nod. "Very much."

And that's how I end up texting Ben to come to Emily's house.

Chapter Forty-Eight

By the time Ben turns into the driveway at Emily's, I'm fighting back every instinct that screams panic attack. I breathe. I do grounding exercises. I pick five things around me to focus on.

The soft moss green of the curtains. The firmness of the stripped pine floorboards under my feet. The scent of Emily's fresh-baked scones. The foam of the sea as seen from the windows of the entry. The sound of Emily talking to Carys in the background.

Through the window of the front door, I watch Ben get out of Posh Van. He has black and purple streaks in his hair and is wearing his familiar beat-up leather moto jacket. He pauses to take in the sea view. Probably to take a breath of the ocean air too.

My heart lands in the vicinity of my mouth as I watch him.

Do I stay here and wait for him to come to the house? Do I go to him?

Instinct takes over and I head outside into the crisp

afternoon air. The sun peeks through breaks in dove gray cloud banked overhead. Walking past the hedge, lush even at the end of January, I approach Ben. My stomach careens.

Why does the man cause a full systemic reaction?

He looks just as tentative as he approaches me, but he brightens as he searches my eyes. What he's looking for, I don't know. If he's seeking a man who can't even talk, he's found it right here.

"I've missed you." Ben's voice wavers.

I gulp. Shit. He's supposed to be the composed one.

"Missed you too," I say. I press my fists inside my overcoat pockets.

Wind ruffles our hair, the splatter of rain like slices of ice. Even so, neither of us moves. Neither of us dares. Like this moment is sacred as we take stock of each other.

Ben's face is drawn, white under freckles. Like the man's not been sleeping well, he has shadows beneath his eyes.

It's hard to remember a time before Ben. The promise of him, the tease of him so close like a fire that burns underground in winter, waiting for the promise of spring. But I'm fairly certain we can turn our own seasons.

At a loss for words, we stare at each other while rain splatters.

"It's good to see you," I admit at last.

"So good to see you, too." Words spill quickly from Ben's lips, as easily as song. God, what I'd give to have those lips pressed hot against my ear, whispering filth and promises and more.

"Emily said I've been a bit of a prick."

Despite himself, Ben laughs. He rakes a hand through his hair. "Aye?"

I nod. "I keep thinking it's a choice between you and Carys. Emily says it's not like that at all."

He swallows hard, his gaze steady. "What do you think?"

he whispers.

"I...I'm nervous." I fidget with the cuff of my coat, trying to channel Emily's earlier assurance. Or Ben's usual confidence. Right now, he looks like a man who has everything to lose. It wrenches my guts.

"Fair," he acknowledges. "I'm nervous, too."

"Let's walk," I gasp, zipping my coat to my chin. Ben tugs on a wool hat. Together, we make our way along the path that overlooks the sea below, dry stone walls separating fields. Before us is the raw Welsh coast. Solitary and enduring.

We get a distance away before we stop. I give him a sidelong look.

Do I dare ask? I mean, I have to.

"Tell me more about Maximus St. Pierre. Please?"

A sound like a wound escapes Ben, something primal and sad. "Ach, Charlie. He was my boyfriend, once. But he's not any longer. Please believe me. And I don't want him to be, no matter what he says. He had his chance but ended up dropping me for someone else. I'm not going back to him, even if he's left. Even with all of his grand gestures, like back in Liverpool. I told him that he's wasting his time."

I nod, absorbing this. "I'm sorry you've been through all of that."

He shrugs. "It was difficult at the time. But that was then, and this is now. And ever since I met you, it's been...well, it's been brilliant. You're hot and funny and brave and so very Charlie. I love how devoted you are to Carys and Emily. I have to say, though, the thought of no longer having you in my life...it makes me sad. But that's not for me to say, if you don't want me, I'll have to accept it—"

"Of course I want you," I blurt instantly.

Wanting Ben has never been a problem. I've always wanted him.

He chews his lip, faltering.

God, what's he thinking in this silence that strikes like a gut punch? We're silent for a long, awkward moment that someone could drive a Posh Van through.

"Just…are you sure you want me, though? I'm just a barista. And a student—a fucked-up one at that—who also happens to have a little daughter and a complicated situation. And I guess I'm scared too, because, well, I want you so much."

"I want you, too. So much. I want all of it, all that makes up your life. If…if you'll let me in, Charlie."

I gulp. I'm not sure if it's the ice rain that stings or the slice of threatening tears. Storm warning, out here. Everything I am lies exposed to the elements. To Ben. Like an offering.

"Seriously?" I whisper. "Just like this?"

"Aye, so." Ben also looks on the verge of tears. "Just like this."

"You barely know me, though. How can you be so sure?"

"I know enough, lovely. I love that you're so fiercely protective of your daughter, of your responsibilities. And that you're grand to be with. What's not to want about that? I promise not to mess you about. And…I promise I understand that you must put Carys first. And, maybe someday, you'll let me put her first, too." Ben smiles, bittersweet with tears in his eyes. "I would love to find out what it's like to be a stepdad far off down the road. If that's what you want."

I tremble at the thought. God, I want him. I want a future together with Ben so badly.

There's a long moment that passes in gusts of wind and slants of rain. The tease of sun casts a soft winter light. A seagull skims along the shoreline. Seagrasses wave. It could be a trick of my imagination, but there's a hint of rainbow against the blue-gray storm clouds beyond.

And it's about then that I step forward. To the promise of Ben.

"You've never answered my question." Ben gazes at me. "About letting me in."

"I know." I hesitate. "I...I can't answer yet."

"You don't need to."

"Soon. I promise."

I probably shouldn't, but I pull him tight to me. Our mouths meet in the bracing winter cold. His arms are mine, and mine his. In a kiss, we drown. And God, I've missed him, missed everything Ben has to offer.

Out here, time stills, and the world is ours.

Chapter Forty-Nine

We climb the steps to the stone cottage. Wet wind slices the afternoon, our hair plastered against our foreheads as the rain lashes us.

"I miss snow," gasps Ben as we tumble into the small entry of the cottage, the wind at our heels.

"Hell, yeah," I say, uncoiling my rain-damp scarf. "God."

Emily comes up the hall, holding Carys. Carys is torn between fascination and angst at spotting Ben, a stranger in our midst. Further proof that she's my daughter.

I gulp. Here's the whole jumping off of a cliff bit, the collision of worlds. Something I imagined in recent sleepless nights.

Emily joins us, bouncing Carys slightly in her arm.

"Hello," she says with a smile for Ben. It's like I'm seeing her for the first time too, long sandy hair in a wavy plait over her shoulder, an oversize sweatshirt that falls off her shoulder, gray leggings. Carys has big green eyes, her dark hair newly released from her ponytail so it floats like a cloud around her head. She peers shyly up at Ben.

And Ben's transfixed by Carys too. He smiles at her. To my relief, she gives a tentative smile back.

"Right, introductions," I say gamely, springing belatedly into action. No time to panic, not me. Sadly, there's no tables handy here to flip as a distraction, just a small shelf firmly secured to the wall in the entry for keys and a dresser for gloves and accessories.

"Emily, this is Ben Campbell. My, er, friend." I gulp. Not exactly smooth. But it doesn't have to be smooth. We just need introductions. A beginning, more than anything else. "The man I've been seeing."

It's hard to know what to call him at this point. Boyfriend? The man I've been dating? A friend? Especially when we don't know what's ahead.

Her grin widens. She's clearly taking stock of him. Of me, too. We're all crowded together in the small cottage entry, coats on hooks on one side of us, a painting of the sea by Emily's gran on the wall opposite, and a rack of shoes on the side.

"Ben, this is Emily. And this is our daughter, Carys." I smile encouragingly at Carys.

She smiles back again at us before promptly hiding her face in Emily's shoulder.

Emily smiles and smooths her hair. "She's a bit shy with strangers," she explains. "Charlie's spoken highly of you. Great to meet you. Welcome."

"Cheers. Very happy to meet you," Ben says earnestly.

As usual, my face is on fire.

Breathe. Just breathe.

If I can remember to breathe, everything will be all right.

"May I offer you some tea?" Emily looks from Ben to me. "Not sure what your plans are?"

"Oh, I don't want to impose or anything." Ben, it has to be said, looks highly appealing with his blue eyes and lean jeans. The most sensible thing to do would be to lick the rain right off him, but Emily would probably not be into watching the precursor to a public mating ritual.

"Let me put Carys down for a nap. Charlie, you can figure out if you want to put the kettle on," Emily says smoothly. "No worries if you want to head out to the pub or something for a drink instead."

We look at each other, and for a moment, we share the same thought.

"No, let's stay—" says Ben.

"Doesn't seem right to leave you behind—" I say at the same time.

And so fully agreed, we stay in with Emily. Soon, we're set up by the fire, everyone curled up with their own blanket and tea. Somehow, it feels familiar, like we've done this before. They're both relaxed, and it's helping to put me at ease.

I can trust this, can't I?

"How long have you known Charlie?" Ben asks Emily.

"Since forever and a day," Emily quips. "Probably longer."

He flashes that grin which makes me swoon like a Victorian heroine, each and every time.

"Since school," I say when I regain something akin to my senses, or a reasonable facsimile. "At least…five years?"

"Seven." Emily grins. "Keeping track of time isn't your strong suit."

"Tell me about it," I agree.

"We bonded over suspicious school lunches." Emily laughs, shaking her head at the memory. "Was it pasta or potato that day?"

I shudder at the memory too. "Jury's still out, and the world's leading scientists are still saying the results are inconclusive."

Ben laughs. "Friends ever since?"

"Yeah," I agree. "Luckily Emily's stood by me through a lot of things."

"That's what friends do," she says easily.

She really has been an amazing friend through my ups and downs. And, of course, with Carys.

"Emily's my true family," I offer to Ben. "I mean, we have our daughter. But Emily and her gran, Katherine, have always been brilliant to me."

Ben smiles. "It's important to have someone who has your back."

"So, how good are you at cards?" Emily asks lightly. "I'm terrible."

"Ah, I never play cards," Ben says solemnly.

"Me either," I agree.

And then it's on.

We settle in for ferocious card games, and a couple of rounds of tea. Eventually, Ben has to go back to Swansea for the night. I promise to join him tomorrow so we can talk some more. Before he leaves, his kiss on the front step is salty with the sea air.

Something's caught inside me, in the crash of the sea. Something out there that threatens this fragile thing between Ben and me, and our not quite finished conversation outside the cottage, leaving him waiting for an answer.

I can barely sleep, anxious for Swansea, thinking of everything I want to say to Ben. To let him know what he means to me. And more.

That I love him.

But Swansea doesn't work out.

Chapter Fifty

"Motherfucker." I stare at the text on my phone as I stand in the kitchen. Beside me, Emily makes tea, stirring cream into her mug and mine. Carys is down for a morning nap. Momentary sun between squalls floods the small kitchen, the whitewashed walls dazzling.

She glances over, looking concerned. "What?"

I groan and shake my head. "They have to leave earlier than planned to make their next gig in time for interviews and sound check."

Em frowns, pushing blond hair back over her shoulder as she gives me my tea.

I nod thanks, still staring at the phone as if the words blur. My jaw clenches.

Sorry Charlie. Gone to Edinburgh for radio and sound check. x

"He's headed to Edinburgh, the arsehole."

In the fifty versions of today that I rehearsed in my head during the sleepless night, Ben not being in Cardiff wasn't in any of them.

"Edinburgh?" Emily looks startled too, and I feel vindicated. "Shit, Charlie."

"Yeah, exactly."

With a thump, I lean against the counter and sigh, considering Em as I carefully sip the steaming tea. Luckily it didn't slosh.

"Bloody inconvenient too," I grumble. "How am I supposed to talk to him now and sort things out? These things are better in person than over the phone. And God knows when he's next in London. I get that the show's gotta go on and all of that, but seriously."

"That's what comes of falling in love with a rock star," Emily teases over her tea. "They leave town for the next show. Like the sun sets."

My scowl deepens.

God help me. I really need to see him.

"What am I supposed to do?" I ask plaintively. "Just go to Edinburgh?"

"Yes." Emily considers, then nods. "That's exactly what you need to do."

Aghast, I stare at her. "You're supposed be the practical and sensible one here. So much for being my rock."

"I'm dead serious, actually."

"Em, that's…that's impossible."

"It's not impossible. People travel to Edinburgh all the time. There *are* trains and roads to Scotland, by the way." Her eyes dance merrily. "Also, Ben's dreamy and if I were you, I'd get moving. Boyfriends like that don't come along very often. Whatever troubles you've had, I bet you can sort it out. I saw the way you both looked at each other yesterday like you've each made an amazing discovery."

There's a surprise lump in my throat, making it tough to swallow all of a sudden. "Yeah. There's that. But also, there's so much to consider. He's famous. Which probably means being in the spotlight. Not just him, but me and you and Carys, too. What if there's press on your door?"

"We can deal with things one day at a time," Emily assures me. "Don't worry."

"I just want to make sure you're safe."

"We're safe." Emily smiles affectionately at me. "But I love that you're thinking of us like that."

"I can't help it. I need to think of everything, about what it means having Ben in my life. In our lives."

"Do you work tomorrow?" she asks.

Tomorrow's Saturday.

"No, I got this whole week off for the trip to see you because you were sick. Including the weekend. I wasn't sure how long you'd need me here, so I thought to put in for a few extra days."

Emily looks terribly pleased. "Brilliant. And you're not ill?"

"I felt a little off on Wednesday, but I think I'm cured now."

"Then go."

"Em, how's that practical? It's going to take me all day to get to Edinburgh. Plus, the train's going to be too damn expensive without the advance ticket." She should know, more than anyone else, about how hard I save money to send to her.

"Are you telling me you *don't* want to see Ben?" She peers at me over her mug, her fingers carefully wrapped around the top. She sips.

She's ruthless.

"No." I frown. "I want to."

"Then go. Take my car if you want."

"No, no. I can't," I say hurriedly, shaking my head. "You need that for Carys and your work."

"I can use Gran's."

I draw in a deep breath. "You're sure this is a good idea?"

"More than. It's a worthy cause. The only thing I expect are updates. Frequently and often." Her grin is radiant. "I'm invested now."

Despite myself, and my nerves, I laugh. "'Kay. Fine. If this goes pear-shaped…"

"Unlikely. I'm into probabilities and that would be very low, babe. Go."

Now or never.

"I'll pack and call a taxi to take me to the station. I can't take your car all the way to Scotland. I don't know when I'd be able to get it back to you. I'll take the train."

When the taxi comes half an hour later, after I've kissed Em and Carys goodbye, I slide into the back, watching them stand together on the front step to see me off. Wind tousles their hair.

"Don't forget to text him that you're on your way!" Emily can't keep from shouting dating tips into the wind.

Laughing, I nod and blow them a kiss, shutting the door. And I'm off.

Chapter Fifty-One

Getting to Edinburgh from Swansea is no mean feat. With the taxi and waiting at the station, it takes ten hours and two trains to get into Waverley Station by 8:00 p.m. Overhead, its high glass ceiling soars. It's colder here—a lot colder, more than cold enough for snow, ice, and the rest. I flip up the collar of my black wool overcoat and wrap my gold scarf against the biting wind that waits outside.

We exchanged texts. Ben knows I'm coming, but there's the not insignificant fact that he's performing right now. After a round of debating whether I should meet him at the venue or elsewhere, Ben suggested at his home, swearing off any afterparties. I break into a cold sweat at the thought of meeting his mother alone, but Ben's provided assurances that his mum is excited to meet me, which helps put me a little more at ease.

Getting out of the latest taxi, I tell my nerves to fuck off. I ring the bell at Ben's family flat in one of the grand Georgian sandstone tenement buildings in Stockbridge. And Ben's mother answers.

And then I'm standing at the doorway, met by Ben's mum. She's younger than I expected, with black glossy hair flowing down her shoulders. She's in a striped knit jumper, and I swear I recognize the wool from Ben's stash.

"And you must be Charlie. I'm Dani. I've heard so much about you. Come on in—it's freezing out here." Dani stands about to my shoulder. Tiny but fierce. I get a better understanding of Ben already. She ushers me in and gives me a big hug, which helps settle my nerves, much to my surprise. I didn't expect such a warm welcome.

I'm dying inside though to imagine what he's said about me. Or God—how horrible my family was to him. Will she grill me while I'm here waiting for Ben? He wouldn't hear of a hotel and insisted we stay here tonight.

"Thanks so much for having me. I don't want to impose."

She waves me off, gesturing at wall hooks where a collection of coats hangs. "Nonsense. Here's a place for your things. And you can leave your bag here for now. We'll deal with that later."

"Thanks for having me here before Ben gets in," I tell her, grateful. "It's been a long day. But…I needed to see my boyfriend."

And fuck, it feels good to say that. I can't help but grin.

"I understand." Her smile is broad, so much like Ben's that it lets loose the riot of butterflies having their own afterparty in my guts. When my stomach rumbles, Dani laughs. "Let's get you something to eat, then."

Before long, I've shed a few layers, though still chilled from the train journey and the cold, leaving my gold scarf on over my black jumper. Everything's so casual here that it wouldn't be seen as an odd thing to do. His mum insists on feeding me soup from dinner, which is delicious. This feels like a proper home, and Dani's putting me at ease.

"So, Charlie. Ben tells me you're a musician too. And

that you're going to uni for literature and that you met at the coffee shop where you work. And that you have a little one that you were just out to see in Wales."

I nod, so impressed that he's spoken about me to his mum. Obviously, they're close. I can't imagine what that's like. "That's all true. She's two."

"Ach, bless. That's a lovely age."

I pull out my phone, pleased to have had such a warm reception, and I'm always eager to talk about Carys to people that matter. And Dani matters. A lot.

"She's the spitting image of you." Dani pats my arm.

And we talk about the journey up and about Carys, and my life back in London. The funny thing is, it doesn't feel weird at all, like I'm visiting family. And I suppose I am. I'm so damned lucky that she'd welcome me after what poor Ben went through at my parents' place. Their home isn't grand, but it's well cared for, and loved, and I can feel that here.

When Ben arrives late, calling his hello from the entry, I excuse myself and beeline to see him.

His cheeks are pink with cold, his striped scarf around his neck, green hat freshly tugged off, leaving his blond hair looking especially wild. And he's so damn gorgeous.

"Ben." I brighten at the sight of him.

His face lights up.

"Come here." I tug him close with the scarf still draped around his neck. When we kiss, he's heaven, his mouth soft and delicious, his lips cool against the heat of mine.

"Mmm." He slaps my arse for good measure before we straighten at last, leaving us both spinning.

"You've met Mum."

I nod. "She hasn't fed me to any bears."

"Any shortbread so far?" he teases.

"Not even a single piece," I lament.

"I heard that, Charlie," Dani calls, though I hear the

smile in her voice. "Both of you, quit making out back there and have some tea."

We grin at each other and steal another kiss. And it's thrilling to take his hand in mine and join her while Ben has a late meal.

And it's later still by the time we retreat to his childhood bedroom for the night. Thankfully there's a double bed, which means no one—me—has to sleep on the floor. And Ben shuts the door and turns to face me.

We stand there, taking in the sight of each other, excited and nervous and everything at once.

"I came to see you," I say unnecessarily. "I needed to see you."

God. Lame.

Ben nods, giving me a fleeting smile. The moment's passed for a hug or kiss as greeting, and we're instead left with the weird whatever this is that hangs between us. Emotion is caught raw in the air around us, fragile.

"Cheers," says Ben. Yesterday's question is in his eyes.

"I missed you," I whisper. "Last night. And the night before that. And the one before too."

He swallows hard.

"I didn't sleep last night," I confess. "Thinking of you. Of Emily and Carys. Of my life. Of the future after uni finishes."

"Sounds…sounds like a lot."

"Yeah, but I needed to have some space to think. To figure out for certain what I want. What's possible. Dealing with the idea of being on the edge of your fame, and what that might mean for Carys and Emily, too."

Ben shifts, hands in his leather jacket pockets. "The fame thing, though—Charlie, you know that's not real, right? Though the paparazzi are a problem now and again, I won't lie to you about that. But I can help and so can my team."

We're still standing. Today's jumper is moss green mohair.

Softer than air by the look of it. It's stunning, just like him. Another of his creations, I'm sure.

I gulp. Every hair on my body's electric. Goose bumps cascade across my skin. I stare at him. And then words tumble out, shocking us both.

"I had to come to Edinburgh to tell you something important." I stand tall, take his hands. "I love you, Ben."

Ben's quiet as he stares at me, a riot of emotion across his face. Now it's his turn to look torn between joy and panic and despair.

"And?" he whispers.

"And, if you'll have me, I want to be your boyfriend. To wake up to you. To imagine being with you even after winter goes. That I'll wake up on some sunny summer weekend and you'll be there. That you'll be part of my life, every bit of it—"

And then, right then, Ben catches my face between his hands, kissing me so reverently, so urgently, that I lose my bearings. We could be anywhere, just us.

We're pressed against the wall, our kisses fierce. Ben doesn't seem to know whether to laugh or cry, his eyes suspiciously wet.

"I figured you wouldn't want me. That it was too complicated," Ben gasps between kisses. "With everything you have on."

"It is complicated, but I realized I fell in love with you. And that's something I can trust. I know I can trust you."

Our kisses blaze. We stumble to the bed, all fingers and kisses and rawness. We practically fall into it. My hands under that jumper might have been the final straw, my fingers tracing his abs, the curve of his ribs.

I kiss Ben thoroughly.

"Charlie?"

"Yes?"

"You know I love you too, right?"

The reminder warms me from the inside out. I catch his face between my hands, kiss him lingeringly.

"I love you too, you numpty." It's exhilarating to say it out loud.

Now we're giddy, unable to stop laughing, a clumsy tangle of half-frozen fingers and adrenaline as we undress each other. When I help him out of his cloud of a jumper, his pale skin is warm against my body. We tumble together onto the bed.

Together, we're all kisses, hands tracing each other's bodies like we map a new landscape. Like our bodies know that it's a homecoming.

Ben, down to his shorts, pauses between kisses. "You really do want me?"

"Of course. Of course," I murmur against his skin, pressing him down against the bed, pressing his wrists to the down of the pillows. "So much, Ben."

He gasps as my teeth rake the softness of his shoulder, his skin hot against mine. With every tease, every nip, every kiss, he surrenders more.

And Ben laughs, and he cries. And I do too.

"I thought you wouldn't. I really thought you wouldn't…"

I pause to hold him tight, to gaze into the comfort of his eyes. "I always wanted you. I just figured you could do better than me. And I needed to take care of Carys. But Emily's helpfully reminded me more than once that I can have a relationship and be a good dad, too. That I can have both."

Ben nuzzles my neck. I shiver.

"I know your family comes first."

"I think…I think you've become my family too, Ben. You slipped under my skin when I wasn't looking."

His smile is huge. "Aye. I'm prone to do that. Watch out."

We laugh, holding each other.

"I don't know what everything will look like," I say. "But

I think…I think we'll figure it out together."

Ben kisses me. We give over to the urgency of our bodies, keeping as quiet as we can. He's hard against me. I tease him while he shivers and I savor every response, no matter how little. Before long, his head's thrown back against the pillows, lost in pleasure as he's nude on the covers.

I kiss the inside of his wrists, his elbows. His nipples. The cascade of freckles over his shoulders.

When I take him into my mouth, he groans with ecstasy. "Don't stop."

I don't stop. His shudders only urge me on, the taste of him sweet on my tongue. And I tease and suck. And Ben whimpers until desperate words tumble muffled into his arm. "Oh God—Charlie, I can't—"

So fucking hot. As he comes, I watch with frank admiration. That he can lose control so completely and give himself over, this incredible man who's somehow fallen in love with me and me with him. What a funny thing this universe is, how unpredictable. But I can't get upset, because it's brought me Ben, like the snow that falls again beyond his window.

After another round, we wake up into a bright late morning, as though in a dream, a cascade of white drifting down beyond the window. Disoriented, with Ben in my arms, I wonder if we're back in December, in the dream of Ben's London bedroom. We are in his bedroom again, another city and month away. His skin is warm against mine. I've wrapped myself around him, the blankets sheltering us.

"So much for breakfast," I whisper, kissing his shoulder.

Ben laughs sleepily. "They call it a nooner. Except at 3:00 p.m."

"You're a fount of information, Morrissey."

"I aim to please."

I hold him tight against my chest, trying to imprint this moment in time.

"Is this really real?" I murmur my question against his ear.

He shifts so that we're looking at each other across the pillows. "Totally real, lovely. The realest."

We lose ourselves in kisses, wrapped close.

"I can't wait till you're back in London," I admit. "I've missed you."

He flashes a grin. "Soon. I've missed you more than I can say. Only a couple of weeks more."

"Mmm, good news."

"Aye. Good thing, too." Ben gives me a serious look.

"Why's that? You miss me already?" I tease.

"Naturally. And it's not even Valentine's Day. Brace yourself."

"You're going to need a musician-repellent for Maximus St. Pierre," I say solemnly. "I'll give you a bouquet of garlic."

Ben laughs and I laugh too, and we're lost in gales of laughter together. Imagining a string of days like this with Ben ahead lifts my spirits. Like we'll be able to navigate the year ahead, to the end of my uni and beyond, all of the way to Emily and Carys coming to London.

Together, we drowse in kisses and bask in bed beneath the crisp sheets till we're starved and at last ready to take on the day, which Ben has off. When we emerge from our private cocoon, Dani's gone out. Eventually, we too go out into the snowy world, hand in hand.

When we reach outside, everything stills in the quiet evening white blanketing Edinburgh. We linger for a kiss, the promise of everything that lies before us hopeful and new.

Epilogue

Chewing my lip at my reflection—neatened dark mop of hair, freshly shaven, green eyes like my daughter's—I finish adjusting my tie in the mirror. There's wrapping and neatening up, my fingers knowing the routine by instinct from years of school days and uniforms, appropriate for today's long-awaited graduation. This day took a lifetime to come. My shirt is crisp and white, the red tie standing out as a splash of color that my mother will doubtless find scandalous.

Carys, perched on the counter against me, reaches for my tie. "Want."

I glance down at her. She's already in her spring dress and gives me a curious look as she alternates between watching me get ready and playing with her full skirt.

"You'd need a suit, then, darling. Like mine. Ties tend not to look right with dresses. You don't have the collar, for starters."

Carys considers this. "I want suit."

"I'll get you a suit for my birthday," I promise, already delighting in the scandal that will bring to the slew of Renfrews gathered for the occasion in a couple of weeks' time. Summer also means we'll get to Scotland—all of us—in Posh Van: me and Ben, Carys and Emily. We'll go on a week's holiday and get Emily to finally meet Ben's mum.

It's early summer, the start of July bringing heat to London. Last year's fears about the change in seasons taking Ben away were just a manifestation of my anxiety. We've been together now for six months.

"You might even need a suit when you start school." I give her a serious look. In England, children start school at age four. Carys's just turned three, and it's hard to imagine she'll be in school in a year's time. She's got loads of opinions about everything, and I'm thrilled to hear them, even when I can't understand what she's saying.

"Let's go meet Ben, shall we?"

Carys takes my hand, leading me through Ben's Marylebone mews house—now our family home for all four of us. Molly and her partner have moved to their own flat to let Emily and Carys have the extra space. This way, Carys can have all of us in her life, and we can help Emily finally get to uni, too.

Posh Van takes us to meet everyone else at the Royal Festival Hall, where UCL always has its graduation. The imposing Southbank Centre overlooks the Thames, the sweeping sprawl of London before us.

I'm ready for the future, for a life after uni. But now, looking back, I see that my future arrived several times before today. One future is the arrival of little Carys, held in my arms as we head to the promenade overlooking the river where we're all to meet. Another future was coming clean from drug abuse and getting help for my anxiety and moving on from self-medicating. And the third future, which brings the other futures together, is meeting Ben while slinging lattes at the café.

And there, standing against the backdrop of the blue sky, blond hair ruffled by the breeze, is Ben. He leans on the railing in a black flamingo shirt, sleeves rolled up, tie being tossed around by the wind. Goose bumps cover my arms at the sight of him.

"Ben!" shouts Carys. She wriggles in my arms and I set her down. Breaking free of me, she runs to him.

And he turns and gives her his best grin, the one that melts me inside. He crouches and she flings her arms around his neck like she would do when I visited in Wales. He's on a tour break for a couple of weeks before rejoining festival season, fresh in from Glastonbury. He got in late last night and had a meeting with his agent this morning before meeting me for my graduation.

He scoops Carys up, much to her delight. Beaming, he comes over to me.

And God, what it does to me, to have Ben and Carys and Emily all here.

Then he stands in front of me, in his matching tie, because apparently we've become that sort of couple.

"I've missed you," I manage unevenly. Joy careens through me, an emotion I didn't know or trust until Ben taught me to trust it, that I learned to trust myself too. He gazes at me, all smiles and impish grin. As we kiss, Carys laughs.

I never imagined a day like this one would come for me, but it has, and the future has me and Ben in it.

"Mummy! Granny!"

Carys brings us back from our kiss. Katherine's traveled from Wales to see us for my graduation. Emily's elegant in a blue wrap dress, silver bangles on her wrist. She kisses my cheek, then Ben's in turn. Dani's come down too and joins us shortly after more hugs and kisses.

We're a happy knot of people.

Emily grins and gives me a bouquet of flowers, an amazing display of roses and broad daisies and other beautiful flowers. "We saw this and we texted Ben and we all thought you should have these."

I chuckle. "You've never bought me flowers before. Any of you."

"It's a shame because you've bought me flowers," Ben teases affectionally.

I laugh and reach out to adjust his tie. He preens and runs a hand through his hair.

"I'll never let you live it down, Morrissey," I say gruffly, but I'm smiling.

"Shall we go meet Michael and Jenna and head in?" Emily asks me. "Now that we've found each other here?"

I nod.

A year ago, I couldn't have dreamed of where my life would lead. This summer, I'll join Ben on tour to open a couple of his shows with my band, a big break for us. Then I've got an editorial internship lined up while Emily starts uni.

It's here, the future. I'm living right now with Ben and all of them. As we all walk, I grab his hand and we pause, hanging back from the others for a moment. His gaze doesn't waver, all for me.

"I love you so much, Ben."

"Love you to the moon and back," he murmurs before stealing another kiss.

We kiss like nobody's watching us, like we're the only ones in a city of millions, just me and Ben and our new family—together.

Acknowledgments

This novel has been a journey, starting from a short story several years back. Many people have helped develop this story along the way, in all of its different versions.

Special thanks again to my editor, Heather Howland, for working with me and believing in Charlie and Ben's story. Many thanks to the Entangled team for bringing this novel to life and supporting it behind the scenes. Thanks again to Amy Acosta, Bree Archer, Riki Cleveland, Meredith Johnson, Liz Pelletier, Heather Riccio, Debbie Suzuki, Jessica Turner, and apologies to anyone I may have inadvertently missed. And thanks again to LJ Anderson of Mayhem Cover Creations for another beautiful cover.

Several critique partners and beta readers have read versions of this story, providing great feedback and encouragement. A big thanks to my original critique group partners Ambrose Hall, T.M. Delligatti, C.N. Steinhour, Tonia Markou, Claudia Clarke, Evelyn Canto, and Theo Popov, who have encouraged my writing and development as a writer over the years. Without you, this story wouldn't exist.

Early versions of this story were also critiqued by T.L. Brassey, David Hawthorne, Jon Carl Lewis, Gary P. Priest, Jon Oldblood, and Dylan Wylde. Sincere apologies for anyone I have missed.

More recently, Anita Kelly, Avione Lee, Chandra Fisher, Molly Steen, and Jen Tarr have read versions of this story and provided plenty of encouragement and assistance, along with the fantastic Writing Folks family, who never fail to inspire.

Special thanks to Gwynne Jackson and Andy Palanzuelo for believing in me as a writer and in my writing.

Big thanks for the support from the usual suspects: Cynthia, Charlotte, and Joel.

Thanks always to my family, who have listened to a lifetime of stories.

And thanks always to the readers, for choosing to pick up this novel and escape for a few hours in this imaginary London. If you want to keep up on my news and books, please visit http://www.haydenstonebooks.com.

About the Author

More animal than mineral, Hayden Stone is a writer of fun queer fiction, especially with kissing. He currently lives in Victoria, Canada, and has previously lived in Vancouver, Canada and London, UK. He likes strong coffee and is owned by two cats. You can find out his latest news on Twitter or Instagram, or at his website: haydenstonebooks.com

Also by Hayden Stone...

AN UNEXPECTED KIND OF LOVE

Discover more romance from Entangled...

Tinkering with Love
a Rock Falls novel by Aliyah Burke

As if losing her dream job as motorcycle mechanic after moving all the way from San Francisco to the midwest wasn't bad enough, Dawson finds out that her replacement job as a car saleswoman is now holding teambuilding event in the mountains. And between dodging murderous chipmunks and dreamy dates under the northern lights, she's now falling for the charming ex-pro hockey player Tully Faulkner—the very guy who stole her job.

Playing it Safe
a Sydney Smoke Rugby novel by Amy Andrews

Donovan Bane loves playing rugby for the Sydney Smoke. And if that means he has to keep his sexuality a secret, that's a sacrifice he's prepared to make. Until one man suddenly changes everything... Beckett Stanton is out and proud—and not looking for a guy who isn't. Still, Beck can't resist being the man to show Donovan everything he's been missing. And for the first time, Donovan doesn't want to play it safe.

His Holiday Crush
a novel by Cari Z

One meeting away from making partner, Max Robertson is guilted into coming back home for Christmas. The plan is to go for just one night, but a wild deer and a snow bank wreck everything. Former Army Sergeant Dominic Bell of the Edgewood police has his evening turned upside-down when he gets called out to a crash—and it's his one and only high school crush. Everyone deserves a present this holiday season, right?

Rough and Tumble
a novel by Shae Connor

My name's Grant Clark, and I managed to screw up my entire life. In triplicate. I fell in love with my best friend, I thought he was straight, and because of number two, I didn't make a move until it was too late. Or is it? When I accidentally interrupt him with another guy—and he turns out to be the worst—well, I think it's time I finally make a move. Don't you?